LOVE IN THE WILD

A Tarzan Retelling

EMMA CASTLE

EMMA CASTLE

Dark and Edgy Romance

ISBN: 978-1-952063-16-9 (e-book edition)
ISBN: 978-1-952063-17-6 (paperback edition)
ISBN: 978-1-952063-29-9 (hardback edition)

For Dian Fossey, Jane Goodall and the others who have worked tireless to protect wildlife around the world. The world is a better place when we believe in the magic of the wild.

FOREWORD

"AFRICA IS MYSTIC; IT IS WILD; IT IS A
SWELTERING INFERNO; IT IS A
PHOTOGRAPHER'S PARADISE, A HUNTER'S
VALHALLA, AN ESCAPIST'S UTOPIA. IT IS
WHAT YOU WILL, AND IT WITHSTANDS ALL
INTERPRETATIONS. IT IS THE LAST VESTIGE
OF A DEAD WORLD OR THE CRADLE OF A
SHINY NEW ONE. TO A LOT OF PEOPLE, AS TO
MYSELF, IT IS JUST 'HOME.'" – BERYL
MARKMAN

This is a retelling of Edgar Rice Burroughs's classic story *Tarzan of the Apes*. I make no claim that I have written it better, but I believe that this version will find a home with modern readers who love adventure and steamy romance.

When I set out to write a modern version of Tarzan, there was one thing I wanted to do, which was tell a love story. As Burroughs always said *"There is no Tarzan without Jane."* That quote always stayed with me, and I wanted to make sure that the readers saw my heroine Eden for what she is, a partner to Thorne, my vine-swinging hero, someone who is his true other half.

You will find that much of *Love in the Wild* varies from Tarzan not just names but also the location which here is set in Uganda rather than coastal Africa. I have emphasized real towns, real jungles and researched thoroughly the society which characters like Thorne's friend, Bwanbale lived in, to make an accurate portrayal of the current culture. The friendship between Bwanbale and Thorne is a crucial one. Thorne representing ancient man who thrives on instinct and Bwanbale representing the nobility and open-heartedness of modern man. Eden is also crucial to Thorne's character. She represents the outward manifestation of his heart and soul. I enjoyed playing with symbolic imagery, such as the power of water to represent healing and rebirth throughout the novel. The themes of gold and power are also important to consider as you read. At the end of this book, you will find a small group of book club discussion questions to engage in further discourse with your fellow readers.

I wanted to make a more mystical connection to the jungle than the original story. The ancient tribe from the jungle that speaks to Thorne is fictional, but the ancient tribe of the Batwa which is mentioned within the novel is real and the members of that tribe have been displaced from the jungle which was their home for thousands of years. I chose to give the animals of Africa a voice, as seen through brief glimpses of the character Keza, the gorilla who raises Thorne. I believe it is important that the reader see these animals as powerful and important forces in the world by giving them a voice within these pages which I hope will inspire readers to care more about them in the real life.

I hope as you turn the page and begin this journey you will sit back, enjoy the story, and let yourself believe, for a moment, that magic still exists in the world...

"Get on your knees," a cold voice commanded.

Eden Matthews sank to her knees. Half a dozen men and women next to her did the same. One woman was sobbing, and a man was begging for his life. But Eden saw no mercy in the eyes of the man who stood in front of her holding a gun to her head.

All around them the jungle was quiet. Even the animals and insects seemed to have sensed the danger and elected to stay still. She stared at the barrel of the gun, her gaze fixed on the circular black hole, then forced herself to look her soon-to-be-murderer in the eyes. The man was unshaven, mid-forties, his clothing splattered with blood and mud. Behind him were four other men with stony, empty black eyes, all armed. They were a mix of white and black men, and the heavy weapons they carried meant they were most likely rebels. Or worse—poachers.

"We were supposed to be safe," one woman whispered to herself. "This is a national park. We have permits . . ."

Permits didn't matter to men like these—these were the true monsters of the jungle.

"Keep your mouths shut," the leader snapped. She didn't dare take her eyes away from him. His gun swung a few inches to Eden's left at the older woman who'd spoken.

Eden's heart was beating so fast she was amazed she hadn't had a heart attack. These men wouldn't let them go. They were going to kill them and leave their bodies in the Ugandan jungle, never to be found. The gorillas she had come to photograph had fled before these men had arrived, as if they had sensed the danger. If they were poachers, and the gorillas had been their intended target, Eden at least hoped the majestic creatures were far away and safe.

"Cash, what we gonna do with them, eh?" one of the men asked their leader.

"Shut up—I'm thinking," he growled. His eyes swept over the group of visitors and their two Ugandan guides.

"The boss wouldn't like witnesses," the other man added.

"True." The one called Cash stroked his beard, and then, with terrifying slowness, he swept the gun to the forehead of the man at the far end of the tourist group and fired. Eden jerked as his body fell face-first onto the leaf-covered ground.

Several more bangs echoed in the small clearing, and more bodies fell.

Eden wasn't able to close her eyes. Fear had so immobilized her that she simply couldn't move, couldn't breathe. She could only watch.

"Maybe we keep one alive?" Cash volunteered to his men with a cruel laugh. "These other bitches were old. But this one, she's fresh and young. We can have our fun with her first. The boss would never need to know."

Lungs burning, Eden sucked in a breath, her back aching from being stiff on her knees.

"Yes, I think we'll keep her." Cash lowered his gun, but Eden didn't relax. Whatever hell was about to come next for her would be far, far worse than a quick death.

Blood roared in her ears, so loud that the trees actually seemed to tremble and the ground to vibrate.

Wait, no. That sound wasn't in her head. It was coming from somewhere else, somewhere distant, but near enough to frighten the men closest to her.

"What the fuck was that?" Cash demanded.

"*Mnyama,*" one of the men murmured in Swahili. "*Mnyama Anakuja!*"

Eden didn't speak much Swahili, but it sounded like he said, *The beast is coming.*

"A silverback?" Cash asked.

The man shook his head. "No. The pale ghost."

"Pale ghost? What the fuck are you talking about?"

Two of the men exchanged glances and just ran. They vanished into the moss-covered hagenia trees that formed the canopies high above them.

Cash spun around, firing shots in their direction before he turned back toward Eden. The roar echoed again, sending birds into flight and small monkeys in the trees scampering away.

"We should go!"

The other men clambered away at once, but Cash shouted at them. "Not until I kill this one." He pointed his gun at her again.

Eden closed her eyes tight. She imagined her parents' faces back in Arkansas, could see the door of her childhood home. She choked down her despair and longing to be there in that moment and not here—anywhere but here.

The gun went off. Eden experienced a second of stunned surprised because she still felt the jungle air thick with moisture and smelled the heavy scent of sweat around her. She was dead, so why did she still smell the jungle?

"Ah!" Cash's scream came a millisecond later, followed by a sickening crunch.

Eden didn't dare open her eyes as she heard the sounds of violence—screams and snapping bones.

The beast was here. Her stomach churned as she

swallowed down the rise of bile in her throat and her breath escaped in rapid pants of terror. She would be next. The long silence that followed made her brave enough to open her eyes, slowly taking in the scene of carnage. Cash lay dead a dozen feet away, his neck twisted right around. That was something.

The other tourists she had come with were all dead, but they had been left untouched by the beast. She swallowed hard as tears blurred her vision.

The sound of footsteps behind her and a huffing noise caused her to flinch and close her eyes again. Body heat and hot breath on the back of her neck sent a chill down her spine and stirred her hair. The beast was still here. She was next.

Please, let it kill me quickly.

A grunting noise, similar to the ones made by the gorillas, came from behind her. Something touched her ponytail. She gasped and threw herself to the ground on pure instinct, her hands crunching into the leaves beneath her. The beast moved somewhere in front of her. When she dared to look, her lips parted but no sound escaped.

A man crouched in front of her, ten feet away. His tan skin was covered with blackened, drying mud, making him look more monster than man. His long dark hair hung in loose tendrils down around his shoulders. His eyes were a vivid dark blue, and they narrowed on her as his full lips pressed into a hard frown.

In one hand the man held a blade. His other hand was curled into a fist. She watched the corded muscles of his forearm ripple as he shifted and moved. There was a lithe grace to his nearly naked body as he shifted back and forth on his bare feet. A loincloth of animal skin covered his groin but left his legs bare to her view. He chuffed at her softly, like a jaguar. But the strangest thing, perhaps, was a band of gold that rested on his brow like a crown, the precious metal shaped into small leaves like a laurel wreath.

He gestured with his balled fist to the man on the ground and grunted again.

Eden blinked, unsure what to do or say. This man had saved her. But who was he? Where had he come from? Why was he grunting instead of speaking?

"Hi," she whispered, and he halted in his gestures. "Do you understand me?"

The man tilted his head to the side, and his nostrils flared. It was hard to read his face with the mud streaked across it.

"Hello?" She tried to greet him again. The word *hello* was also used in Swahili, in case he spoke that rather than English.

He slowly straightened to a towering height, and she got to her feet as well. Eden kept her distance, not knowing what to expect with this wild man.

She tried some Swahili and continued to stare at him. *"Kiswahili?"*

Suddenly his head turned, and he scanned the forest. It was still eerily quiet. Eden knew his attention was focused elsewhere, yet she had a sense he had missed nothing, including her movements. The man threw his head back and let out a roar, the same roar that had sent Cash's Ugandan men running for the hills. They had known the danger of whoever this man was.

She asked him if he spoke Swahili. "*Unaongea Kiswahili?*" Unfortunately, she didn't know enough of the language to truly have a conversation.

Her savior shot her another distracted look before he grunted again at the forest and whistled sharply. There was an answering whistle far to her left. The man turned her way, and with lightning-quick reflexes, he grabbed her.

Eden screamed, but a second later the air was knocked from her lungs as he threw her over his shoulder. He began to run, dodging through the trees and leaping over the taller bushes and vegetation like an Olympic hurdler. The impact of his feet jarred her and sent a punch to her stomach. She was going to throw up if he kept this up much longer.

Where was he going? What was he going to do to her? Why didn't he communicate? He acted . . . well, he acted more like an animal than a person. A wild man. It made no sense.

Eventually he stopped running. He rolled her off his shoulder and onto the ground. She couldn't stop it—her stomach emptied its contents, and she lay gasping on the ground at the base of a particularly thick-rooted hagenia tree. She clawed at the ground, trying to catch her breath and stop the shaking of her arms and legs.

Her head spun, and she gazed up at the distant light, barely able to make it out through the trees above. She saw something jutting from the base of the tree, going all the way up. Small pieces of wood, like tiny steps in the trunk, created a path all the way up the tree. The wild man grasped her hand and pulled her to her feet. He then gestured for her to climb onto his back. Was he kidding?

She shook her head violently. "No, no, I'm not—"

He lunged for her, and she shrieked, holding up her hands.

"Okay!"

He pointed at his back, and he faced the tree, waiting patiently.

It was weird climbing onto this stranger's back, but she did it. He used the wooden steps the way a mountain climber would use footholds. She nearly closed her eyes as they reached ten feet and kept on going. The tops of the trees looked to be another ten or fifteen feet away.

As they reached the heavy foliage above, the man pushed upward, and the foliage moved away in a nearly perfect square shape, just large enough to accommodate their two bodies. He continued to climb, and Eden gasped.

The tree went up another fifteen feet, through a hole in the roof that was sealed with mud. All around them was wood—chopped timbers worn smooth into planks, forming a structure around her and the man like a tree house.

A tree house? Here?

He crawled across the floor and tapped her legs. She slowly let go and touched her feet down. The wooden floor was as solid as a rock. Eden stared around at the tree house. It had to have been built nearly twenty feet off the ground. The bottom of it was completely camouflaged from below.

"What is this place?" she asked, mostly to herself. She saw a wooden door with a simple flipped latch made with thick rope. A small window-like opening allowed for some minimal light.

The man grunted at her and pointed to a corner of the little structure. Eden saw nothing there. The man moved toward her, and she immediately backed into the corner he pointed to. She fell back, landing on her bottom, and he held up a palm and made that soft chuffing noise again. Did he want her to stay there? He opened the trapdoor and started to climb down the way they had come up.

"Wait! Where are you going?" She started to move, but he grunted and huffed at her, and she halted. He pointed to the corner, and she shifted back to the corner wall, clutching her camera to her chest. He gazed at her a long moment, those blue eyes solid and inscrutable as he watched her. Then he disappeared from view, pulling the trapdoor down behind him.

Eden wasn't sure how long she sat there staring at the door. After what felt like forever, her muscles relaxed and the tension in her body slowed and seeped out of her. She slumped onto the floor on her side. Her body trembled, and a rush of tears came hard. She cried as the recent events all came back to her. The dead faces of the men and women who'd traveled deep into the impenetrable forest with her. Everyone eager for the experience of a lifetime.

Sweet Maggie, humorous Harold, and all the others whom she'd formed a bond with in so short a time. All dead. Their lives had been snuffed out because they had been in the wrong place at the wrong time.

And what about her? She was alive, but was she ever going to get out of the jungle? And who was the beast of the forest who'd saved her? Who was the pale ghost?

1

TWENTY-TWO YEARS AGO

Amelia Haywood sat in the small Cessna, her tiny son, Thorne, in the seat beside her.

She grinned and pointed at the dense miles of spreading Ugandan forest far below them. "See? Look at the jungle." Thorne squirmed and stretched up in his seat to peer out the oval window. Amelia stroked a hand down his dark hair. It was silky as a baby's, even though Thorne was three years old as of last week.

Thorne pointed a tiny finger at the window. "Mummy!"

"Yes, Thorne, that's the jungle."

"Monkey!" He looked down at the child's picture book in his lap, where it said, *M is for monkey.* Then he focused back on the window.

"Jacob, how much farther is it?" Amelia asked her husband.

Jacob turned to face her from the seat next to the pilot. His dark hair and vivid blue eyes were a mirror image of their son's. Thorne looked like her a little too, around the mouth, especially when he smiled. That pleased Amelia, because Jacob always said it was her smile that he dreamed about whenever he closed his eyes. Amelia had never imagined she could love someone as much as her husband, but she did. Jacob and Thorne were her entire world.

"We've got about another hour until we get to the airstrip," Jacob guessed.

Charlie, their hired pilot, nodded. "He's right, about an hour."

"Tomorrow we'll see the monkeys," Amelia said to her son. She turned the book's pages until she got to the letter *G*. A picture of a gorilla was below the letter.

"Gorilla." She spoke the word slowly and clearly.

Thorne planted his palm on the picture and said loudly, "Monkey!"

"Gorilla," she said again.

The child turned serious eyes to hers and then said, "Go-willa."

"Close enough." Amelia chuckled and reached up to finger the necklace at her throat. It was a small gold chain with a gold ginkgo leaf. Jacob had given it to her on the night he proposed. She'd gotten a ring, of course, a lovely princess cut diamond that was a family heirloom, but Jacob had said he wanted to give her a gift that was special, and this most certainly was.

From the beginning she and Jacob had been a perfect match, both in love with wildlife and conservation. Because of his family's wealth, they had been able to build a center near Bwindi Impenetrable Forest for park guides and guests to rest and relax before making the trek into the woods to see the gorillas.

They had also donated a large sum of money to support anti-deforestation efforts and a police force to protect the shrinking population of mountain gorillas. For the first time since she had been pregnant with Thorne, they were able to return to Africa, the cradle of civilization.

For as long as Amelia could remember, she had felt a pull to this beautiful continent. It was one of the few places that still held mysteries unseen by human eyes. It wasn't a desert plain—it was mountainous, with depressions and shallow lakes, waterfalls, and rivers.

Amelia had studied the varied geography on the continent while at university. The mountains fed the major rivers, causing the waterways to bleed into undulating savannas until they fell in a series of rapids and waterfalls into narrow gorges and coastal plains.

The rivers themselves were not navigable for any great distance. Travelers, traders, soldiers, and explorers from ancient times to present day had all failed to penetrate the interior heart of Africa.

Amelia could feel that heart beating, steady as a drum, calling her to come closer, to seek out answers deep in the misty mountains. Legends were born and made here. Amelia wanted to be among them, to explore and discover, conserve and protect.

Thorne continued to turn the pages of the book, speaking the words softly to himself in his toddler voice that was sometimes more gibberish than real words. He was a quiet child. He spoke little, but she knew he was smart. He was already learning to recognize the letters and their sounds, and he was even sounding out a few simple words in his picture books.

The plane suddenly dropped a little. Amelia's heart jumped in her chest, but then she chuckled. Thorne squealed in delight.

"Heavens, what's the matter, Charlie? You didn't let Jacob take over flying, did you?"

Charlie held tight to the controls. "No, we seem to have hit a draft."

The plane jerked, and Amelia checked her seat belt and Thorne's, making sure they were secure.

"Are you buckled in?" Jacob called back to them.

"Yes."

"Good. Hold on—"

The plane's engine suddenly sputtered, and the plane tipped down. The engine reengaged for a brief few seconds before giving out again. But it was too late. The plane dropped out of the sky toward the jungle below.

The next few seconds happened in flashes. *Smoke—screams—plummeting—trees—crash—silence.*

AMELIA COUGHED AS SHE WOKE IN THE THICK darkness. For a second, she couldn't remember what had happened. She strained to see anything as her eyes adjusted to the dark. A soft whimper beside her made her flinch.

"Mummy . . ." Thorne's voice came from somewhere beside her.

"Hold on, darling," she said and unfastened her seat belt. The inside of the Cessna was becoming clearer as her eyes adjusted to the darkness. They must have landed below the canopy of hagenia trees.

She unclipped Thorne's seat belt and felt around his tiny face. "Are you hurt, my love?" she asked, searching for any injury. He shook his head.

"Jacob! Charlie!" she called out.

There was a cough at the front of the plane. "Darling?" Jacob's voice, rusty sounding, came back to her.

"Charlie?" she called out again, but no sound came from the pilot's chair. A massive tree had pierced the window between the two seats in the front of the plane.

Her husband reached over and clapped a hand on Charlie's shoulder, giving the man a gentle shake. He didn't respond. Jacob picked up the man's wrist and put two fingers against his skin.

"No pulse," Jacob said. He turned Charlie's head slightly, exposing the part of his skull that had been caved in by the tree limb. "Christ . . ." Jacob closed his eyes briefly and exhaled a heavy sigh.

Amelia covered her mouth with her hands as grief squeezed her heart. *Poor Charlie.*

Jacob unclipped his belt and climbed through the narrow aisle over fallen luggage toward them. "Are you and Thorne okay?"

"Yes, we're all right." She pulled Thorne onto her lap. "What happened?"

"The engine gave out." Jacob ruffled a hand through Thorne's hair and kissed Amelia on the forehead. "Thank Christ you're all right."

Jacob turned to the door on the side of the plane and twisted the handle. After a few seconds it groaned and gave way. A wave of heat and humid air filled the cabin. Jacob stuck his head out into the jungle.

"I think we're still a long way from the airstrip. It looks like the plane made it all the way to the ground, but we won't have to worry about it being unstable if we move about the cabin." He pulled his head back inside and glanced around. "Look for the first aid kit. There might be a flare gun and some supplies."

Amelia tucked their son back into his seat and helped Jacob search the cabin.

"At least we have food," she said. They had brought a few weeks' worth of provisions. She had insisted on having dried edibles packed on the plane before they left London.

"I found the satellite phone," Jacob said with a relieved sigh. "I'll call Cameron." He dialed his younger brother's number back in London.

"Damn. It went to voice mail," he muttered. "Cameron, it's Jacob. Our plane crashed somewhere west of the Bwindi airstrip. I need you to call the number of the forest guides that I sent you in an email last week. Have them start looking for us right away. Make sure—" Jacob stopped abruptly. "Bloody hell."

"What's wrong?"

"The message shut off." He ended the call and turned off the phone to preserve the battery.

Amelia located the first aid kit and Jacob's handgun, which was safe in its case with a box of ammunition.

"I want us to sleep inside the plane. It's the safest place. I'm going to move Charlie's body outside and bury him, if I can. When they find us, we can retrieve his remains then. I'll find the multitool. It should have a pickax on one end."

Amelia nodded in agreement. She didn't like thinking about Charlie's body being out there where it might attract animals and insects, but they had to stay safe. A corpse close to them would only increase the risk of predators, not to mention infection and disease.

"Let me help you." Amelia checked to make sure Thorne was in his seat. She cupped his face and gazed into his big blue eyes. "Stay here, honey. Mummy and Daddy will be right back."

She joined Jacob at the front of the plane. The cockpit window was smashed into fractured pieces like frosted glass. Charlie's limp body sagged back in the seat, and Jacob leaned forward and hugged him as he lifted him up. Then he moved the body toward her. Amelia shivered as she took the man's wrists and backed her way out of the plane's door. She and Jacob carried the pilot a good distance from the plane, but they kept the plane in their sight as they laid him down.

Jacob dragged his fingers through his dark hair and met Amelia's gaze. "We can't dig a deep grave, not without shovels. The small ax will have to be enough. It has a sharp-edged scoop on the other end."

Amelia had no words. It was an unspeakable tragedy to leave their pilot's body to the elements and wild animals, but what choice did they have?

She reached out and clasped her husband's hand and squeezed it. "I'm sorry, Jacob." She could see the pain in his eyes. He was a man with a heart deeper than the ocean. He loved all living things and valued all life.

Jacob led her away from Charlie's body back to the plane. They stopped just outside the cabin, listening to the cadence of the jungle, the hum and chirp of insects, the blend of wild, exotic birds and monkeys, oblivious to the disaster that had just happened. Jacob and Amelia exchanged a long, meaningful glance. It was as if the jungle was beginning to swallow the plane and the three surviving passengers whole.

Jacob gently gripped her hips, pulling her to him, and she wound her arms around his neck. He embraced her, hugging her to him, and brushed his hand up and down her back.

"We're going to get through this. Cameron knows were alive. He won't stop looking for us. Until then, we can have a proper family adventure. Just think: Lofty and Cameron would have a good laugh if they were here with us."

Amelia chuckled shakily. "Lofty thinks everything is an adventure." She thought of Jacob's old schoolmate, the Earl of Lofthouse, whom everyone called Lofty, and the idea did give her a bit of spark back. Lofty was a delightful man with a sense of humor and a taste for expensive brandy. He, Cameron, and Jacob had been thick as thieves as boys.

She nodded. He was trying to keep things light, but emotions rolled through her like a building storm. Her husband and child were in an ancient forest, possibly unreachable for any rescue, and she didn't know how to protect them. Danger was everywhere.

THE NEXT TWO WEEKS OF LIVING IN THE DOWNED plane were not easy. Jacob Haywood kept a close eye on his wife and child, making sure they were safe at all times.

He also purified their water from a nearby river by mixing it with a solution that contained iodine and chlorine dioxide tablets, which killed off some giardia parasites. Thorne always made a face when he had to drink the tablet-treated water, but he would look at Jacob, and with a little weary sigh he would drink the water. The boy never complained, even when his small belly grumbled with hunger. Most days Jacob felt like a failure. He and Amelia both had staved off eating whenever possible to give more food to their son, but it was time he started trying to hunt. Uganda had an antelope species called the kob, which lived in these forests. With any luck he could find some, or fish in the river that he'd found not too far from them.

"Darling?" Jacob retrieved his gun from the case inside the cockpit where he'd hidden it out of Thorne's sight for safety.

Amelia was sitting in one of the seats with Thorne, reading the jungle alphabet book to him. "Yes?"

"I'm going to go hunting, and maybe I'll fish in the river. Stay here with Thorne. I should be back in a few hours."

She stood and lifted Thorne into her arms. "Jacob, I don't know if that's safe."

He was almost too big to hold like that, but Jacob had the sudden urge to have his child in his arms. He held out his hands, and Amelia passed him the toddler. Thorne rested his cheek on Jacob's shoulder as he cradled the boy, pressing his own cheek on the child's head.

A realization dawned on him as he swayed the little boy in his arms. Someday he would be holding Thorne for the last time. At some point the boy would be too big, too old for this. Was *this* the last time? Would Jacob even be aware of it when that last time he held his son came and went? A chill crept along his arms and the back of his neck. It felt like someone had stepped over his grave.

He held Thorne a moment longer before he gave him back to his wife. Amelia offered him a wistful smile, but her eyes were heavy with concern.

"I'll be back soon," he promised and kissed her quick and hard.

"Be careful," Amelia warned as he stepped into the jungle that awaited him outside the security of the downed Cessna.

The trek into the jungle took nearly an hour. He glimpsed a few simian-shaped shadows above him, swinging or jumping between the trees. But he didn't aim his gun at them. He knew the dangers of ingesting monkey meat, so he would only kill them as a last resort. He climbed over the rocks, wound his way through tightly growing moss-covered trees, and chopped down thick vegetation with a machete they had brought along on the plane.

He was nearly at the river—it was only another quarter of a mile—when he heard something moving through the brush. There were some low-level foothills that had caves nearby. He had discovered a cave a week ago but hadn't gone too far in. Ebola was often found in African caves. He didn't want to risk contracting that virus.

Whatever was heading toward the cave was definitely big. It might be a kob. He abandoned his path toward the river and followed the sound at a safe distance.

When the sounds ahead of him stopped near the black cavernous entrance to the cave, he halted, holding his breath, but a second later, he exhaled in a rush as he heard human voices.

"This is the one, Holt," a man said. "I saw the gold myself."

Gold? Jacob wondered how they had found gold here.

"Bloody natives," one man grumbled. "Burying gold in a bleedin' cave. What's the point of it? Well, get to work. I want to see it."

Jacob peeled a branch out of the way of his face and saw a group of men entering the cave. They didn't look friendly. The guns they were carrying and their general unkempt appearance, added to their talk of hidden gold, made them dangerous. They were not the sort of men Jacob could ask for help.

He slowly backed away, but not before he saw one man emerge from the cave carrying a crate. A dozen golden objects—from plates and cups to other unidentifiable items—were visible as they jutted out of the top of the wooden crate. The man set the crate down nearby, and when he left, Jacob crept closer and grasped the nearest object he could find and ducked back into the shelter of the bushes and examined it. It was an uncut diamond as big as his fist.

Good God.

Whoever these men were, they had stumbled upon an archaeological find of great importance, and they were looting it dry. The items they were stealing belonged with the descendants of the people who had put them there or, if such people no longer existed, in a museum.

I should leave now, Jacob's inner voice warned him. But the thought of such injustice . . . no. He had to leave. He couldn't put his wife and child at risk. Not for this. He was about to put the diamond back into the crate when he felt it go warm beneath his palm, and a strange humming filled his head. Flashes of light, whispering . . . voices he couldn't quite understand, but he sensed what they wanted.

Keep the diamond. Run now!

He sank back into the foliage, tucked the diamond in

a pocket of his cargo pants, and turned to run, only to barrel straight into a man. They both stumbled back. Jacob saw the man loosely clutching a rifle, and he acted fast. He threw a punch that would have made his boxing days at Cambridge look tame. The man hit the ground, out cold, and thankfully not having attracted any attention.

Jacob shook out his fist, stretching his fingers before he leapt over the fallen body and started to run. Once that man woke up, he would tell the others to come after him. Jacob had to get to Amelia and Thorne.

Jacob had gotten a quarter of a mile away when he heard faint shouts behind him. He picked up his pace. Above him, birds were chattering madly and monkeys screamed in warning. It was like the entire jungle was crying out that danger was coming.

He reached the plane and burst inside. "Amelia, grab Thorne! We have to get out of here!"

His wife grabbed their child. Jacob threw the remaining protein bars and water tablets in a bag and slung it over his shoulder. They had made it a hundred yards from the plane when they stumbled right into the path of a silverback gorilla. It thumped its chest with its fists, making a loud *pok—pok—pok* sound as it snarled and charged them.

Jacob shoved his wife behind him and bowed his head.

"Don't look at it. Keep your gaze down," he warned Amelia.

She covered Thorne's head with one hand as they backed up. The male gorilla advanced a few more paces. Jacob's breath came fast as he tried to think and remain calm. The gorilla was pushing them back toward the plane—back toward the gold thieves. He reached a hand behind him, and Amelia laced her fingers in his in silent support.

Suddenly the gorilla's attention lifted above them to something behind them. His lips curled back in a fresh snarl, and he started to charge at whatever he'd seen behind them.

A volley of bullets struck the animal's chest. Blood misted in the air, and the beast collapsed dead at Jacob's feet.

"No!" Despite their current peril, his heart ached for the gorilla's life. With horrifying dread, he and Amelia turned around to face the true danger of the jungle.

"Jacob," Amelia whispered, her hand still in his and her other arm holding their child to her chest.

They faced the group of armed men. A white man, young, possibly twenty or so, seemed to be the one in charge. His pale-blue eyes were so cold that they made Jacob shiver. Jacob knew that he and his family were not going to survive. There was no mercy in those eyes, only cold calculation.

"Please," Jacob said. "Please leave us alone. We won't

tell anyone anything." He moved protectively in front of Amelia and his child. He would, without hesitation or thought, give his last breath to protect them.

"How did you get this deep into the forest?" the young man asked. "The tours don't come this far east."

"Our plane crashed. We were headed for the airfield near the forest guide station." Jacob nodded toward the direction they'd come from.

The man jerked his gun at them. "Show me."

Jacob took Thorne into his arms, and Amelia stuck close to him as they walked back to the crash site. He and his family stood with the Cessna at their backs as the armed men conversed in hushed tones.

"Amelia, we aren't getting out of this alive." He shot her a quick glance before facing the men again.

"Why can't they just let us go?" she asked.

"Because I saw the gold and diamonds they were looting from a cave." He caught her gaze and put a hand lightly, almost casually on the slight bulge of his pocket where he had the diamond.

"Gold?" she echoed. "All of *this* is for gold and diamonds?"

The greed of men ran deep, like the fissures of rocks that exposed the veins of the gold they coveted so badly. And with every ounce of greed, twice the blood would be spilled. Jacob knew better than to bargain with men like these.

The thieves faced them again. The youngest one, the one with the cold eyes, raised his gun at Jacob.

"We've had a little vote. You aren't worth leaving alive." That was Jacob's only warning before the gun fired.

"Jacob!" Amelia cried out.

The bullet tore through his chest. He reached up slowly and touched the wound as his blood bubbled over his hand. Amelia's voice was distant to his ears now as he fell back against the side of the plane and sank to his knees.

Above him, the exotic birds shrieked a warning that came too late. He choked. The sense of drowning was so frightening, yet he couldn't move, couldn't speak. His vision paled at the edges rather than darkened, as though he was slowly being surrounded by a light, soothing mist. Dimly, he wondered if that was why a person's eyes clouded. It was like death stole over them like an inescapable fog.

It was so hard to think now. He clutched at the last few seconds of his life, and his mind drifted to thoughts of autumn leaves caught upon the wind, carried to places far and away.

AMELIA SHOVED THORNE BEHIND HER. THE CHILD WAS stiff and silent with fear. Jacob lay motionless a few feet away. The light in his eyes guttered like a candle in a mighty wind and finally went out. She had no time to grieve—her maternal instincts overrode all else.

"Please, we won't tell anyone. My son's only three. I need to take care of him." Thorne curled one arm around her leg, holding on for his tiny life.

"It's nothing personal. No loose ends."

"Please don't. Not my baby!"

The man almost smiled. "Don't worry, love. I don't kill children."

The man with blue eyes raised his gun again, and Amelia stared him down, defiant to the last as he fired. She collapsed to the ground, Thorne hugging her arm, sniffling as he tried to stay quiet.

"Please don't. Not my baby . . ." She tried with her dying breath to shelter Thorne at her side. It was so hard to breathe. So very hard . . .

"A mother's love—how touching," the man mused thoughtfully as he gazed down at the child. He met Thorne's gaze, and then looked toward Jacob's body. "Search his pockets. I don't want to leave anything someone could use to identify him."

One man searched Jacob's pockets and held up the fat uncut diamond. The man with blue eyes holstered his gun and took the diamond, holding it up with a possessive gleam darkening his eyes.

"Put their bodies inside the plane. I don't want anyone to think they survived the crash, assuming anyone even finds the wreck." He walked away, and the remaining men came toward Jacob.

"What about him?" one of his men asked and nodded at the toddler.

The man with the blue eyes turned back. "He is not to be harmed. Put him in the plane with his parents. I don't kill children, but he'll die out here soon enough. Let nature run its course." Amelia was breathing shallowly now, her limbs cold and numb.

"Don't touch . . . him!" she gasped, choking on her own blood as the men lifted up her beloved husband. "Don't . . ."

Then they came for her. She was already slipping away. Such a funny thing, dying. Once the pain faded, all that was left was quiet silence, like falling asleep on a sunny Saturday afternoon. But it wasn't easy, letting go—not when she left her child behind.

ADROA OKELLO HELD HIS RIFLE LOOSELY, A CANVAS bag of gold slung over one shoulder as he stood inside the crashed plane. Others had carried the bodies in and set them in the chairs. But the boy, the helpless child, wouldn't be parted from his mother. He sat curled on her lap, one hand resting on her lifeless arm, his body trembling as he murmured, asking her to wake up over and over.

Adroa wanted to help the boy. He was no killer, but he'd been paid good money by his boss, the Englishman called Archibald Holt, but who he called Death Eyes in Swahili when he was out of hearing. Adroa had a wife and his own children to feed and he couldn't risk crossing Holt.

The child sniffled, his vivid dark-blue eyes so wide and full of tears that Adroa could not bear it. He was the last of Holt's men inside the plane now. No one would see what he was about to do. He swung the canvas bag off his shoulder and removed one of the gold trinkets they'd stolen from the cave—a gold circlet of leaves like a crown. He held it out to the child. Holt would never know a piece like this had gone missing. And perhaps the gold would distract the child for a little while.

"Be good now," he told the little boy in English and patted the child's silky dark hair. "Stay inside, you hear? Someone will come for you." He didn't want to lie, but what else could he do? Save the boy, and Death Eyes would kill him. Kill the boy, and Death Eyes would kill him.

The boy gazed up at Adroa mutely, his tiny fingers curling around the leafy golden crown. A sudden eerie feeling stole through Adroa. He felt the presence of his ancestors in the shafts of light penetrating the canopy above. Many thousands of years ago, his people had lived in this jungle. They'd built great cities among the trees, and the cave had held their sacred treasure. All of that had been a myth to Adroa until he'd set foot in the cave with Holt and the others a few weeks ago. The glint of gold beneath their pale flashlight beams had almost blinded him. And he'd sensed the anger of the ancient ones in the cave, felt their righteous fury deep within his blood and bones. But they were dead, dead and gone, and had no use for treasure now.

Perhaps it was his imagination, or perhaps it wasn't, but he was sure that he heard a whispered warning among the trees as he left the crashed plane. The whispers murmured that a ghost would rise, crowned in gold, a lord of the jungle returning to avenge his family.

Adroa stumbled back and raced into the jungle to catch up with Holt and the others. He tried to banish the image of that child from his mind, but he knew it would haunt him for the rest of his life.

2

Half a mile away from where the Haywoods' plane had crashed, a band of gorillas paused at the rush of strange noises in the distance. The rapid sounds were harsh and violent to their ears. Their leader, the silverback Mukisa, had been far ahead of them, scouting the unfamiliar area to ensure their safety. But Mukisa had not returned.

Keza, a young adult female, carried her new infant Akika, one of Mukisa's children, in one arm as she followed the others, trailing Mukisa's scent.

The smell of blood now drifted to them on the wind, and the band grew agitated. Keza held her child tight, ready to run or climb to protect her baby. They continued to track the scent deep into the jungle until they came upon Mukisa's body. He lay facedown, one black palm reaching out in the dirt.

Keza was the only one brave enough to approach her mate's body. She touched his fingers, feeling the coldness, the unnatural stiffness already settling into him. She prodded at his shoulder next, but she knew, as all animals did, that her mate was gone. Their leader was dead.

Sunya, one of Mukisa's younger sons, came forward and grunted softly, declaring himself the new dominant male. He faced no opposition. He led them forward, in the direction Mukisa had been taking to reach the river, where they could find water.

Strange new smells filled Keza's senses—an animal she did not recognize, along with an acrid burning scent that left her jittery and anxious for the safety of her infant, Akika. They soon entered a clearing where a great white shape lay in the underbrush.

A sharp cry came from within the white mass. Most of the gorillas stepped back, pressing their knuckles hard against the ground, ready for an attack. The cry came again, and something deep in Keza's breast tightened. This was the cry of a child. A cry for help. Her mothering instincts were strong with her first child, and she would respond to any call in need. She approached the white shape alone, still cradling her sweet Akika to her chest. When the cry came again, Keza pushed her way carefully into the dark hole.

Her eyes adjusted to the dim light, and she halted as her nose picked up the scent of death again, and that strange animal smell she didn't recognize. She moved closer. It was a sound of distress, not unlike her own babe's feeble cries.

A white-faced creature was looking at her, its eyes blue like the sky. Keza tilted her head, puzzled. She had never seen a creature like this. It had no hair covering its body, just some on the top of its head. The babe held out something that glinted in the dying light, but that object held no interest to Keza. She hooted softly at the baby creature and reached a finger toward it.

The child dropped the shiny object and curled tiny fingers around her thick black digit. In that instant, Keza bonded with the strange child. She reached for him, curving her other arm around his small body, and nestled him beside her little Akika. The child shifted, sniffled, and then grew quiet. She could hear his belly growl with hunger.

Sunya might not wish for this infant to stay in their band since he was not Sunya's child, but she was older than Sunya and fierce with a mother's love. She would kill him if he tried to harm either of her sons. Even across species, a mother and child could love without question. There were many harsh rules that governed Keza's world, but one ruled above all, and that was a mother's love.

THORNE CLUNG TO THE MOTHER GORILLA, HIS BELLY growling. He didn't understand why Mummy and Daddy did not wake up, no matter how much he asked them to or cried. But the black beast from his favorite book had answered his cries.

G. Gorilla.

The gorilla had crept toward him, and he'd stopped crying. He nuzzled his face against her dark bristly hair and gazed wide-eyed at the baby gorilla next to him. The baby's reddish-brown eyes were wide as he gazed back at Thorne.

As Thorne was carried into the jungle, his ears took in the rustle of leaves and the buzz of insects, the exotic sound of birds and monkeys. The blend of sounds turned into a gentle symphony that lulled him to sleep between the warmth of Keza's chest and the humid jungle air.

The band of gorillas stopped after several hours and settled in a safe, dense spot to feed and rest. Mist rolled in around them, thick and cooling to the skin. Thorne was kept within reach of Keza, who set Akika down beside him.

The little human boy watched the gorilla who had carried him to safety, her black and silver fur blending to a burnished bronze at the top of her head. In that moment she was beautiful to him, more beautiful than anything he'd ever seen before.

She was his mother now; he understood a mother's

caring touch as she brushed her fingers over his head, and his tiny heart filled with infinite love for her.

KEZA PUZZLED OVER HER NEW CHILD'S TINY FINGERS, similar yet not quite the same as Akika's. She ruffled a hand over the dark hair on his head. It was soft, far softer than her own. She plucked gently at his ears, checking for mites. He made a gurgling noise, baring his teeth, but it didn't seem threatening to her.

She curled her lips back, showing her own sharp white teeth, and he clapped his tiny hands together. The little smacking sound was odd. Keza wondered if he was trying to show his strength at so young an age. She curled her fist and gave a powerful smack to her chest. The noise startled the child, and he grew still. But after a moment, he curled his own fist and slapped it against himself in imitation. Keza hooted in approval. He learned quickly. That was good. The jungle held many dangers, and the quicker this hairless ape could learn, the safer he would be.

The other gorillas in the band warily watched the young child. Sunya snorted and bared his teeth, but one quelling look from Keza and he came no closer toward them.

"I'm Thorne." The child spoke with a strange tongue. She grunted at him.

He tapped his chest. "Thorne." Then he climbed up her legs and perched on her lap and tapped her chest, gazing deeply into her eyes as though waiting for her to respond. She seemed to understand that he wished to know her name.

"Keza." She spoke in her own language, and he repeated the sound. Then he gently placed a hand on Akika's tiny arm, his questioning eyes so full of yearning that Keza became spellbound by him.

"Akika . . . brother . . . friend." She spoke to him in her tongue, and he replied, imitating her. Though their sounds were merely a pleasant noise to Thorne at first, the thoughts behind those noises grew ever clearer. In time he would learn their language more clearly than the one he had been born into.

He was quick to learn a dozen words that first day. She taught him which plants to eat, like stems, bamboo shoots, and fruits. He favored fruits the most, and she let him eat those. At first he was not strong enough to hold on to her back like Akika, but after a few weeks he could curl an arm around her neck and hold on just as well as her other son.

As the days passed, Keza settled into her life as a mother to her two children. The band of twelve gorillas she lived with were always tolerant, and often indulgent to both Akika and Thorne.

It soon became clear that Thorne had deft control of his hands and could peel bark on trees and could climb with the ease of the younger apes. He was slow to grow and did not prefer to walk on his knuckles, but Keza let him do as he wished. She saw in her own way as he grew stronger that his balance was better when he was upright. Every now and then Keza would walk upright with him, holding Thorne's tiny hand in her right and Akika's hand in her left.

Joy filled her whenever she saw her children playing together, wrestling and growling. She hooted and huffed in encouragement. Akika, the child of her body, and Thorne, the child of her heart. She could not be happier.

When Akika was nearly a year old, he fell climbing and a nasty set of spines from a bush below were embedded in his arm. Keza could not pull them free. But Thorne, with his slender fingers, stroked his knuckles over Akika's face and head in a gentle, soothing motion before he began to ease the spines from the distressed gorilla.

Akika watched his pale-skinned brother with soft, loving eyes, and Thorne bared his teeth in the way that Keza now understood was not a threat, but his way of showing joy. Keza knew she had made a good decision taking the hairless ape into her arms that day, and her love for him became infinite.

THIRTEEN YEARS LATER

Thorne stood at the edge of the still pool that fed into a small waterfall below. His family drank handfuls of water hesitantly at the edge. Gorillas could not swim easily and kept well away from it for fear of drowning, or the other dangers that might lurk within it. But Thorne did not fear the water. He was drawn to it, fixated by the way the canopy of moss-covered trees reflected perfectly in its glassy surface.

He crept up to the shore of the pool and peered into the water, glimpsing his face reflected back at him. This was not the first time he had looked into the water, but it was the first time he truly noticed how different he looked compared to his family.

Thorne's face was narrow, with a thinner mouth, and his eyes were the color of an evening sky. A scruffy layer of dark-brown hair grew around his jaw and his loins but not over the rest of his body. His limbs were sleek, his muscles defined and yet so different in so many ways from his brother.

Thorne studied the different shape of his fingers compared to Akika's. Even his feet were different. He'd never been able to grasp things with his toes as gracefully as his brother could. He'd been too afraid and ashamed to compare his body to the others. He knew what they called him in their grunts and huffs. *The deformed hairless ape.*

Perhaps he was not deformed after all. Perhaps he was formed as he should be, and he simply was not an ape? The idea, once formed within him, gave him a greater curiosity, a need for answers. Some nights when he lay alone, a little way from the other gorillas as they slept, he let his mind wander, and strange dreams came in that moment just between sleep and waking. Dreams of apes who looked like him, their voices soft, full of love . . . and other strange dreams of a world that in this lush jungle land seemed impossible.

Perhaps they were dreams born of fevered nights when the humidity threatened to choke him and he sought refuge high in the treetops, thrusting his head above the canopy to feel the wind on his face.

One truth that always came back to him, no matter how much it hurt him to think about it, was that he had not always been a gorilla. Once, long ago, he had been something, *someone* else.

Thorne touched the surface of the water, creating ripples that distorted his image in the pool. A quivering took hold of him as for the first time in his young life he accepted that he was truly *not* like his family.

G. Gorilla . . . A soft voice spoke to him through the mists of time. The forest around him almost seemed to hum in response.

He knew that he was something else. But what? Thorne's heart grew heavy with shame at not being Akika's true brother, but there was a glimmer of curiosity that defined his species—though he did not yet know he belonged to that species.

Thorne stared at the surface of the water.

If he was not a gorilla, then perhaps he could swim the way he'd seen the leopards do when they crossed rivers and lakes. They moved slowly, sleekly through the water, pawing their front legs in forward circular motions and kicking with their back legs. Thorne was not as big or as heavy as his kin, so perhaps he could do the same? He'd noticed he had a different mobility in his body, so it was entirely possible that he was capable of swimming. There was only one way to find out.

He flung himself recklessly into the pool. Keza's scream of terror was muted as Thorne sank beneath the surface. He opened his eyes, seeing the murky depths of the watery world around him. His bare feet touched the bottom of the pool. He coiled himself tight and pushed up until he surged into the light and gasped sweet air. He moved his arms, testing their effectiveness, and soon he was pulling himself toward the shore, where his mother was pacing and wailing in panic.

Thorne, a little weary after such a new activity, crawled out of the water, breathing deeply. Keza rushed to him, balled a fist, and thumped his side with one hand, her touch gentle even as she reprimanded his behavior. Then she grasped his head and pulled him around, looking him over for injury.

He hooted in reassurance at his mother and grasped her large solid hands with his own, holding them to his skin. Gorillas thrived on physical touch, they lived for contact with one another, and Thorne was no different. He craved his mother's brushing caresses over his hair and the light thumps of her loosely balled fist against his chest in greeting.

He glanced back once more at the pool, and a deep longing for more answers and more truths filled him. But he would have to return when his mother was not there to fuss over him.

The band finished drinking and worked their way into a group of fruit trees to eat their evening meal and rest. Thorne climbed the nearest mango tree; he alone among his family was still the most comfortable at such an activity. Once gorillas aged, they stayed closer to the ground.

Thorne plucked some ripe-smelling fruit from a tree and tossed them down to the gorillas below, where they divided the food. But he did not join them. He clutched a pair of mangoes in his hand and climbed higher in a hagenia tree until he leaned against the thin branches that formed the canopy. He pushed his head through the spreading branches and looked out over the tops of the forest that stretched for hundreds of miles around. Above him the sky was inky black, with a vibrant spread of glittering stars.

Stars . . . He knew what they were. Well, not exactly, but he knew the word. *Stars.* The word felt different on his tongue. It was not from the language of the birds, the leopards, or the gorillas. It was a language that was softer, clearer, yet just as beautiful as the languages he spoke now with love in his heart. The word *stars* remained inside him like a well-kept secret, spreading a warmth he could not explain as he ate his fruit and gazed upon the expanse far above him. There were feelings, not quite memories, that churned within him, calling in soft whispers.

Remember who you are. Remember . . .

THOUSANDS OF MILES AWAY

Cameron Haywood stood at the window of his study in Somerset Hall, the ancestral home of the earldom of Somerset in England. He held a glass of scotch and gazed upon the same stars, though muted somewhat by the distant city lights.

Thirteen years. Had it really been that long since his older brother, Jacob, had been lost in the Ugandan forest with his wife and child? It felt like a lifetime ago. He had never wanted to become the Earl of Somerset. He would give *everything* to have his family back.

Thirteen years ago, he had done all that he could to find his brother. He had sent search parties, tried to locate the plane, and bribed every official for any information. He'd flown there a dozen times, scouring the impenetrable forest, even calling the names of his loved ones until he lost his voice.

Cameron went to his desk, turning his back to the stars. The sounds of a party going on in his house downstairs gave him no joy at the prospect of mingling among the powerful men and women of England. Today would have been his nephew's sixteenth birthday.

"Cameron." His wife, Isabelle, stuck her head into his office. "Our guests are waiting. Duty calls, I'm afraid. Lofty is entertaining everyone with tales, but you know he can't do that forever. Well, he can, actually, but we shouldn't let him." Isabelle almost smiled. Jordie Lofthouse had been the only one who could make Cameron or Isabelle smile in all these years.

"I'm coming, darling," he sighed. He touched the faces of Jacob, Amelia, and little Thorne in a framed photo on his desk before he went out to meet his wife.

"You look pale," Isabelle murmured in concern. She looked up at him with those lovely gray eyes of hers, eyes that had bewitched him long before Jacob's death. Isabelle had married him before he knew his life would change forever. She hadn't wanted their sudden change in circumstances any more than he had. They'd both wanted to be free, to live a life without the constraints of the titles that had been thrust upon them.

"It's Thorne's birthday today. He would have been sixteen." Cameron rubbed his eyes with his thumb and forefinger. Isabelle brushed his dark hair back from his face with her fingers.

"I know. I remembered this morning. Why don't I

send everyone away and we can have a quiet night together by the fire?"

He almost chuckled. "Banish the peers of the realm from the halls of Somerset? As tempting as it sounds, I don't think that's a good idea." He pressed a kiss to her temple. "I shall just put on a brave face and get on with the night. It won't be the first time."

Cameron and his wife descended the grand staircase into the waiting crowd below with diplomatic smiles. But his heart, at least part of it, still searched for answers in the dark heart of the jungle in Africa.

Four years later

Thorne heard the creatures long before he saw them. Three animals stumbling through the underbrush of the forest. Their disregard for leaving evidence of their passage left an easy trail to follow. The sounds they made, a unique mix of complex utterances, were musical, like birdsong rather than the deep vocal chorus-like language of the gorillas.

Curious, he crept along the massive stretching branches of the trees above these creatures as he sought a clearer look. They continued to vocalize in their nonsense language as they stopped and sat down at the base of the trees.

He slid lower, using thick vines to support his body

as he tried to see their faces. They wore strange animal skins, very different from the kob deer pelt that covered Thorne's vulnerable parts.

His gorilla family wore no such skins. Their bodies were more compact, and their posture lent them far more natural protection. Thorne felt exposed and vulnerable, so after killing his first deer, he began to wear animal skins as a way to protect himself. He wasn't quite sure how he'd come by the idea—except perhaps to say he'd dreamed it. Visions of animals like him wearing gleaming pieces of something on their necks and arms. They'd showed him in wild, quick flashes in these dreams how to hunt deer, how to use the shale rocks to skin them. He'd been ashamed to hunt in front of the gorillas, who did not eat deer, so he had gone much deeper into the forest to hunt.

He'd refined his technique now to have a dried bit of leather from the deer with which to fashion himself a way to tie the pelt tight around his waist without worry of it falling off while he swung from vines and climbed.

The creatures he stalked now were almost fully covered in such skins.

One of the creatures removed a covering from his head, and Thorne's mouth parted in shock. These animals were like him, yet not. Their skin was dark, like the rich bark of a mahogany tree and just like the creatures in his dreams who'd taught him how to survive. Their hands and limbs were not formed like the gorillas'.

They were exactly like Thorne's. For the first time in seventeen years, he was staring at a face like his own.

"Gorilla."

The word was the only one that he recognized in the stream of sounds pouring from their lips as they spoke to one another.

A sudden, painful flash of memory, an image of a gorilla upon wood. No, not wood—*paper*.

A face like his gazed down at him, a female with a bright smile and golden hair . . . smiles . . . How had he forgotten what a smile was?

His lips curved into a grin, and he huffed excitedly until he saw one of the creatures lift a long brown stick, pointing it at a small monkey perched on a tree branch not far from Thorne.

The creature held the stick close to his face, and there was a violent *bang!* Thorne was so startled that he lost his grip on the vines and plummeted to the forest floor. He landed catlike on the ground, not ten feet from the creatures. One of them screamed and pointed at him. The male who held the loud stick turned it on Thorne, hollering. There was another deafening *bang!*

Pain knifed through Thorne's arm, and he howled with rage as he stood to his full height. He curled his fists and beat savagely on his chest, bearing his teeth as he'd seen Sunya do a thousand times before. The creatures shouted back, but fear widened their eyes and they scrambled away. In their haste to flee, one tripped, his head hitting the base of a knotted tree as the others left him behind.

Thorne stopped a short distance from the body and crouched, studying him. The creature had different feet than him, and his face held no hair along his jaw and mouth like Thorne. He reached out, his fingers touching the male's face. His skin appeared smooth, but beneath his fingertips, Thorne felt the bristle of hair, much like his had felt when he'd been younger. Despite his size, perhaps he was not yet grown?

Suddenly the male's eyes snapped open, and he stared in horror at Thorne.

"Gorilla." Thorne repeated the word, finding it easier to say than he expected. He tapped his own chest and repeated. "Gorilla."

"What?" the man said. "No. Not gorilla."

Not. That word Thorne recognized too.

The male looked him over, as amazed by Thorne as Thorne was by him. Eventually he nodded and tapped his chest.

"Human," the male said. "Man."

Thorne stared at him, bewildered as the tongue that he had been born to speak came back to him in hazy flashes.

"Boy," he said.

B is for boy. You're a boy, Thorne. A female's face flashed in his mind, the woman he'd glimpsed in his mind with sunlight-gold hair who smiled.

"G is for gorilla." Thorne whispered the words, his voice rasping. He had not used his vocal cords like this in years. It almost hurt to speak.

"You speak English?"

"Ing-leesh?" Thorne murmured the familiar word.

"Yes, English," the male said with excitement, smiling.

"Yes," Thorne echoed. He pressed his calloused palm on the man's chest, their eyes locked on each other. Around them the jungle murmured softly, and Thorne smiled as he looked at the man.

"Friend?" Thorne asked. There was something about the man's face, a kindness and quick intelligence in his eyes that made Thorne trust him.

The man nodded, now solemn. "Friend."

3

UGANDA—PRESENT DAY

Eden Matthews grinned at the people nearest her as she got in line with a small group of visitors at Bwindi Impenetrable Forest National Park. For $600 and a park entry fee, she was about to have the experience of a lifetime, hiking her way deep into the mountainous terrain of the jungle to see the mountain gorillas.

At twenty-four, she was one of the youngest photographers to have made the journey for *National Park* magazine. For as long as she could remember, she'd been obsessed with conservation. Her parents had taken her to zoos and aquariums when she was a child, and seeing those animals, knowing their natural habitats were being destroyed, had changed her life.

She swung her camera bag over her shoulder and tightened the elastic hair tie holding her blonde hair out of her face. She had been warned more than once about the humidity and the steepness of the climb she was about to make, but it would all be worth it.

"Everyone, stay close, please," one of the guides called out. "We are going to start the hike now. Stay in pairs if you can, and please watch the forest floor. Beauty may be above you, but danger will be below you."

"Goodness, that sounds ominous, doesn't it, Harold?" one of the older women asked her husband.

"He's probably talking about snakes, Mags." Harold put an arm around his wife's shoulders. "They have those snakes here that if they bite you, you can take ten steps before you keel over dead."

Mags whipped her head up to look at him in shock.

Eden bit her lip, trying not to laugh. It was clear Harold was teasing, but his wife seemed too anxious to realize that.

"We'll be fine," Eden told her. "Just watch where you walk. I'm Eden Matthews."

"Maggie Fitzpatrick. This is my husband, Harold. Are you from the States?"

Eden smiled. "From Arkansas. You?"

"Phoenix." Maggie plucked at her soaked tank top. "I'm used to the heat, but not so much the humidity."

"Arkansas is humid, but nothing like this." Eden pulled out a cute bright-red elastic headband and slid it on the top part of her forehead to catch sweat.

"Follow me," the guide at the front called out. The

second guide fell in behind the line of tourists as they started into the jungle.

As Eden and the others began their trek, a light rain began to fall. Her hair and clothes were soon soaked despite her rain slicker because of the humidity and sweat. She wore a long-sleeved T-shirt and hiking shorts and boots with tall socks past her ankles to protect her legs. The smell of bug spray and sweat seemed to follow them wherever they went. The light rain turned into a heavy downpour only a few minutes later.

"Welcome to the jungle!" one of the younger men ahead called back. Everyone laughed, and the tense excitement of the moment eased a bit.

"What made you come here, honey?" Maggie asked as they kept pace with each other. Harold was ahead of them, carefully pushing aside branches for them.

"I'm a photojournalist for *National Park* magazine." She paused, thinking over the real answer. "But honestly, I am just passionate about the jungle and conservation. Gorillas have been one of my favorite animals since I was a kid."

It was hard to put into words what it was that Africa made her feel. The dark jungles, the sun-streaked savannas, and the majesty of a continent that refused to yield to human civilization. It called to something ancient inside Eden. Uganda was called the Pearl of Africa because of its lush jungles, which sheltered the wild gorilla population. The habitat was so ancient it had survived the last ice age intact, while the other forests of Africa had perished.

Their path toward the mountains continued, steep and slippery. Eden had been warned that finding the gorillas could take anywhere from thirty minutes to five hours. The jungle thickened after the second hour, forcing everyone to resume their single-file marching order. The guides and gorilla trackers cleared the path ahead as best they could with machetes. The higher they climbed, the heavier Eden's breathing became, and her thighs grew tight and strained. She turned to hold out a hand to Maggie and Harold on the rougher parts of the ascent.

"Jesus, the kids won't believe we did this," Harold laughed, catching his breath.

Eden gripped Harold's palm as he hoisted himself past a steep branch. "You have kids?"

"A son and a daughter. Both in their thirties. They bought us this trip since they knew Mags liked that Dian Fossey book, *Gorillas in the Mist*."

"I love that book too." Eden's heart twinged when she thought of the conservationist Dian Fossey, who had been brutally murdered in the mountains. Wherever there were people determined to save something, it seemed there were even more ready to kill or destroy it for a profit.

The plant life around the tourists changed along with the elevation. Bamboo shot up in thick, towering stalks all around them, forcing them to squeeze between the tall stems. After another hour, the forest changed around them again. They entered the Hagenia Zone, named for the spectacular moss-covered trees that gave the jungle an enchanted feel. An ancient magic seemed to hang in the air, mixing with the wild birds' chorusing. The branches above them were thicker than her body and stretched twenty or thirty feet on either side. It was easy to see how monkeys could jump between the trees here.

The rain suddenly stopped, yet you wouldn't know it from the way the water continued to drip off the trees around them, the waxy emerald leaves of the plant life gleaming in the intermittent shafts of light slicing through the canopy. Eden and the others removed their rain slickers. She crushed hers into a ball and stuffed it back into its pouch before tucking it into her backpack.

The strong smell of damp and decaying vegetation overpowered her senses, masking the other aromas. Misty clouds hung low around the distant peaks and filled the valleys between the mountains ahead. Mist poured down toward their group, making the ground almost invisible. Eden tripped over a large root, but she caught herself and continued on. Maggie tripped behind her in the exact same spot, cursing the root as Harold helped her up.

"Everyone drop your bags, get your cameras out, and

follow me," the guide at the front announced quietly. "The gorillas are just up ahead."

Eden held her breath as they moved together. Within a minute, the mist revealed a band of twelve gorillas. A young juvenile nearest them was lying back against the roots of a tree, a piece of fruit held lazily in one hand as he gazed at the intruders.

Eden was transfixed by the sight. His reddish-brown eyes were calm, a hint of caution mixed with curiosity. He was probably used to seeing humans, but no one here except the guides and trackers had ever had the chance to see a gorilla in the wild before. A gorilla shrouded in mist.

She raised her camera and framed the juvenile in her sights and snapped a dozen photos. The gorillas continued to eat and socialize. The juveniles wrestled, and a few of the mothers held tiny infants to their breasts.

It was moving to see how these creatures were like humans in so many ways, that they cared for and nursed their young, that their children played and the adults touched each other with gentle affection. She watched two mothers with infants who stood upright and toddled a little farther away, but it was the way one mother put her hand on the shoulder of the other, like friends, that stole Eden's breath. She took a dozen pictures of that moment alone.

The tour group had an hour to watch. When they

had only ten minutes left, the gorillas seemed to sense they were free to move, and as though summoned by the magic of another realm, they blended back into the jungle as silently as they had appeared.

"My God," a woman whispered to Eden and the others. "Did you see them? They were just like us."

"Did you see their hands? They were huge." Another man held up his own hand, looking at it as he recalled the size of the hands of the dominant silverback who had prowled, not threateningly, but protectively, around the other gorillas.

"All right, everyone, we're going to have a quick lunch and then head back down. Be sure to have your rain gear ready," one of the guides warned.

Eden crouched down by a tree and unzipped her bag, but she paused when she sensed movement in the jungle near where the gorillas had gone. She got her camera ready again and waited, bringing the rustling plants into focus. But the face that emerged was not a gorilla, but a man. A man with a grizzled beard and flat eyes. He scanned the forest and spotted her, suddenly smiling.

Then came the screams, the shouts, the guns being fired in the air.

Poachers. Poachers had been tracking the gorillas.

Eden huddled next to Maggie and Harold as they were shoved into a jumbled group. They were forced to walk deeper into the jungle, well beyond the boundaries where any guides or trackers would come looking for them.

"Oh God, Harold," Maggie whispered.

Her husband put an arm around her shoulders. Eden tried not to think about where they were headed or why and instead focused on anything that might help them find a way to safety. All their bags had been left behind, but Eden still had her camera bag slung across her chest.

"Here's good, Cash," one of the poachers said.

"It'll do," Cash said. His British accent was rough, uncultured. "Line 'em up," Cash ordered, and the tourists, including Eden, were all pulled into a line.

"On your knees!" one of the men shouted, and they started shoving people down. Eden sank to her knees on the muddy forest floor. Her heart raced as the man called Cash raised his gun and pointed it right at her head.

No one was going to save her, or the others. They were going to die like Dian Fossey and all the others who had given their lives to protect the wilds of Africa.

LOUNGING ON THE LIMB OF A TREE, THORNE HEARD his gorilla family send a warning howl in the distance. They were a mile away, but the sound carried. Birds screamed in response, and Thorne leapt to his feet, listening for any hint of what had caused the commotion.

"*Danger, danger,*" the animals of the forest warned him, but Thorne never let danger hold him back. He raced swift-footed along the tree branches until he saw a sturdy vine and in one flying leap grasped it and swung. It had been this way for many years. When danger threatened his family, he was the one who faced it. Sunya and the other males viewed him as weak, and Thorne had lived his entire life proving to them he was not. Now swinging headlong into danger was but second nature to him.

Moving through the jungle, vine to branch, branch to vine, he reached the source of the disturbance in a mere few minutes. He was a hundred yards away when the sound of guns went off.

Guns. He hated them.

He had learned from his friend Bwanbale how to speak English and Swahili, and in the last five years he had gained some knowledge of the world beyond his forest. Guns brought pain, suffering, and death to all that he loved in the jungle.

Rage surged through Thorne, roaring like a fire within him as he swung toward the small clearing. Some humans were kneeling on the ground, and others were shooting guns at them. It was easy to see who were the predators and who were the prey as the bodies fell.

Thorne filled his lungs with air and let out a wild roar that echoed across the jungle.

The predator men screamed and ran, but one stayed behind, his gun pointed at the last remaining prey. Thorne launched himself from the nearest tree and tackled him to the ground. They rolled half a dozen feet, and the moment Thorne had his bearings, he gripped the man's neck and snapped it. Then he chased down two other men, killing them and leaving their bodies where they fell. The forest would take care of them.

He returned to the small clearing and crouched behind the survivor, and his breath caught in his throat.

This human was *female*. He had never seen a human female before, at least from what he could remember aside from puzzling dreams of a female who'd held him in her arms and sang to him. He'd refused to come near the part of the forest where Bwanbale had said humans visited. His only experience with other humans had been violent and dangerous, aside from Bwanbale.

But now he wished he had ventured closer to other humans much sooner. This female's hair was the color of sunlight. He ached to touch it. He crept closer, staying crouched lest she attack. Female gorillas would some-times snarl and attack males who crept up on them when they did not wish to mate.

He grunted in the tongue of his gorilla family, hoping to reassure her that he meant no harm. Thorne leaned in, smelling the air just above the back of her neck.

Something about her scent—a mixture of sweat, fear, and fruit—appealed to the deepest male part of him, but he didn't want her to fear him. Her hair, bound up in a strange way, brushed against his face, its silky texture tickling his nose. He reached up. His fingers trembled now when they had never trembled before. Thorne curled his fingers in the sunlight of her hair.

The female gave a soft gasp, almost a sound of distress, and flung herself to the ground. He was so startled by her sudden movement that he leapt around her prone body to see her face. She was in a submissive pose, but he wanted . . . *yearned* to see the face of this female. The one he had saved, the one whose scent called to him like nothing ever had before.

In that moment he was overcome with bone-deep loneliness. He had always been alone. Though Keza and Akika loved him, he knew he was not truly one of them. Now he had a chance to end the ache that had dwelt inside him for years.

She slowly lifted her head to look at him.

He remained hunched, his knuckles pressed into the ground as he studied her eyes, eyes the color of leaves. Her face was delicate, her nose small and curved up slightly. There was a hint of something secret and wonderful in her pale skin and the way the blood tinted it the soft color of ripe fruit.

His heart beat an unsteady rhythm against his chest. Looking upon her filled him with a dozen hungers that he barely understood. Bwanbale had spoken of human mates, of women, but Thorne had not been able to imagine such a female.

This female was *like* him and yet *unlike* him. She was smaller, her body soft and curved as opposed to the hard, angled lines of his own form, yet he found her enticing in a way that made him want to let out a low rumbling growl of pleasure like a jaguar would when filled with contentment.

At the thought of jaguars, he made a chuffing noise as he curled one fist around one of the few human weapons he possessed—a knife, one Bwanbale had given to him. He wasn't sure how to speak to her, because the English he'd been taught seemed to have fled his mind in the presence of this female's beauty.

Thorne balled his fist and pointed an arm toward the dead men and grunted. He wanted her to know she was safe, that he'd killed the predators and now she would not be harmed. The words Bwanbale had taught him still wouldn't come to him.

The female continued to stare, swallowed hard, and then spoke to him.

"Hi."

It was a greeting. He stopped pointing to the dead men.

"Do you understand me?" she asked.

Thorne did understand, yet he was too fascinated by her

soft voice, which was the sweetest birdsong he'd ever heard. It prevented him from responding. He tilted his head to one side and inhaled deeply. He could feel the river mud he'd painted on his face and body a few hours ago drying and growing stiff against his skin. It kept his skin protected when he went into the sunlight and helped him camouflage himself the way other beasts did when they wished to hunt or go undisturbed in the jungle. Was she startled by his appearance? He must look fierce to her—or at least strange.

She got to her feet. "Hello?"

Thorne stood up to his full height. The female did not approach him, but stayed where she was, her eyes lifting from his feet all the way up to his face, her lips parted as she inhaled softly. Then she seemed to recover herself and spoke again.

"*Kiswahili?*"

She spoke Swahili, but his focus was soon diverted. The forest had grown quiet around them again, just as it had when he'd fought the predators. *Something* was out there. It was not safe for his female. Thorne's keen ears heard the jaguar's footfalls, and he issued a warning by throwing his head back and bellowing. He had killed jaguars before, but he would not now, not when he had a female to protect. Caring for others was one of his responsibilities. Yet when he thought of caring for this creature, that duty became a sacred thing. Keza would praise him for it.

"*Unaongea Kiswahili?*" The female asked him if he spoke Swahili.

Thorne cast her a glance before he gave a sharp whistle into the jungle, calling for the birds to be his eyes and warn him if the jaguar came back this way. The birds whistled back, and he faced his female again. There was no time to try to find his tongue to speak. She needed to be taken to safety.

He grabbed her and threw her over his shoulder. Hers was an easy weight. When he'd seen fourteen winters in the jungle, he had been smart enough to battle dominant silverback males who'd tried to chase him away from his mother and brother. He had speed and agility in other ways, and his ingenuity had proved the most useful skill he had in battle against an opponent bigger than him. He had proved to those males then that he could and would fight back. But he'd also grown strong, strong enough to fight almost any beast in the jungle, and where his strength wasn't enough, his cunning was far better.

Those adult gorillas had backed off and let Thorne and Akika as grown males stay in the band when adult males were expected to leave to form their own bands with other female gorillas. By the time he had seen seventeen winters in the jungle, Thorne had killed the jaguar who had stalked his family and attacked the infant of another mother. That beast had been twice the weight of this female.

Thorne ran at a quick pace deeper into the jungle, far away from the areas where the men of Bwanbale's world went. He had his own place, a home he had built that was close to the waterfall and the river. The female would be safe there.

He reached the network of trees that formed his private home, and he set the female on the ground. She rolled to her side and vomited. Thorne's chest ached because he wanted to soothe her, but when animals were sick they often felt weak and did not want to be touched. He didn't wish for her to lash out at him.

When she seemed to have recovered, he held out his hand. She placed her palm in his, and something shot through his body, as though for the first time in his life he was *awake*. Her green eyes met his, and for a second he wanted to speak, wanted to tell her all that lay in his lonely heart, but for the first time since he was a child, he was afraid. What if this beautiful female did not wish to hear the words from his soul? He pushed away the riot of new feelings swirling inside him and pointed to the tree before them, then gestured for her to climb on his back.

"No, no, I'm not—"

He lunged at her, planning to throw her over his shoulder again, but she threw her hands up in submission.

"Okay!" She pointed at his back.

Good, she understood his commands. He faced the

tree, his breath strangely quick for being so still. Her soft hands touched his shoulders, and her legs wrapped around his waist. Excitement burst through him like a sunrise. He wanted her to be in front of him, to feel her body against his, but he could not climb that way. This need to feel her against his body was both strange and exciting.

Thorne used the footholds he had made in the tree and climbed up to the concealed entrance of his home. He moved the branches covering the entrance aside and crawled into the tree house. That was what Bwanbale had called it when Thorne had brought him here. He had marveled at Thorne's series of three structures connected by vines wound carefully around and through wooden planks to make pathways in the air.

Thorne was not sure how he had first envisioned building his home. Perhaps it came from the murky depths of the past he could not remember or the wild and beautiful dreams that came often when he fell into the twilight of sleep. Once he'd learned he could use vines and the pieces of wood from fallen trees, he'd used pieces of broken shale rocks to smooth the fallen wood into flat planks.

He'd shown Bwanbale his home, and the other male had helped him refine the buildings and his technique even further so that his home was hidden from the ground. But from above, it truly was a home in the trees. Bwanbale had left him tools, a machete, a long knife, a short knife, a spear with a sharp arrowhead, and other things that had helped Thorne. In exchange, he'd shown Bwanbale how to hunt and how to find his way through the forest that Bwanbale called *impenetrable*.

He had made a home here. In recent years he had felt the need to be apart, to live away from the gorillas. It wasn't simply because he didn't belong, but it was more the need to feel he could survive alone, define his own space and life apart from his family. The gorillas of his family belonged to the ground, but Thorne did not feel comfortable sleeping below where animals might strike out at him. So he'd built this place, a haven in the trees.

He visited Keza, Akika, and the others often, but he did not worry them with his presence. He longed to explore the jungle more, and he strayed farther and farther north, deep into the mountains and caves where even the gorillas did not tread.

The female took her first tentative steps on the wooden floor. "What is this place?"

Thorne grunted, wanting her to stay in the safe corner. When she didn't immediately understand, he herded her into the spot he wished her to be and she fell back onto her backside and gazed up at him, a hint of fear rolling off her skin.

He had to return to the place with the other humans who were dead so he could search among what they had left behind. If he was to have this female, he needed to prove to her he could provide for her and protect her. Keza had taught him that to love was to care for others. Maybe then this female might consider being his mate.

In the many years of being here, he had never had the chance to mate. It had left him with an undeniable loneliness that had been slowly hollowing his heart from the inside out, but now . . . Now he might have a chance to have someone who belonged to him. He started toward the trapdoor to leave.

She moved toward him. "Wait! Where are you going?"

He bared his teeth and growled. She needed to obey him for her own safety. Bwanbale had warned him that human females could be stubborn. Their gazes locked as he waited to see if she would challenge him again. She stayed put, her green eyes still full of fear and uncertainty. Only when he was certain she would not try to follow him did he slip down the tree and leave.

Thorne raced back to where the attack had happened. As he reached the small clearing, he peered through a tangle of foliage at the bodies still lying upon the ground. He rested his palms on the latticework of vines that ran like pale veins through the vast emerald sea of the trees.

A heavy stillness settled around this place of death. It reminded him of the place where old gods dwelt in the cavern full of fallen stars. Bwanbale often spoke to Thorne during their time together about his gods. The spirits had dwelt in the forest since before the dawn of man. Only Thorne was brave enough to venture into those places. His curiosity drove him to explore that which his animal brethren would not. The quiet cave had called to him, and he'd answered.

In those explorations, Thorne had discovered a cave that held the dust of the gods in the walls, like striated stars shot through with sunlight, and glittery stones that covered the floors in numbers too high to count. The crown of leaves he wore when hunting rested upon his brow now. He believed it to be the crown of one of the gods of the jungle. He had offered it to Bwanbale as a parting gift. Bwanbale had curled his hands around Thorne's, making Thorne clasp the circlet tight.

"This belongs to *you*, Thorne, Lord of the Impene-trable Forest. Wear it with pride. A man like me deserves no crown. I am but a hunter. And even that, I am no more."

Thorne thought of the times Bwanbale came to visit him and the fantastical tales he told of the world beyond. Bwanbale had asked him once, "Where do you come from, my friend? Who are your people?"

But Thorne had no answer. He had no people, not in the way Bwanbale meant.

Yet now he gazed upon the remains of what could be his people. Their deaths filled him with a disquieting sorrow. He was no stranger to death, and he did not fear it. Yet he feared when death came for those he cared about. Each death among his gorilla family tore at Thorne's heart, just as it did with these strangers. Their cold bodies lying still on the forest floor twisted his stomach with dread.

Only after some time had passed did the forest begin to speak again. The songs of waxbills with their chattering and the rasp of crickets as dusk approached. Thorne now moved among the fallen humans, inhaling the stale scent of death until he found an object that smelled like his female. He lifted it carefully to his nose.

It appeared to be made of a strange animal skin that was coarse beneath his fingers. He carried it away and began to hunt for fruit. The best trees were a mile from his home, so it took a little time for him to collect enough fruit for them both. He also had his water skin that Bwanbale had showed him how to make. He would take it to the waterfall and fill it with water for her.

He was halfway back to his home when an idea struck him. He wanted to give his female more than mere food and water. To be her mate, he should give her gifts. He could think of only one place that held things that might interest her. The dark cave of the gods. Thorne moved swiftly, taking the quickest path to the cave, and with his knowledge of the dark, he crept into the black heart of the gods' dwelling.

Deep past the stalagmites and stalactites that had been formed by water dripping inside the dark realm over the eons, Thorne found his way to the chamber of sacred objects. There he searched, fingers touching the objects carefully until he found something that could hang upon her body. A strand of gold that tumbled in snakelike fluidity in his palm and warmed to his touch. It was large enough for him to put over his head and hang from his neck. Satisfied, Thorne finally returned home.

As he lifted the entrance to his house, he spotted her shape in the dim light from the small opening. She was curled up, asleep. He crept silently through the entrance, set her animal skin pouch down next to her, and then removed the necklace from his body and laid it close to her face. He set the fruit down on a large wax leaf and held his breath, waiting for her to wake.

She sighed, soft and sorrowful, one of her hands resting beneath her cheek, fisted as though she had been plagued by awful dreams. But after a moment, the tightness of her features vanished and she relaxed.

Thorne was enchanted by the sight of her. Now that she was still, unafraid, and unaware of his scrutiny, he could study her at his leisure. He counted her lashes and memorized the shape of her nose, her lips, her winged brows that arched above green eyes that were still closed.

It was good he was here. She needed protection. To sleep so deeply and not sense danger or even hear his return? She was helpless.

I will care for you. But he could only think the words. His tongue was still tied by some invisible force, trapped by a foolish fear that he would not be able to communicate with her if he tried to speak.

Thorne nestled in behind her to rest. He kept one ear trained to listen for any sounds of danger, but after a while he calmed enough to relax. He came closer, wishing to hold his future mate. He should have washed himself clean of the mud on his skin. Perhaps she did not fully see that she was the same as him. Tomorrow. Tomorrow he would show her. He would take her to the waterfall and begin his courtship. Until then, he would give her body the comfort of his presence.

He pulled her closer with gentle hands, tucking her into the curve of his own body. She moaned and settled against him, tucking her head under his chin. Warmth swept through Thorne's body, and a sense of contentment he'd not felt since childhood overwhelmed him. His eyes burned as he held his mate in his arms.

You are my future, my mate, my destiny. My everything.

Outside, the jungle plunged into the depths of twilight, its sable mantle lying over the impenetrable forest.

4

S *creams. Gunshots. A mighty roar. Deafening silence.*

Eden jerked awake as the nightmares broke through her sleep. She gasped when she found herself unable to move. Was this another nightmare? She glanced wildly around the room, trying to make sense of where she was, and found herself staring into the brightest blue eyes she had ever seen. The mud-streaked face from her nightmares was real.

She gasped again and tried to pull away. He held tight a moment before loosening his grip, clear disappointment in his eyes.

Eden scrambled back, and something behind her tumbled across the floor. He sat up and moved around her to collect whatever it was she had disrupted. In the gray light of early morning, she saw him put pieces of skinned mango on a leaf that was bigger than his two hands cupped together.

He grunted, chuffed, and even whistled at her as he held out the mangoes. Eden stared at the food, her stomach grumbling on cue at the sight of the fruit. His mouth curved into a smile, and he nodded to her in encouragement. She reached across the space between them and took a mango, trying not to stare at him. Much of the thick mud from earlier had fallen away to expose his body to her view, but his face was still darkened with it, making it hard to fully see his features aside from those wildly blue eyes.

The trauma of yesterday was still in the back of her mind, but she could now focus on her mysterious savior, this wild and strange forest god. And a god he was. There was a mighty strength to his limbs, and he had a noble bearing that held her fascinated—and more than a little frightened. She was helpless against this man. If he desired it, he could take whatever he wished from her. Yet he gazed upon her with gentle eyes and offered her mangoes.

She took another piece of fruit and was floored by the devastating effect his responding smile had on her stomach, which suddenly filled with butterflies.

"Thank you," she said, only she felt silly doing so, since it was obvious he didn't understand her. She bit into the fruit and sighed at the sweet taste. He watched her eat two more pieces before he finally ate one himself. Then he reached for something on the floor and held it out to her.

Midday sunlight caught on the bright gold of a long necklace. It was an ancient-looking necklace with a huge diamond pendant hanging from the center.

"Oh my God . . ."

She was almost afraid to touch it, but he pushed it into her hands before she could refuse him. He curled her fingers around the necklace and patted her closed hands with a tenderness that left her feeling breathless.

"Thank you. It's beautiful." She stared at the necklace, and he watched her expectantly. Eden did the only thing she could think of and put the necklace on. He grunted and smiled, as if satisfied with her reaction, and then he opened the trapdoor in the center of the room. He turned, exposing his back to her, and pointed at himself.

It looked like she was going for another ride. She climbed onto his back, more aware than ever of the heat of his body between her thighs, but the dried mud that coated his body was staining her clothes, and she prayed she could find her way to a river or stream or even a pond to get washed up.

He began the descent, and when their feet touched the ground, he let her off his back. The wild man held out a hand to her, and she took it. It was strange to feel connected to this nameless mystery man, but Eden was beginning to trust him as he led her through the jungle. Besides, what choice did she have?

After about half an hour, at least by Eden's guess, she heard the roar of a waterfall and her heart leapt. She might be able to clean herself off and get something to drink. She glanced back down at herself and cringed at the mud and blood staining her clothes.

The wild man took her straight to a large pool at the base of the waterfall, which poured over a mountainous area nearly two stories tall. The sight was breathtaking. The waterfall was as clear as glass, cascading into a frothy whiteness that settled into gentle ripples across a wide pool that was clear as the sky above.

"Is it safe?" she asked as the man took her to the edge of the water. "I know you can't understand me, but—"

He turned to face her, his gaze solemn and his lips parted as he whispered one word. "Safe."

It was almost a hoarse grunt, as though he hadn't spoken in ages, perhaps ever. Yet she recognized that word, and her world spun as she realized that she might have a chance to communicate with this man.

"You know English?"

He nodded uncertainly.

"How much can you speak?"

He held up his hands and shrank them together in the air.

"Okay, how much can you understand?"

His hands widened apart.

A flood of questions filled Eden's mind, but right now she had to focus on more pressing needs. The kind that pressed against her bladder.

"I need to use the . . . Wait, you probably don't understand what a restroom is. I need . . . privacy?" As embarrassing as it was, she squatted down, miming her intentions.

He nodded toward a clump of trees.

"Stay close," he said in a hoarse whisper.

Eden went over to the bushes and did what needed to be done before she rejoined him at the water's edge.

"Is it deep? I can swim. I'm just worried."

"Deep, yes. Safe." He removed the gold leaf crown from his head and set it down in the grass. Then, without warning, he untied the strips of leather that held his loincloth on and dove into the pool.

Eden had a brief but glorious glimpse of his muscled ass as he disappeared into the water. A cloud of mud circled around where he had vanished, sullying the pretty blue water. Eden waited for him to come up, wondering what he looked like beneath the layers of mud. But long seconds passed and he didn't come up.

Had something happened to him down there? She took off her hiking boots and socks before hastily wading into the water and diving under to search.

Her heart thundered against her ribs as she dove beneath the surface, trying to find him. She opened her eyes, searching, but all she could see was a blue haze and white bubbles from the waterfall. She surged back up to the surface for air and then shrieked as something curled around her foot and pulled her back under.

Water covered her head, and she reached down to claw at whatever had grabbed her leg, but it was already gone. She swam back up to the surface with visions of crocodiles and snakes in her head as she sucked in a lungful of air. The water beside her churned, and the wild man's face appeared. He shook his head, and his long dark hair whipped around his face. He ducked below the water again and came back up, allowing Eden her first glimpse of his face unmarred by mud.

My God.

She couldn't have guessed what lay beneath the heavy coats of mud. The chiseled features of a god matched his muscled form. There was a slight cleft in his chin, and the tan skin of his face made his blue eyes glow even more brilliantly. It was difficult to look away from his face. Dark shapes colored his shoulders. Tattoos? They looked tribal in design. She'd never been into tattoos before, but they only added to the mystique of this man.

He swam slowly around her, his lips curved in a playful smile, then suddenly splashed water at her. Eden gasped and instinctively splashed back at him. He let out a deep, rich laugh that made her melt. They swam and played, not quite touching each other, but close enough that she was aware he was completely naked. Eventually her skin began to prune, and she realized that she was drenched in her only set of clothes.

Now exhausted, she started to go back to the shore, but the man caught her hand and motioned for her to swim toward the falls. She followed him and blushed to the roots of her hair as he climbed out of the water and onto a small rock ledge, leaving nothing to the imagination. Then he vanished behind the waterfall. She gripped the smooth rocks at the base of the ledge and pulled herself up, finding it easier than she expected. Then she followed him behind the glass-like curtain of water.

The cave behind the falls was deep and dark, and she could barely see the outline of the wild man ahead of her.

"Wait! I can't see." Her voice echoed all around her despite the roar of the falls behind them.

A warm hand caught hold of hers, and she was pulled deeper into the darkness before they stopped. Her feet touched something soft. Animal fur? She knelt and touched it. Yes, it was, but what kind she couldn't tell. Hands touched her shoulders, pulling lightly at her clothes as though to remove them.

"Wait . . . What?"

"Too wet," he said in a low voice. "Animal skins need to dry."

"Skins? Oh, my clothes." She glanced around, not quite able to see him clearly. Maybe it would be okay to take off her clothes in the dark? Eden hesitated a second and then peeled off her clothes, even her panties.

"Sit," he urged, and she did, tucking her knees up to cover her body.

"Hey, do you have a name?" she asked the tall, warm man sharing the darkness with her.

"Thorne."

"Thorne? Just Thorne? No last name?" Eden tried to see his face as he knelt down beside her on the bed of furs. Her heart jumped in nervousness at what he might do next.

"Son of Keza," he added quietly.

"Is Keza your father?"

"Mother." The word was spoken with a fierce tenderness.

"Is she here? Does she live with you?"

There was a long silence. "No. Thorne left. Thorne see them sometimes."

Eden nearly jumped when she felt a hand touch hers. Thorne stroked a fingertip over her knuckles, the gentle touch exploring and soothing rather than threatening.

"Sleep," he said in the mantle of darkness. "Thorne protect."

Eden knew she shouldn't lie down in her undressed state, nor should she bury her face in the furs and start to rest. But the makeshift bed was soft against her bare body. It was only late afternoon, but she was indeed tired. She was a little cold, but Thorne soon wrapped the furs around her, and she could smell an inviting masculine scent clinging to them. *His* scent. Clean man and waterfall with a hint of mango. It was a scent she would dream of for the rest of her life, just as she knew she would dream of this wild forest god.

EDEN WOKE HOURS LATER. SHE SENSED THAT SHE WAS alone and crawled toward the distant sound of the waterfall until she saw light up ahead. It would have been reasonable to panic, yet the words "Thorne protect" had left her feeling safe. How that was possible, she didn't know.

As she reached the edge of the waterfall, she found her clothes just out of reach of the water's misting spray. She found they were dry and looked clean of the mud, though there were some rust-colored stains. Blood that would never wash out, but at least she would feel clean.

Eden dressed and carefully walked along the ledge to exit the waterfall. She froze at the sight of Thorne standing waist-deep in the lake. His sun-bronzed skin was taut over his bulging muscles, yet he wasn't built like a bodybuilder. His muscles came from necessity, not vanity, and there wasn't an ounce of fat on him. He was perfect. A little *too* perfect, except for the faint scars that could be seen all over his body. She could not tell their origins, only that they must have been painful. Life in the jungle had to be insanely dangerous.

It was impossible for Eden not to feel the raw animal magnetism that he radiated. She'd never felt so drawn to anyone before in her entire life. Water cascaded down his forearm, and he splashed lightly as he cleaned himself.

Eden, pull it together. You're having a crisis. You cannot get fixated on this guy. You survived a horrible ordeal, and now you're in some jungle-man fantasy that cannot be real.

Maybe she hadn't survived? Maybe this was all an elaborate dream in her own private heaven. That didn't seem like such a bad thing. In fact, spending the rest of eternity in an emerald jungle and bathing beneath water-falls with a forest god sounded amazing.

Eden had always dated guys who wore suits and focused on business. She was drawn to their take-charge attitudes and how they could dominate her in bed in the best possible ways. They were all attractive, nice and fit, but none of those relationships had lasted long. The connection she longed for, like the one her parents had, never existed with those men.

But there was something here between her and this quiet man of the wild. He was like an ancient god who could hold the heart of a star in his palms. His face was focused, predatory, yet compassion softened his features whenever he gazed at her.

Eden moved off the ledge and leapt down onto the muddy bank of the lake, her gaze still locked on Thorne. He stopped washing and stared at her, his palms resting on the surface of the water by his hips, drawing her focus to that V-shaped muscle that always made her a bit dizzy when she saw it on a man. And Thorne's was the best she'd ever seen.

"Thorne, can you take me to the forest guides?" she asked as she put on her hiking boots, which still sat by the lake. It had been the last thing on her mind, but rationality had returned. She needed to get back to civilization, find the police, and tell them what had happened to the tour group. Then she had to call her family and let them know she was safe. After that, she needed therapy. Lots of it.

"Forest. Guides?" He repeated her request but did not seem to understand.

"Yes. The place where we went to see the gorillas."

"Gorillas?" This word he spoke more confidently.

"Yes."

"Thorne take to gorillas," he promised and started to walk out of the water toward her. Just like that, her mind blanked as she got a full-frontal view of Thorne.

Holy shit. He was even more perfect than she could imagine. Eden swallowed hard and forced her eyes back up.

"Wait. Not gorillas. People. *Humans.*"

He paused as he bent to lift his loincloth up from the

grass. "No humans," Thorne replied with a solemn finality. "Not safe. Stay with Thorne."

He wrapped his loincloth around his body and retrieved the gold circlet and placed it upon his head. Eden changed the subject as she touched the diamond pendant around her throat.

"Thorne, where did you find that?" She pointed at the gold leaves adorning his brow.

He removed the crown and studied it, his long fingers curling gently around the delicate band of gold leaves. "White rock."

"White rock? Can you show me?" Maybe if she got him to trust and like her, he would change his mind about taking her to the forest guides.

Thorne's blue eyes focused on the forest behind them with sharp intensity. Birds chattered and monkeys called out. Eden heard nothing dangerous in the sounds, but she had not lived here in the wild the way he had.

He seemed to be both man and animal, belonging fully in both worlds, yet forced to linger somewhere in the middle.

"Is it safe?" she asked.

He suddenly smiled. "Yes. Safe. Come. Meet Tembo."

"Who's Tembo?"

"Come see," he answered with a smile.

Eden gasped as Thorne grasped her hand in his and led her into the forest. They followed a trail that was well worn despite the overgrowth of vegetation. Large circular tracks could be seen in the muddy path.

Thorne cupped his mouth with one hand and let out a reverberating sound that was oddly familiar, but Eden couldn't place it. There was an answering trumpet call ahead of them, and Eden gasped. An elephant!

They quickened their pace, leaping over small rocks and ducking between hagenia trees that grew close together, until they skidded to a stop. Eden bumped into Thorne from behind, but he barely budged.

Just up ahead, seven elephants stood facing them on the path.

"Tembo." Thorne spoke softly, his lips curling in a delighted smile as he looked between her and the elephant.

"Come, meet Tembo," he encouraged and walked toward the elephant who led the herd.

As Thorne approached the bull elephant, he walked right up to him and gently clasped his long trunk in his hands and laid his forehead against it. For a moment, Eden couldn't believe what she was seeing. The man had just walked up to an elephant and was leaning against it the way a person might a very tame horse. But it was a dangerous bull elephant.

Thorne closed his eyes, still smiling. Eden watched him, completely enthralled. He embraced this world with such joy and love. Who was he? How had he come to be here? Eden had to find out.

"Come." He waved to her, and she joined him, her heart pounding as she stood close to him and the elephant.

"Tembo," Thorne said as he patted the elephant's trunk. The elephant lifted his trunk and gently tapped Thorne's chest before touching Eden's cheek and exploring her.

"Tell him name," Thorne said.

"Eden," she said. "I'm Eden." She realized she hadn't told Thorne her name until now.

"Eden," he repeated with a reverence that sent shivers of excitement through her. She touched the elephant's trunk and gazed deep into his dark-brown eyes. The animal had a quiet majesty unparalleled by any other animal on the planet.

"How did you become friends with an elephant?" she asked.

Thorne stroked the weathered gray trunk, and Tembo playfully lifted the end of his trunk, delicately poking around Thorne's neck.

"He was young calf. Two female lions chased him across here." He waved at the meadow. "I stopped them, chased them away. Took Tembo back to his family."

Eden watched as Thorne and the elephant shared a look of gentle, friendly affection that made her heart swell.

"Nature's great masterpiece, the elephant; the only harmless great thing." Eden echoed the old quote by the philosopher John Donne as she was pulled into the bull elephant's quiet, contemplative gaze. Peace like she had never known before settled into her soul.

"What does that mean?" Thorne asked.

"It means . . ." She thought it over carefully before responding. "It means that elephants are not predators like lions. They are dangerous when provoked, yes, like all animals, but at their core, they are kind, they are loving, and as one of the largest creatures on the planet, that is a rare thing, to have power and not use it to hurt others. Elephants are compassionate and gentle." Which made it all the more painful to think of how often these creatures, like the gorillas, were slaughtered by poachers.

"No sadness," Thorne whispered as he brushed the pads of his thumbs over her cheeks, wiping away tears she hadn't even been aware of.

"I'm not sad," she confessed. "I'm full of joy."

"Eden is happy?"

"Very happy." She curled her arms around Tembo's trunk and hugged, unafraid of him now. She laughed as the tip of his trunk tugged on her hair, which was falling loose past her shoulders. The elephant trumpeted, but the sound was soft, sweet.

"Tembo says you have hair of sunlight."

"Hair of sunlight?" She loved the sound of that, but then it hit her what he'd just said. "Wait, you *understand* him?"

Thorne nodded, but he did not explain further. He

reached up to touch her hair, his fingers coiling in the strands. He must have been using the elephant as a means to say what he actually wanted to say. That was it.

Eden knew she had to look terrible right now. Humidity was not her friend. But from the look on Thorne's face, he clearly thought she was beautiful. There was a mix of innocence blended with a primal desire in his eyes that made her tremble. How could this stranger fill her with such a potent longing for things that she didn't think she'd ever find?

Thorne peered down at her, his fingertips moving from her hair to her face. He explored her cheek, her forehead, then her lips. She stared back up at him, her heart beating like a bird trapped in a cage, desperate to be freed. Was he going to kiss her? She wanted him to, as crazy as that was.

"Beautiful female," he whispered. His hand moved to her neck, touching her collarbone, and then slowly moved down toward her breasts. She almost leaned into his gentle, exploring touch but recalled herself and flinched back. He became tense and sniffed around them, as though he expected to find a reason for her pulling away.

"Sorry. It's just, we don't know each other. People shouldn't touch like that unless . . . they know each other, you know?"

Thorne's head tilted to one side. "Thorne know you.

You are Eden." He said her name in that husky tone of his. "Mates."

She blinked, dazed by that simple declaration. He thought she was his mate? *Men.* "Thorne, have you been with a woman before?"

"I am with you," he replied confidently.

"Yes. Yes, you are." She tried not to stare at his muscled chest, which was calling for her to touch it. She wanted to explore his body as he'd been exploring hers.

"What I mean is, have you *mated* with anyone before?" She hoped to God he understood what she meant. Understanding crossed his stormy eyes, and a blush stained his cheeks. He looked away toward the elephants, who had wandered past them.

"No. Eden is Thorne's first mate."

A virgin jungle god. I'm either blessed or cursed. She honestly wasn't sure which.

"Look, Thorne, we are not mates."

"You have mate? I will fight for you." He puffed up his chest, and she couldn't help but notice how tall he really was. The idea of him fighting for her should not have been hot, but it was. No modern woman would ever admit that, but she was in a primal world with a primal man.

"No, I have no mate, Thorne."

The ferocity in his expression softened. "Good. You are Thorne's mate."

Men.

He reached for her face again. Eden caught his hand between hers, holding on to his palm. His skin was rough and calloused, his fingers strong and the backs of his knuckles scarred with faint scratches. She wondered what he had endured out here. Her heart was strangely heavy at the thought of him alone in the jungle for what seemed like his whole life. Where was his family? Why hadn't he stayed with them? He still gazed at her with that sweet, intense hunger. She had to get him off the idea of mating and back to the answers she needed.

"Can you take me to the white rock?"

His eyes narrowed, as though he sensed she was distracting him.

"Thorne take you. Then talk mates."

"Okay, sure." She would agree to that if she could get some answers.

Thorne led her through the forest for almost an hour before they paused at the edge of a small clearing. Eden peered over his shoulder as he pointed to a shape covered in undergrowth but still visibly white. Her lips parted, and she covered her mouth with her hands.

A wrecked plane lay on the forest floor like the skeleton of some great beast. Thick vines hung over it. Rust rimmed the edges of the open door and windows.

"My God . . ." Eden stared at the wreck. It answered so many of her questions—or at least hinted toward the answers. She touched Thorne's shoulder. "How long has this been here?"

He tensed beneath her hand. "Always."

That single word made Eden think. Was the plane connected to Thorne? He acted as though he hadn't spoken English in . . . well, years. Was it because he hadn't? Eden walked toward the plane, even more desperate for answers, but when she realized that he wasn't coming with her, she turned back to him. A wave of apprehension rolled through her, and she saw the stark pain in Thorne's eyes.

"Thorne, are you okay?"

He squared his shoulders and moved with resolute steps toward her and the plane. A tense silence surrounded them as he reached her.

"Is it safe to go inside?" she asked.

He didn't say anything at first. His gaze seemed to go straight through her and into a place where she could not follow.

"Safe," he finally said.

Eden ventured inside first, stepping into the darkness of the plane. It felt like she was entering another world. The humid jungle air left a sickly sweet scent inside the cabin. Eden flinched as she glimpsed two human skeletons, rags of clothing hanging off them. They were slumped in their chairs as though they had fallen asleep a century ago and had left nothing but their bones behind.

"Gods." Thorne nodded at the bones with solemn respect.

"No, those are human," she whispered. "Like you and me."

Eden moved down the aisle toward the bodies and studied them. One had a large, elegant signet ring on its index finger. The other wore a necklace with a ginkgo leaf pendant. She guessed based on what was left of the clothing that one was a man and the other a woman. She knelt by one empty seat and saw a pile of moss-covered cardboard children's books. She lifted one up.

The Jungle Alphabet.

Thorne's eyes focused on the book. His face drained of color, and his eyes widened in apparent shock.

"G is . . . for gorilla," he uttered in broken syllables, as though in great pain.

"Thorne?" Eden stepped toward him, but he fled the plane and vanished into the trees.

"Thorne!" She ran after him but froze as something fell out of the book and onto the grass between her boots. She bent and picked it up.

Her heart shattered. It was a photo of a beautiful young couple holding a small boy between them. There was only one conclusion that made any sense to her. There was no mistaking the truth that came to her in a blinding rush.

The child was Thorne.

5

Thorne couldn't breathe. He leapt over fallen trees and dug his fingers into the bark of the hagenias as he tried to claw his way to freedom from the ghosts that now chased him.

"I'll be back soon." A deep voice came out of the past and into Thorne's heart and mind. Strong arms held him tight, and he was safe. Safe *always* in this man's arms.

"Be careful," the woman said. She smelled like flowers, and her laughter made him smile.

Screams. A black beast with silver on its back. Red mist . . .

"Please . . . Please leave us alone. We won't tell anyone anything."

Thorne came to a stop. His chest heaved as he leaned against a tree that was four times his body width. The ancient wood gave him support, but it could not stop the weight of the past.

"Please, we won't tell anyone. My son's only three. I need to take care of him." Choking fear knifed Thorne's heart as he failed to escape the memories of the past.

"Please don't. Not my baby!"

He remembered now. Remembered holding on to the female—his *mother*—with all his might, but he hadn't understood how to save her or to protect her.

"A mother's love—how touching." The cold voice cut through the memory. That voice. The monster who had killed his mother and father.

Thorne threw his head back and roared. The tree he leaned against vibrated down to its very roots, and the birds above him scattered. Hundreds of wings flapped wildly as they fled from the white ghost and disappeared into the sky far above him.

Thorne sank to his knees, one arm still clutching the tree, and the other hit the earth and he clawed at the dark soil as he started gasping.

A pain he hadn't experienced in many seasons gripped his chest, squeezing the breath from his body. He tried to suck it back again, making a strange sound in his throat. Moisture gathered in his eyes. Tears, like the ones he had wiped from Eden's cheeks when she'd greeted Tembo.

The pain was unlike anything he had ever felt before. He had battled leopards, poachers, and even silverbacks from rival bands to protect his family. He had fought crocodiles, hippopotamuses, and even deadly snakes.

Scars covered his body from his battles, yet all of that paled compared to the scar ripping open inside him now.

"Mummy, wake up." Thorne remembered trying to wake his mother, and the dark-skinned man who held out a crown of leaves to him to stem his crying.

Thorne had visited this place only once before as a child, daring to step foot inside, where he had found the golden circlet on the ground. He had examined the strange thing as he'd backed away from the white rock and returned to the forest. Something about the white rock had left him uneasy all those years ago. Now he remembered why.

This place was a tomb. A grave. A place of ended lives. Tembo and his herd visited their fallen loved ones once a year, at the same place within the jungle. That place was one of peace. This white rock was a place of horrific tragedy. Thorne had not wanted to remember his past—or perhaps he couldn't, until now. But it was still only bits and pieces. Sharp fragments that sliced him deeply.

"Thorne!" Eden's distant shout broke through his rush of painful thoughts. "Thorne! Please come back!"

He got to his feet and, filling his lungs with air, made his way back to his future mate. Eden stood near the plane, still holding the picture book. When she saw him, she dropped the book and ran to him. He opened his arms to catch her, and she wrapped herself around him.

"I'm so sorry—I didn't know. I didn't know," she said and pressed her cheek to his chest.

He put his arms around her slowly, embracing her the way he had embraced Keza as a child, but this was different. With Eden, everything was different. A fierce need to protect her, even stronger than the first moment he saw her, took hold of him now. Deep down, he knew that it was his job to protect this female, to care for her, to cherish her as a mate should be cherished. She raised her head, and he saw tears coating her lashes. The sight tore at him. A mate was sacred, and he'd made her cry, which meant she was in great pain.

He brushed her tears away. "Eden cries . . ."

"Yes," she admitted. "I'm sorry. I didn't know that was your family who . . ." She swallowed thickly before continuing. "I didn't know your family was in there."

"Family . . ." He thought of Keza and Akika, and the others who had raised him. *Keza* . . . Her face came back to him in a new—or rather, very old—memory. She had rescued him when he'd been all alone. She had carried him to safety and made him her son. She was his mother, but not his *only* mother.

"Do you remember what happened?" she asked him. "I found a journal in the cockpit. I only skimmed it, but it looks like your family crashed here and survived two weeks before . . ."

"What is journal?" he asked her.

"It's a book, sort of like a story, but it was written by

your father. It tells people about what happened in the past."

Father . . . Memories of a handsome face, much like his own, and strong arms holding him close. *Safe. Always.* Until he wasn't.

"Do you want to know who they were?" Eden asked. Her gaze softened the tension inside him.

"Yes."

She relaxed and stepped out of his arms, but she took one of his hands, leading him back toward the white rock. No . . . *airplane*. More words, words that Bwanbale hadn't taught him, were coming back. He remembered.

Eden did not go back inside the plane. She retrieved the child's book from the ground and opened it up, removing something small tucked inside.

"This is your family." She handed him the flat object.

He looked down at it, and his heart quivered deep within him, sending reverberations straight to his soul as he saw the faces of his parents for the first time since they'd died. He dared not speak lest he cry again. He touched his mother's face and his father's, then stared at his own tiny self in the magical reflection.

"Amelia is your mother, and Jacob, that's your dad."

He repeated the names under his breath, vowing never to forget them again, just as he would never forget Keza's face or name.

Eden sat down on the grass outside the plane's open door. "Do you remember what happened to them?"

Thorne joined her on the ground, resting his arms on the tops of his bent knees. They sat side by side, looking into the jungle.

"Bad men came. Men with guns." He'd learned that word from Bwanbale while the man had treated the wound on Thorne's arm where a bullet had grazed him. Thorne had demanded to know what the sticks were that made such a terrible noise and caused such pain. Bwanbale had taught him much about the violence of men, and that was why Thorne had never sought them out.

"Men with guns? Did your parents know them?"

"No . . ." Thorne struggled to remember that awful day that had robbed him of a life he would never have remembered if not for Eden. "Father came. Took Mother and Thorne away. Bad men found us, used guns."

"So your parents were murdered?"

"Murdered?" He didn't know that word, but it left a terrible taste in his mouth.

"Yes. Killed by another human."

Thorne nodded. "Murdered." The word tasted bitter upon his tongue.

"How did you survive, Thorne?"

He could feel Eden's eyes upon him, searching for answers. He was silent a long moment, collecting his thoughts. "Keza found me."

"Keza?"

"Mother. *Other* mother. Keza is gorilla."

Eden stared at him. She blinked.

"What?"

"Keza found Thorne. Took Thorne in her arms. Made Thorne safe. Gave Thorne family."

"A *gorilla* rescued you?"

Thorne nodded.

"*Gorillas* raised you?"

Thorne nodded again.

"*Gorillas.*"

Thorne wondered why she was having trouble understanding him.

"Nobody is going to believe this," Eden muttered, scratching at her forehead. "This is incredible."

"What is *incredible?*" He sounded out the unfamiliar word. Eden used so many words he did not understand.

"It means *good*. It means *beautiful*. It means . . . Actually, it means *not believable*, which is pretty accurate, come to think about it. I don't really know how to explain it."

Thorne half smiled. "Thorne understand. Good. Beautiful." He reached over and cupped her face with one hand. "Eden is incredible."

Her cheeks turned a soft pink like the petals of wildflowers that grew in the mountains.

"I'm not incredible," she mumbled.

"Yes. Incredible," he said in that dominant tone of his that warned her not to argue with him.

"You really lived with gorillas all this time?" Eden leaned closer, seeming quite curious. He liked it when she was curious, when she was happy.

"Keza had infant. Akika. Thorne's brother. Thorne learn to climb, swim, live as gorilla." He studied the trees that formed his world with new eyes. His parents hadn't come from here. He looked back to the book she held. "Eden read to me journal?"

"Huh? Oh! Sure." She ducked inside the plane and came back out with a book bound in what looked like smooth brown animal skin. She opened it and began to read.

"My name is Jacob Haywood, the Earl of Somerset. I crashed here with my wife, Amelia, and my three-year-old son when the engine failed. Our pilot, Charlie MacGrath, perished in the crash. We removed his body to the woods nearby. My wife and I face great and insurmountable odds. This part of Uganda, the Impenetrable Forest, is called so for a reason. I fear no one may ever find us. My son, Thorne, gives me hope. He never cries, never complains. He trusts me to keep him safe. The last thing I wish to do is fail him, but I fear that my brother, Cameron, may not find us in time."

Eden stopped reading. There was much Thorne didn't understand in what Eden said, but he believed he understood enough.

"Thorne, you have more family," she breathed. "You have an uncle, Cameron."

"Uncle?" he asked. The word was familiar.

"Your father had a brother. His name is Cameron." She then went back to the first line. "Your father was an earl from England."

Thorne still did not understand. "What is *earl-fromengland?*"

"No, an earl. It's . . . oh, how do I explain that? A man with power, who commands many people. England is where you are from, not here, not Africa."

This Thorne understood. An earl was like the dominant silverback.

"And when a father dies, his son becomes the new earl. That's you. You are the Earl of Somerset."

"Thorne does not want power." He had exactly what he wished for here. The jungle, Keza, Akika, and now Eden. He had no need for anything else. *Power* to a human male meant *death*. He didn't care about that. He had plenty of power here in the forest where he ruled among the animals and kept the natural order. He'd never fought for control of his gorilla family—Sunya was more suited to the role. What Thorne craved most was peace. Death did exist here, power did exist here, but it was all part of the cycle of life. No animal killed others out of a joy of killing. Even gorillas when they fought for control did not usually kill each other.

"Thorne, you must listen to me. We need to leave the jungle and find your uncle."

"No. Not safe." Thorne stood, but his feet wouldn't move. He was rooted in place for a long moment, before he entered the plane cabin again. The two gods—his parents—lay there as silent ghosts. Thorne curled one hand into a fist and placed that fist over his heart. Eden joined him, and she pointed toward the figures.

Eden moved to the skeleton. "Your father has a ring. It belongs to you now." Thorne watched her gently remove a thick band of something shiny from the bony hand. She returned to him and gently took his hand in hers. Then she slid the object around his smallest finger.

"A perfect fit," she murmured. "I think this must be your family crest."

Thorne examined the image on the thing Eden had called a ring. "Crest?" It seemed as though a sun was rising over the trees, the small lines curved simply, yet he knew it was a sunrise, or sunset. He curled his hand back into a fist, feeling the ring around his finger. An unexpected surge of pride filled him. He closed his eyes. A dim memory of lying in his father's arms, half-asleep, touching this ring with tiny fingers.

When he opened his eyes, he looked toward his mother and saw a shiny leaf hanging by a shining thread around her neck. He reached for it. It was like the gift he'd given Eden, the one she now wore around her neck.

"Here, let me." Eden did something to make the shiny thread break apart so it could be removed. She tried to hand it to him, but he reached up and touched her neck.

"You," he whispered. "You have it."

Eden's eyes blurred with tears as she removed the other gift and put this one in its place. She handed him back the heavier gift, which he laid at the feet of his mother's bones in silent memory.

Eden touched the shiny object around her neck. "This looks like a ginkgo leaf, only gold."

"What is gold?"

"This." She touched the leaf and shining thread. "The stuff that's shiny."

"Yes. Thorne has seen much gold." He thought of the cave and the glittering stones. "Bad men take much gold." He closed his eyes, letting those awful memories take hold. He reached up to his head, touching the crown of leaves. "Bad man gave Thorne this. But Thorne let go to hold on to Keza's fur when she took Thorne away."

Eden watched him, a thoughtful expression on her face. "Thorne, would you let me meet Keza and Akika? Would it be safe?" She touched the ginkgo leaf against her collarbone as though it gave her comfort. That thought filled him with a quiet joy, to know that his mother's treasure was pleasing to his mate.

"Eden can see family. First we eat." He held out a

hand. Eden placed her palm in his, and they returned to the jungle.

EDEN SAT IN THE CRADLING ROOTS OF THE TREE BELOW Thorne's tree house, nibbling on fresh mangoes and some kind of wild nuts that Thorne had found for her. He had retrieved her camera bag from the tree house after she had asked him to.

As he lounged nearby, licking the juice off his fingers from his own mango, and Eden couldn't help but stare. The more time she spent with him, the more she seemed to forget the world outside the jungle. She could have gazed at him forever, admiring the lean lines of his muscles, his beautiful yet masculine hands and feet, which held strength and dexterity in them from years of necessity and adapting in this wild, wondrous world. Yet there was something more to it than that. She couldn't explain why, but it felt as though he was here for a reason, not just because of luck and survival.

A butterfly with black wings, marked by two bright-blue spots that resembled eyes, fluttered around Thorne's head before settling upon his shoulder. He held still, his breath even as he carefully moved the butterfly to his finger. Then he knelt in front of Eden and held it out to her. He placed the butterfly on her fingertip.

"Eden stay with Thorne?"

Her throat tightened. She did want to stay with him. If she had no life calling her home, no family, she might have thrown logic and reason to the wind and stayed here forever with this wild man. She couldn't indulge in crazy romantic notions of living in the jungle with him. He may be cut out for the wild, but Eden acknowledged that she wouldn't make it a month without a real shower, shampoo, a hair dryer—the list was endless.

What she needed to focus on was a way to convince him to leave the jungle and find his uncle. Cameron Haywood deserved to know what had befallen his brother's family. But this was still a sensitive subject for Thorne. He did not trust humans, and no doubt he had good reason for it.

"I can stay for a little while, but not forever." She hoped he understood. The butterfly took flight, leaving them close enough that she shivered, but not out of fear. She was lost in the bright blue of his eyes, and she couldn't help but reach out to touch his face. He held still as she explored his dark eyebrows, the lines of worry creasing his brow, down to his straight aquiline nose, and to his lips. They were full and lush, tempting.

Thorne has never kissed a woman. He might not even know what a kiss is. Eden was secretly thrilled at the thought, but she wondered if she would be taking advantage of him. Based on the journal, he was twenty-five, a year older than her. One kiss wouldn't be bad, would it?

"Thorne, may I kiss you?" Eden asked.

This was insane. Kissing a strange wild man who'd been raised by gorillas in the jungles of Uganda. What if he did return her to her people and then disappear back into the forest? The thought of him never knowing the magic a kiss could hold broke her heart.

"Kiss?" He echoed the word, his brows drawn together. He seemed to decide that whatever terrible thing a kiss might be, he would endure it. His reaction almost made her laugh.

"It's okay. I promise. Just . . . close your eyes." She demonstrated what she meant for him to do.

Thorne closed his eyes, his hands clenched into fists as he tensed. It was adorable, the way he seemed to think she was about to mete out some medieval torture.

Eden cupped his face in her hands, feeling the light rasp of stubble beneath her palms. Then she leaned in and feathered her lips over his. She took her time, enjoying the tight heat coiling in her belly and how good it would feel to kiss him deeper if she had the chance. He was as still as stone as she continued to kiss him. Then she pulled back to examine his reaction. His eyes were open, and he was staring at her, soft-eyed, almost dreamy.

"That wasn't so bad, was it?" she asked.

Thorne was silent a moment, and then he licked his lips and scooted an inch closer. "Thorne kiss Eden?" he asked.

She nodded. "Yes, you may kiss me."

He cupped her face and mimicked her movements as he brushed his lips over hers. She opened her lips and flicked her tongue against his mouth. He stiffened a second and then opened his own mouth and touched her tongue with his. A pulse, like a drum, began to beat inside her, burrowing deep as her body hummed with life.

It was so innocent a kiss, but in that moment it was also the most important kiss of her life. Her first true kiss with this jungle lord would be her undoing. It would also be her everything.

This time when they broke apart, Thorne gazed at her with heavy-lidded eyes, the eyes of someone awakened to desire.

"Do mates kiss often?" he asked. The gentle rumble of his question sent zings of arousal through her. At the same time, something softer wrapped itself around her heart.

"Mates?" She was having trouble thinking now because he was so close, and his scent filled her head with wild, hungry, yet sweet thoughts.

"Yes. Tell Thorne about human mates. Please."

He completely destroyed her heart with that plea. This gorgeous, raw, primal man was so desperate to know the ways of his own people. How could she deny him?

"How does Thorne mate Eden?" he asked more specifically.

"Mate?" Eden reached up to grasp his wrists, but she didn't pull his hands away from her face. After everything she'd been through in the last two days, it felt good to be held.

"Yes." He smoothed the pad of his thumb over her bottom lip. "Gorillas do not kiss. The male is . . ." He struggled for words. "Rough. He uses power to convince female to be mate."

"Oh . . ." Eden blushed. She thought of everything he must have witnessed in the animal world. Mating in many species was rough, sometimes even violent. But humans were different, and she sensed Thorne was beginning to realize that such a difference existed.

"Well, people, *humans*, when they both like each other, they decide to date."

"Date?" Thorne listened as if she was telling him the most important secrets of the universe.

"Dating is where two people do things they enjoy, like eating together or having fun. Playing." God, how could she explain this? He had no memories of movies, art museums, or coffee shops, the places where she usually went for dates. "They do it so they can get to know each other. To decide if they want to be mates."

"Eden and Thorne ate together." He nodded toward the remaining mangoes on the leaf nearby. "And play in water?"

"Yes, I suppose we did."

"After date?" he said, pressing on with his questions.

"After? Well, if they like each other, they might kiss."

"Like we kiss?" He brushed his fingers along her throat, the touch so light that she didn't feel threatened.

"Yes." She had to admit that was true too.

"After kiss?" His blue eyes never left hers as he continued his questions.

"It depends. Sometimes they spend the night together."

"Eden spent night with Thorne." He pointed this out with pride.

Heat flooded Eden's face. "We did, but it's not quite the same thing. You see, sometimes they need to have *more* dates before they decide. And sometimes they decide *not* to be mates."

His lips pursed, and he slowly pulled his hand away from her throat. The loss of that connection rang deep inside her like the melancholy sound of a single bell. She hoped he didn't take what she said the wrong way, but he had to understand that there were choices involved.

"Thorne . . ." She honestly didn't know what to say as she reached for his hand. "This is all new to you. *I'm* new to you. Dating . . . *mating* is something you take slowly. Some people rush, but it's better to make sure that you care about someone, that you love someone first."

All her life that's what she'd wanted and had yet to find it with a man. If she could teach Thorne one thing, it was the importance of getting a relationship right. Heaven knows she hadn't been able to get it right yet herself. Thorne watched her eyes, his gaze searching.

"Will Eden take Thorne as mate?"

"We should take our time, see what happens between us." She shouldn't have said that. She had to focus on getting out of this jungle and contacting the authorities about the massacre. Remembering that made her head pound and her stomach churn. It was so easy to forget the awful nightmare when she was with Thorne, but staying here with him and pretending it hadn't happened —it wasn't right. She owed it to Maggie, Harold, and the others to get back into the civilized world and help the authorities track down the men who did this and arrest them. But while she was around Thorne, she couldn't seem to think past the gorgeous jungle god who wanted to *mate* her. If that wasn't straight out of a late-night wet dream she didn't know what was. Any woman on the planet would kill for this fantasy. But this wasn't a fantasy. People were dead, and the jungle was dangerous.

"No other males for Eden?" Thorne clarified, his gaze hopeful and serious.

"No." There were certainly no other men before she'd come to Africa. And after their gentle and life-altering kiss, she couldn't picture herself with any other man.

"Good." He lifted her hand to his and pressed his lips to her knuckles in a way that made her heart flutter. How did he know to do that? Were his memories of his early childhood strong enough to retain some things he'd seen his parents do? He was English nobility, and now more than ever she saw that he was infinitely more than that, with his classically handsome features and the quiet, noble presence of his heart that seemed to hearken to the ancient days of fair ladies and knights riding white chargers into battle.

Thorne Haywood, Lord of the Jungle, was a fairytale prince. Eden was worried she might—no, definitely *would*—fall in love with him. What would happen to her when he finally left the jungle and embraced the destiny that should have been his years ago? There might not be a place for her in his life then. And if he didn't leave the jungle? What place was there for her here?

Eden touched the necklace Thorne had given her, the ginkgo leaf necklace that had belonged to his mother, the one that held such a significance to him now that he was learning who he was—who he might be someday.

He was her wild man, but someday he would belong to the world. If that was the case, she should take advantage of the time when he belonged to her and her alone.

"Could I meet your family?" she asked him. "Keza and the others?"

"Yes, I will take you to them." He helped her to her feet, and Eden followed Thorne into the jungle.

6

Thorne's lips were still tingling as he touched them with his fingertips. If he closed his eyes, he could even relive that kiss.

Kiss.

A strange word for such a powerful experience. He had been certain that she would lash out at him the way many animal females did when going into heat. Yet she'd given him something else instead, something precious: the human custom of kissing. The more he replayed it in his mind, the more he swore he remembered his parents kissing. The memories were hazy, tinged with heartsick longing, but they were there all the same.

They do it so they can get to know each other. To decide if they want to be mates.

He was a little embarrassed at his body's response to that kiss. Before he met Eden, he'd felt no shame about his body, but being around her, a woman from another world, a woman who knew the ways of their people where he did not, did make him embarrassed. Surely a male who couldn't control his body wasn't worthy of being a mate.

Thorne was terrified he would do or say the wrong thing and lose her. In his world, mating was about forming a relationship, a bond of trust and power.

And sometimes they decide not *to be mates.*

If he could not gain Eden's trust, she would never want him. How could she trust a mate who did not know the ways of their world outside the jungle?

Thorne was still puzzling over how he could win Eden over when he scented Keza's band on the breeze that meandered through the dense jungle. They had climbed higher on the mountainside, and the canopy above them had thinned enough to allow the air to ruffle the trees.

"Eden stay behind Thorne," he cautioned. He pulled free of her hand so he could fight any gorillas if necessary. Sunya was distrustful of humans and never let his band travel south where they could be found.

"What should I do?" Eden asked. She removed something small and black that was a little bigger than her hand and held it up close to her face. He wanted to know what that black object was, but now was not the time to ask. He had to focus on the gorillas in order to protect Eden.

"Eyes down. Head down. Stay low."

They entered a small clearing where the gorillas had settled for a late-afternoon rest. They would be more receptive to visitors while they had full bellies.

"Do not go to infants," he cautioned as the first few female gorillas noticed them. "If infant gets close, back away. Mother will come for infant." Thorne was whispering now, and he hoped Eden would hear.

Keza was one of the first to spot Thorne. Her eyes softened, and his heart swelled at the visage of his mother—his second mother. Knowing of his parents from before and how he came to be here, he loved Keza no less. Perhaps he loved her even more than before. A mother's love could go beyond all boundaries.

Keza grunted and huffed as she approached, lumbering on her knuckles toward him. He bent forward and reached out one hand, knuckles bent in kind as he touched her chest, then her head in greeting. Her huffing increased in a way that almost sounded like human laughter. Thorne spoke to her in the language of the gorillas, telling her of the bad men and the many dead humans and how he had found Eden. He gently took hold of one of Eden's hands and pulled her to stand beside him.

His mother turned her reddish-brown eyes upon the young human female he hoped to call his mate. Keza hesitantly reached out and touched Eden's chest, then her head, huffing softly as she did so.

"Touch her like she touch Eden," he encouraged. "Greet her."

Eden's hands trembled as she curled her knuckles and greeted Keza. Beyond them Sunya, the dominant silverback, watched them. His dark eyes were wary, but he knew better than to fight Thorne. Both bore scars from their battles, but Thorne had always won. Though Thorne had no desire to be the dominant male of the band, his very presence put Sunya's authority in question. But Sunya also knew that he could not chase Thorne away from his family. As a result, Thorne and Sunya lived in an uneasy truce.

"This is my mother. Keza," he said to Eden.

"Your mother?" Such love was contained in those two words that Thorne's heart quivered like the chest of a parrot as it began to sing. It was a feeling of joy, excitement, and contentment all at once.

"She's beautiful, Thorne," Eden replied.

Her lips came up in a soft smile, and her pale skin warmed with pink from the heat of the late afternoon. The loose tendrils of her sunlight-like hair tumbled around her shoulders. He wanted to sit behind her and comb his hands through the shiny gold strands and groom her the way mates did.

His brother, Akika, now approached him. His black back was starting to show hints of silver in his fur.

"This is brother. Akika," Thorne said, then he greeted his brother. Akika stood still a moment before launching himself at Thorne, tackling him into the crushed nests the gorillas had been making.

Thorne grunted at the impact, then laughed as he wrestled with his brother the way they had since they were small. Akika laughed as well, in his own way. He panted hard and lightly knocked Thorne's shoulder as Thorne got to his feet.

Eden raised the black object in her hands up to her face and held still. He didn't know what she was doing, but he didn't worry. It made a clicking noise, but it was not upsetting any of the gorillas around him. They were content to rest. Several new infants sat in their mothers' laps and watched Thorne with bright, curious eyes. Thorne greeted each of the band. Akika followed close behind, showing his support of his brother. Then Thorne returned to Eden.

"You and your brother were playing?" she asked him.

"Yes. Most males do not play when they are older like me. Too much competition for mates. But Thorne not competition."

Eden was holding that black thing up to her face again. "That makes sense. Does Keza have a mate?"

"No. He died when she found Thorne. Akika is son of dead mate. Sunya is dominant male now." Thorne pointed at the prowling silverback who had just settled into his nest, grumpily watching them. "He is oldest son of Keza's dead mate, but different mother."

"Is it unusual for a female not to have a mate?" Eden

joined him as he led her into the shade, and they sat down in a soft bed of grass.

"Most females find new mate, but not Keza. Taking Thorne as son made no males want her." He watched his mother settle down and Akika play with his own juvenile son, who had recently been weaned from Akika's mate.

He pointed at Akika and his child. "Akika's son." Thorne called to his brother, who hoisted the infant on his back and walked over to them. The tiny black gorilla infant squeaked and hooted in excitement as Thorne took the child from his brother's back and held him in his arms.

"He's adorable," Eden murmured. Her eyes grew bright as she spoke again. "You are his uncle."

Uncle . . . The word he had learned for the brother of a parent.

"Yes. Thorne good uncle." He handed the infant back to Akika.

"Uncles love their family," Eden said, her tone heavy with meaning. "Your uncle, the brother of your father— he would want to meet you."

Thorne didn't want to think about his human family. It was too much for him to understand. He tried to distract Eden by pointing at her black object.

"What is this?" he asked as the box clicked again.

Eden scooted closer to him and turned the object around. Something on its surface reflected his image back at him, like a lake but brighter. Only it wasn't reflecting what he was currently doing, but rather it showed him pointing at himself. She pressed something, and then the box showed him wrestling with Akika. It was as though she had captured the past. He touched the image with one finger, only to find it had no depth. Its surface was hard.

"This is a camera. It takes pictures. Pictures are images of what you see." She pointed to the screen and then touched the camera. Suddenly he could see grass moving beneath them.

"Here. Hold it like this and point it at me." She helped him hold the camera so he could see her face in the hard surface.

"Then press this." She touched the silver circle. "When you hear a click, it will take my picture."

Thorne held the box in his hands, steady and quiet. Eden smiled, and he pressed the circle. A click sounded. He stared at the picture of her, frozen in place. He could have stared at it forever.

"Like my parents and me." He was focusing hard on the language again. He spoke full sentences when he thought about it, and he was trying to use different words like Eden did. He wanted to sound like her.

"Yes, remember the picture we found in the white rock? A photograph. Someone took that of your parents and you."

Thorne looked at her picture in the camera before handing it back to her. "You have picture of my family?"

"Oh, right. Yes." She opened the dark animal skin pouch that she used to carry the camera. He saw his father's journal tucked inside. She opened the journal and handed him the photograph. He gazed down in fresh wonder at his parents' faces, and then he looked around at the gorillas resting in the shade.

Two families. Two different fates. The life he should have had, and the life he had been given. His throat tightened as he wondered what his life would have been like if he'd never met Keza and hadn't been raised alongside Akika. Yet at the same time his heart burned with rage that he would never know his human parents or have a life with them.

He wiped angrily at the tears that coated his cheeks. He didn't want to feel so helpless, so hurt by the knowledge of what he had lost. Eden gently took the photo from him and placed it back in the journal. She then curled her arms around him, resting her cheek against his shoulder. His arms went instantly around her in return, holding her close.

A shiver of need ran through him. He *wanted* this female, wanted her in ways he barely understood. The weight of her body leaning into his and the sweet scent of her skin and hair left him breathless.

Had she been a gorilla, he would have known how to show his interest in mating her. He would have held her gaze and stayed close to her, offering his interest and protection until she chose to accept or reject him. But

Eden was from another world, one he understood only a little, and what little he knew frightened him.

She moved so she could sit across his stretched-out legs and tucked her face against his throat. Her warm breath fanned against his skin, and he was blissfully tortured by the need to touch her more. Perhaps she would kiss him again. But even if she didn't, it felt good to simply hold her.

He caught his mother's eyes. Keza hooted softly in approval. He hooted back, and Eden lifted her head, their eyes holding each other.

"You're speaking to them, aren't you?"

He nodded.

"But how? The noises you make, are they words like what we're using?"

It took Thorne a moment to understand her meaning. He shook his head. "No. Not like us. Sounds, looks, moves all have meaning. Thorne understands."

It was difficult to explain. He understood the animals of the jungle in a way that human words could never convey, and they in turn understood him. He did not know why, since the gorillas could not speak to the birds or elephants the way he could. He simply could.

"And what is she saying?" Eden asked.

"Keza is happy."

"Is she happy because of me?" Eden's lovely leaf-colored eyes seemed to glow.

"Yes. Keza has waited a long time for Thorne to find a mate."

Eden's face darkened to that pretty shade of red he saw so often. He reached up to brush the backs of his knuckles over her cheek.

"Why do you turn red?" he asked.

"What?"

"Your face is red."

"Oh . . . That's called a blush."

Thorne noticed that this blush happened to Eden a lot. "Why do you blush?"

She laughed, the soft sound filling his heart with light.

"People blush when they're feeling shy or embarrassed, or excited."

"Shy?" He wasn't familiar with that word.

"Shy is . . ." She paused. "When you're nervous about doing something or being around someone."

Thorne brushed his fingers down her throat, caressing her soft skin. "Are you shy with me?"

"Sometimes. A little. We've only just met, and we're strangers."

"Strangers?"

"We don't know each other. Not really," Eden explained.

Thorne understood. "So we date!"

Eden looked shocked at this, but Thorne remembered her words clearly: *Dating is where two people go do things they enjoy. They do it so they can get to know each other.*

She must have remembered as well, because she suddenly laughed. "Yes! So we date."

"Tell me. Make us not strangers," he commanded.

Eden's fingers slid sensually over his bare chest now. "Just tell you everything, huh?" Her nose wrinkled, and she giggled. The bubbly sound delighted him.

"Yes. Everything." The deep heat of need settled low inside him, but he was still uncertain what to do. Despite her touching him, he knew she was not yet ready to mate. She would tell him; he was certain of that.

He could have gazed upon her forever, listened to her talk as he stroked her skin. The forest around them grew quiet in a peaceful way as the birds of the air and the beasts upon the ground settled down as the evening skies purpled above them.

"I grew up in a place called Little Rock. My father is a teacher, and my mother is an engineer. Um . . . she makes things."

Thorne already had questions, but he kept quiet, content to simply listen. She spoke of a quiet life, a happy childhood, a desire to see the world, a love for animals and the need to protect them. *Conservation*, she called it.

The more she spoke, the more Thorne saw a tapestry of this woman's life being woven. She was as brave as any lioness, loyal as any gorilla, and wise and thoughtful as any elephant.

"My coming here was supposed to help the mountain gorillas. But everyone died, all those wonderful people. Those poachers killed them, Thorne. I would be dead too if you hadn't saved me." She burrowed closer, her body trembling.

"Death comes to all," he replied softly. It was the way of the jungle. Death was a part of life, and everything from the tiny ants carrying leaves on their backs to the powerful Tembo understood that.

"But not like that, Thorne. There was no reason for it. It was murder."

He nodded. "They kill not for food or protection. They kill for the joy of death." In his world, amid the bamboo shoots and the moss-covered hagenia trees, the joy of death held no place. As long as he lived, he would stop bad men like them. He would protect the impenetrable forest and all that lived in it.

Thorne didn't want Eden to be sad. He cupped her chin and lifted her face to his. He studied her eyes, such a bright green, and he saw something there that called for him to act. He lowered his head to hers, kissing her. Her lips were like the petals of a flower. He liked what she had taught him, this way of kissing.

He gently bit her bottom lip and then kissed her again. His arms tightened around her as a hum of satisfaction came from her lips. He wanted to purr like a lion at the delight he felt of pleasing his mate. He may not have claimed her body yet, but she was the mate of his heart, the mate of his soul. He knew little of the world outside the jungle, but he knew this: Eden was his true mate.

Eden pressed closer, moaning as he cupped the back of her head and fisted his hands in her hair. He liked this, holding her still so he could enjoy the taste of her. He'd held back his dominant side while he was learning to navigate this unfamiliar type of mating. Now he was confident, and with that confidence, his dominance was returning.

He nuzzled her neck and stroked her back as he explored her body, but when he pulled at the white skin she wore over her torso, she gently held his hand still.

"Not yet."

"More dates?" Thorne asked.

"More dates," Eden confirmed.

She burrowed close again, and he sighed as he held her in his arms while she drifted to sleep.

"Thorne dream of having mate for many years," he whispered to her, unsure if she was awake enough to still hear him. "Thorne has wish . . . wish for love, for mate to cherish and care for always." He wanted to tell her how much love he held in his heart for her already.

He brushed a hand over her cheek, unable to stop smiling. "Thorne give all that Thorne has to have Eden, to keep Eden."

His body was a riot of hunger and needs. He didn't know what to do, at least not fully. His male parts ached with the need for release, a thing he had done often enough alone, but now that Eden was here, he wanted to ease the ache with her and give her pleasure in return. But she wasn't ready yet. *More dates.*

Twilight stole over the clearing, casting shadows on the sleeping gorillas, making Eden's pale hair glow like moonlight. The leaf necklace around her neck glowed a dark gold.

He closed his eyes. Memories, bright and beautiful, cut through his heart in an equal mix of joy and pain.

His tiny hand curled around the leaf and held tight as he fell asleep on his mother's lap. Thorne could hear their voices, Mummy and Daddy, their words too soft to hear precisely. But the sound of it, the familiar cadence, was a comfort that made him feel safe and loved.

When Thorne opened his eyes, he was back in the jungle, the place that had been his home for almost all his life.

He swept his eyes over the sleeping gorillas. Was Eden right? Did his human uncle care about him the way he cared about Akika's son? If he did, did Thorne owe him answers?

His heart told him yes, but he was afraid to leave the only world he understood. Bwanbale had tried to explain the world of men once, but it had confused and fright-ened him, so he had stopped.

But if he didn't leave, he might lose Eden. This was not her world, and he couldn't make it her world. He had nothing to offer her except himself, but would it be enough?

JEAN CARILLET STOOD OUTSIDE THE OFFICES OF HOLT Enterprises in Fort Portal, about a hundred miles from Bwindi Impenetrable Forest National Park. Night was falling. His shirt was soaked in sweat, mud, and blood. His hands still shook. He had spent two days trying to find his way out of the forest and getting a ride to Fort Portal.

Without Roger Cash to guide him, he was lucky to still be alive. Jean shuddered. All of the men from Holt's treasure team were gone, Cash included. Slaughtered by some wild creature. Jean wasn't sure what worried him more—hearing that animal's roar reverberate across the jungle or breaking the news to Holt that they hadn't found the treasure cave.

He squared his shoulders and entered the lobby. It was expensively decorated, but it was empty now, given the late hour. Jean scanned the mahogany furniture and valuable works of art on the walls. He had been here once before when he had flown in from France to work for Holt Enterprises as a gemologist. He was supposed to assess the value of the diamonds recovered from the jungle cave. The amount of money Mr. Holt agreed to pay him for his silence was staggering. Jean was no fool. What Holt was doing wasn't legal, but Jean was human like anyone else, and agreed to forget the legalities and focus on the prize.

He hadn't signed up for slaughtering tourists who had just come to take pictures. Moreover, he hadn't signed up for being slaughtered in the jungle by that creature. Half-mad with delirium, he had thought that it looked almost human. But no, it had to be some strange form of mountain gorilla.

Holt's office was open. The door was slightly ajar, and gold light cut through into the darkened lobby. Jean stopped at the threshold of the office and knocked.

"Come in," a deep voice commanded.

Jean stepped inside. Archibald Holt was in his mid-forties, the age where a man either retained his physique or promptly lost it. Jean was thirty-seven and already felt the changes in his body, the signs that it would be a battle to keep thin and fit. Holt had made his own choice clear. The man was tall, his dark-brown hair was cut short, and his tailored suit fit the muscular thickness of his form like a second skin. He looked lethal.

Holt rose from his desk. "Mr. Carillet. " His cold blue eyes swept over Jean's bloody, sweat-soaked clothes. "I see that there's been a problem?"

"*Oui.*" Jean wanted to collapse in one of the expensive leather armchairs facing Holt's desk, but he stayed where he was.

"What is it?" Holt demanded. His tone was still calm, but that worried Jean even more.

He cleared his throat. "Monsieur. Cash was leading us toward the cave, and we came upon a group of tourists, mostly American, who were there to see the gorillas."

Holt did not speak. He merely waited, still as a lion, eyes unblinking.

"Well, Mr. Cash gathered them up and shot them."

Jean shouldn't have been surprised by Holt's lack of a response to this news. But of course, Cash hadn't gone rogue, had he? He'd followed orders.

"And?"

"He killed all but one."

Holt's face finally expressed an emotion. Mild disgust. "He took a hostage, didn't he? Let me guess—a woman? That bloody fool thinks of his cock and nothing else. The man is supposed to be a professional."

"*Oui*, a woman. But there was a sound from the jungle. Some of the men began speaking of a beast. A pale ghost." Jean cringed at the memory of the tree shaking with the echoing roar. "We started to run. Monsieur Cash stayed behind to kill the woman, but the *beast* killed him and the others. Only I escaped."

Holt's eyes somehow managed to frost even more. "Cash is dead?"

"*Oui*. The beast snapped his neck. It killed like no other creature I've seen. For a moment I thought . . ."

"You thought *what?*" Holt asked, his voice dangerously low. The gilded furnishings in the office suddenly took on an ominous feel. A stuffed gorilla looked on menacingly from the corner in the muted lamplight.

"I thought the beast looked human, Monsieur Holt. But that cannot be. No one lives that deep in the forest."

Holt slowly sat back down at his desk, storm clouds gathering on his brow. His gaze turned distant for a long moment. When he refocused on Jean, the Frenchman's stomach roiled with nerves.

"Go and clean yourself up at the hotel across the street and rest the night there. Charge it to my account. Tomorrow we will speak again about this ghost."

"*Oui*, monsieur. Thank you."

Jean fled the office and rushed into the growing dark, only to hear a bellow of rage and the smashing of something behind him. Whatever lurked in the branches of the jungle wasn't the only monster in Uganda. Another lived right here in the city, wearing an expensive suit.

7

Eden stretched and yawned as sunlight began to warm her face. For a moment she didn't remember where she was. Then she felt soft grass rustle beneath her, and her eyes snapped wide open.

She dimly remembered falling asleep near the gorillas, but she wasn't lying in a nest on the ground. She was lying in a bed of soft grass that covered a mass of palm fronds from banana trees, which formed a gentle cushion the size of a king bed. She was in a tree house, much like the first one Thorne had brought her to. But that one had been small and closed off except for the trapdoor and a small window. In this one, the walls were carved with strange symbols in beautiful patterns, some of them matching the tattoos on Thorne's shoulders.

This tree house was bigger than her small one-room

EMMA CASTLE

efficiency apartment back in Little Rock. This place was *huge*. The beautiful bed of long soft grass and fronds was in one corner. There were five large windows with thatched reed coverings that could drop in place, held up by vines used like rope to hold them during the day. In one corner of the room, a pile of glittering stones and gold objects rested in beautifully arranged displays. Eden's eyes widened.

Eden wanted to know where Thorne had found those. They had to be from a lost civilization. If there were more, archeologists would consider it the find of the century.

Her camera bag lay close to the bed. Thorne had removed her boots and socks and draped a blanket of fur over her body. It felt like deerskin. She gently pushed it off her body. A small, roughly carved wooden cup held fresh water, and a palm frond that sat within reach was piled with more peeled mangoes, nuts, and wild celery.

Eden wanted to explore this new home, but she needed to satisfy the rumblings of her belly first. She drank the cool water and ate, then got to her feet and padded on the smooth wooden planks to the nearest window. How had he made this place? The craftsmanship was still rough in places, but not everywhere. It was clear that Thorne had gained his knowledge of woodworking from someone. The question was *who* and *how*? She peered out and gasped when she saw how high up they were. In the distance, a waterfall spilled into a pool. Was that the waterfall he had taken her to yesterday?

The jungle shook with a distant roar, one she knew belonged to Thorne, but it was not a warning call. It was something else, a sound of happiness and a challenge to the jungle at the same time.

Then she saw him. He swung down below on the vines and came up toward her with the lithe grace of a jungle cat, landing on all fours in a perfect crouch. Then he straightened, walking confidently along the branch, only a foot wide, toward the ladder that led up to the tree house. His lean, muscled legs were a sight to behold. Eden kept convincing herself that she had imagined the sheer perfection of his body, and yet it wasn't her imagination. He was gorgeous.

She took a moment to watch him unobserved. A flutter in her belly was followed by a slow-burning desire. She'd been trying to slow things down, but damn if he didn't call to something primal inside her. He spoke of mates with such a sweet earnestness that it nearly broke her resolve. He would become a masterful lover, she was certain. Eden had always had a healthy love of sex, but sex with Thorne would be beyond anything she'd ever experienced before, and that was a little bit intimidating. What if she fell in love with him? What if there were simply too many what-ifs when it came to this beautiful wild man?

Thorne suddenly appeared in the window, beaming

at her. "Eden is awake."

"Yes, *I* am." She chuckled, pointing to herself as she emphasized the pronoun. "And it is '*You* are awake.' Not 'Eden is awake.'"

Thorne pointed to himself. "Me." Then pointed to her. "You?"

"Yes, exactly."

His brow furrowed as he considered her words before he vanished and then opened one of the large wooden doors to the tree house.

"*You* are awake," he said more confidently.

"Yes."

"You eat?"

"I have eaten, yes." She corrected him again. Last night she'd noticed him doing his best to correct his speech, and she'd decided to help him.

"I *have* eaten." He looked to her, and she nodded in approval. He brightened. "You take more pictures?" He pointed to her camera bag.

"Can I? I would love to take pictures of the elephants and the waterfall." Her gaze flicked to the gold and diamonds and the carvings on the walls. "And maybe the place where you found those?" She would take pictures of his display as well. She wanted to be able to document everything as best she could.

His hand rose to the leafy crown on his brow, and he frowned.

"Would that be okay?"

"Yes. But cave is dark."

"Not a problem." Eden knelt by her camera bag and pulled out a flashlight. She clicked it on and shone the light on the wooden floor. Thorne tensed, then suddenly smiled at her.

"You carry sunlight."

"Sort of." She motioned him forward and handed him the flashlight. She showed him how to flip the switch to turn it on and off. He did it several times, grinning. Even jungle-raised wild men loved technology, it seemed.

"Can we leave now? I would like to take some pictures." She put her camera bag over her head and slung it across her body.

Thorne glanced at the empty palm fronds he'd left by the bed, then agreed. It was weirdly cute that he was so thoughtful about her needs.

She climbed onto his back, and he stepped out into the webbing of thick branches.

"You hold me," he instructed. One of his hands tapped her knee as if to remind her she needed to keep a tight grip on him.

"I'm holding on as tight as I can," she assured him.

Thorne grabbed the nearest thick vine, his muscles bulging as he wound his fingers around it.

"We aren't climbing?" Panic rocketed through her as she realized what he meant to do. "Oh no, no-no-no—!"

He leapt off the branch before she could finish, and

her words turned to a shriek as she closed her eyes. The pit of her stomach dropped as they entered a brief freefall before the vine Thorne held caught their weight. She heard the chatter of birds and felt the breeze whip her face and hair as they swung. She dared to open her eyes just as Thorne caught another vine and they swung yet again. They were flying, or close to it, and Eden suddenly laughed.

For a few glorious seconds, her past life no longer existed. There was only this moment with Thorne, the jungle, the humidity clinging to them and the wild world ahead with its endless beauty.

Their swinging slowed, and Thorne dropped down to the ground with panther-like grace. She had to practically peel herself off his back from the sweat. She plucked at her clothes, more than a little embarrassed, but Thorne watched her with a sweet, knowing smile that held a hint of mischief.

"What?"

He shrugged and started walking toward the open trail where they had first seen Tembo and his herd.

"Tell me!" She rushed to catch up to him. "Seriously, what?" She reached for his hand, and he turned amused eyes on her.

"You like to hold me with your body." He spoke the words carefully, getting better at his English every time he practiced.

"I do not," she lied.

Thorne merely smiled wider. "You do. We are dating. I am pleased."

He was indeed—he practically gleamed with pride. Eden was torn. He had never had a human companion, at least not since he'd lost his parents, but now he had her. And part of her, a far too big part of her, loved the idea that she was the first woman he had ever kissed and that he wanted to be her man, to care for her and cherish her.

Last night as she fell asleep, he had spoken to her softly about mates and how he had dreamed of one, and how he would give everything that was his to have her. He'd spoken of love, too, but what did love mean to a man raised in the wild? Did he understand the intricacies of falling and staying in love? It was possible here in the jungle that it was easy to love, but in the modern world it seemed infinitely more difficult.

He slid an arm around her waist and pulled her close, so their bodies were flush against each other. He cupped the back of her head and brought his lips to hers. She groaned against his mouth as his tongue played with hers. He was becoming a master of this, seducing her slowly and exquisitely into a state of wild arousal. Eden wanted him to never stop touching her and never wanted to feel his mouth leave hers unless it was to kiss other parts of her. By the time he was done, she'd completely forgotten whatever they had been talking about. Her body was vibrating with the need for more.

"Good kiss?" he asked, his face flushed.

"*Very* good. I'm regretting that I taught you how to do that." She chuckled and bit her lip as though to hide a smile. He looked almost bashful, and that made her flush with wild hungers that would have embarrassed her, but Thorne didn't make her ashamed of her body or what it wanted.

"I like kissing you. It pleases me." He swept his gaze over her body in a way that made her fully aware of where his thoughts were headed. Hers weren't far behind.

"Thorne—"

Whatever she'd been about to say was lost as a trumpeting sound rang out. She turned toward the sound, and Thorne answered the elephant's call with one of his own.

They had traveled to a place where the forest spread out into a beautiful savanna. It was a rare thing to see this small patch of land exposed to the sky in the midst of the jungle. A herd of elephants lingered on the open ground in front of them.

Two younger elephants were playing. The elders watched in quiet enjoyment. Eden could *feel* the love the elephants bore for one another, like an invisible cloud that filled the air with hope and adoration. For a second, Eden thought she could almost hear them—hear words within their sounds and see them within their movements. Was she going crazy? Or was what Thorne had told her about how he spoke to and understood the animals just starting to make sense to her?

"You take pictures," Thorne suggested quietly. "You must see Tembo's infants." He led her closer, but they still kept a respectable distance away until Tembo recognized Thorne. With the beckoning weight of his trunk, Thorne and Eden were welcomed into the elephants' circle.

"This is Tembo's daughter." He pointed to the smaller infant. "And that is Tembo's older son."

Eden noted the size difference between the two baby elephants. The younger one stayed close to her mother and would hide beneath her belly. The older of the two was far braver and ventured close to Eden, letting her touch his head and trunk. Eden must have snapped a hundred photos of them before she turned her lens toward Thorne. He stood illuminated in the afternoon light, the sun glinting off his golden leaf crown. He faced Tembo, smiling as he held his friend's trunk. Eden was struck by the power of that image.

Like two lords, meeting in peace and respect.

Eden's heart fluttered as she watched him speak to Tembo like old friends. There was a magic to Thorne and the way he interacted with the animals around him. He wasn't bound by any laws of men. He held no fear, only love and understanding. Then Thorne hugged Tembo goodbye and came back to her.

"You show me pictures?" he asked. She showed him

the photos, and when he saw himself and Tembo, his smile vanished. "That is me," he said, his tone hushed.

"Yes." It wasn't the first time he'd seen his own picture, but she sensed there was a question lurking behind it.

"Thorne is—*I* am a good male for females?" His troubled look as he stared critically at his own face was oddly endearing. He had no idea how beautiful he was.

"Thorne, you are very handsome."

"Handsome?"

"Pleasing to females, *very* pleasing," she explained. Then she added to herself silently, *A little too pleasing.*

He grinned again, his confidence restored. Tembo suddenly trumpeted, and Thorne tensed.

"What is it?"

"Tembo says danger is near. The herd must leave. We must go." Thorne's eyebrows lowered, and his mouth hardened into a line as he searched the meadow. Eden turned off her camera and shoved it back in her bag.

"Come now," Thorne urged as the elephants began to huddle and move across the meadow in a solid group, the two infants between them.

Eden kept close to Thorne as he led her back in the direction they had come. Thorne stopped and ever so slowly put her behind him as he faced the meadow. His body seemed almost to expand as he made himself appear larger to whatever threat he sensed was out there.

Then she saw it. The golden shape creeping toward them in the tall wheat-colored meadow. A male lion. Eden knew enough about lion prides to know that female lions hunted together, not males. This male lion was likely without a pride and therefore probably desperate for food.

Eden was paralyzed with fear. She'd seen what damage a big cat's claws could do.

"Eden," Thorne whispered, "when lion attacks, you run."

"I can't leave you." Even if it got her killed, she wouldn't leave him.

"You will. I fight lion before."

Eden felt helpless as she saw him advance toward the shape in the grass. He removed a small dagger from the waistband of his loincloth, but it wouldn't be enough, not against a lion.

Thorne began to sidestep, circling the beast as it tracked them toward the thick jungle. Eden kept behind him, not out of fear for herself, although she was beyond terrified. No, she stayed with him because she *wouldn't* leave him, no matter what he said. Thorne shot a look toward the trees behind him, his face shadowed with a dark scowl of ferocity.

"Eden, run!" he shouted just as the lion leapt at them from the grass.

Eden didn't run, but she did move out of the way. Thorne lunged to the side and grasped a vine hanging from a tree. He swung it around the lion's neck. The lion shrieked in rage, slashing its claws in the air toward Thorne as he spun around behind it, closing the noose of the vine about the creature's neck. He held the knife and wound the vine tight around his arm until the lion ceased struggling. Then it went limp. Thorne held still a moment longer before he let go. With careful hands, he loosened the vine. The lion's eyes fluttered as it started to come around.

Thorne rushed toward Eden and grabbed her hand, pulling her as they ran back into the jungle. It was only then as she fell in step behind him that she saw the slashes across his back from the lion's claws. Thorne was bleeding.

"Wait, you're hurt." She tried to pull them to a halt, but he was too strong.

"Must keep going. Lion is not dead." Thorne continued to jog through the jungle with her at his back. He didn't stop until they reached the waterfall close to his tree house. Only then did he pause at the edge of the falls, breathing hard. He still held her hand and finally looked down at her.

"Come into the water with me."

The more time she spent near him, the more she felt her instincts sharpening. If she came into the water with him and let her adrenaline and her heart rule her, she would make a choice that could not be undone.

Yet this choice had been decided long ago, before

she'd ever set foot in Africa. From the first moment she'd seen the solemn faces of the gorillas in a zoo as a child, she'd been set on this path. She'd never given much thought to fate or destiny—until now.

Eden pulled her hand free of his and knelt to remove her boots and socks. Thorne unfastened his deerskin loincloth and let it fall to the ground before he set his crown next to it. Then he walked into the water and stopped when he was chest-deep. He had his back to her. The blood from the lion's claw marks drifted down into the pool, but they didn't seem that deep. Eden removed her clothes and waded into the pool behind him until she was neck-deep in the cold water. As if sensing she was ready, Thorne turned around and moved closer to her.

"You are safe," he said softly. "I will *always* protect you." He cupped her face in his large, strong palms as he gazed into her eyes.

"Why didn't you kill the lion?" she asked. She was glad he hadn't, but she would have understood if he'd needed to.

"I kill when there is no escape. Today I could escape. All life has a purpose. All creatures have a purpose. From ants to elephants, we all belong here, we all fight to survive. If I can save a lion's life, I will. He will find food elsewhere. I do not hate the lion because it hunts. We do what we must to survive."

Eden trembled as a chill traveled across her skin.

"Are you cold?" he asked.

"A little." She moved in closer to him, and his focus drifted from her face down to her naked body.

Eden put a hand on his chest and stroked the hard-muscled front of his body.

"I like when you touch me," he murmured, closing his eyes. "No one except Keza or Akika has touched me with love, and not like this."

Eden swallowed hard. She wanted to show this beautiful, kindhearted, brave man what it meant to be loved, to be cherished. In that moment she made her decision.

"Touch me, Thorne."

She curled her fingers around his wrist. His hand moved down to her neck, his fingers gentle as he touched the hollow of her throat with one thumb. Then he ran the backs of his fingers over her collarbone. His lips parted as his hand moved below the water to cup one breast. His eyes were full of fire and innocence, a mix that called to every part of her.

"You are beautiful," he said. His voice held a roughness that heightened her excitement that much more. What would he be like when he lost control and took her with his primal roughness? She shivered at the thought, but it was one of those deliciously *good* shivers.

"Take me to the cave behind the falls," Eden said.

She had made her choice. She would show him what it meant to make love, and she vowed she would have no regrets about it. Not here. Not with him.

8

Thorne's heart pounded wildly as he and Eden swam toward the rock ledge that would lead them behind the falls. He wanted to nest, to build her a proper spot for whatever came next, but he was too nervous to focus on anything except getting behind the curtain of water.

He climbed in first and turned to help her up. The light hit her body, baring her to him, and his heart stopped. She was exquisite, beauty beyond words. Her breasts were full and soft, her nipples a lovely dark-rose color that made his body stiffen all over. The full flare of her womanly hips, so different from his own, called for his hands to touch. He wanted to feel her body pressed to his, feel their skin touching everywhere at once.

Eden stood up on her toes and kissed his parted lips.

The heat of her in his arms was so unexpected and wonderful that he sighed against her mouth.

Thorne wrapped his arms around her, his hands sliding down her back to cup her bottom. She moaned against his lips, and her breasts rubbed against his chest. His cock was hard—too hard. It was actually painful. He pulled away, ashamed. Maybe something was wrong with him.

"What's the matter?" Eden asked.

"I hurt," he confessed with humiliation.

Her hands stilled on his shoulders. "Your back?"

"No, here." He guided one of her hands down to his cock.

"Oh . . ." She gently touched him, wrapping her hand around his shaft. "Sometimes there are good hurts, when mating."

She had said it. *Mating*. Had he proven to her that he was a worthy mate? His heart leapt with hope.

"Thorne, I want you to mate with me. Do you know how?" Eden inquired.

"Yes." He stepped back. "Stay here." He rushed deeper into the cave and collected a thick pallet of furs. He set them down near the lit entrance of the cave behind the falls, just out of reach of the spray of the water. He wanted to see her and not be lost in the darkness. He arranged the furs carefully, leaving the leopard skin on top since it was the softest. It would also show his prowess for defeating such a fierce predator. When he was done, he gestured for Eden to get on the fur nest. She knelt and then lay down on her back. He was confused at her position. He got down on his knees beside her and tried to roll her over so he would be behind her while she was on her hands and knees.

"Not like that, at least not the first time," she said. "Like this."

His gaze moved over her body to between her legs, and as she parted them, he stared at her feminine folds, which were a dark pink.

"Lie on top of me. I'll show you. There are many ways to mate—this is one way." She held her arms out to him, and he crawled up her body, lying in between her bent thighs. She cradled him, held him gently. It felt good to have her soft, giving body beneath his own hard one.

Eden coasted her palms up and down his arms, soothing him with soft murmurs before she slid one hand between them. He gasped as she touched his shaft. He lifted his hips as she guided him toward her. The instant he felt the wet heat of her body wrap around him, he sank into her, feeling a state of bliss he had never imagined possible. He gasped softly, the surprise of the sensations almost too much.

"Oh God," Eden whispered. "That feels incredible."

Thorne would have smiled, but he was too lost in the heaven that was Eden's body. Instinct took over as he began to move, gently at first, learning the feel of her body beneath him, trying not to hurt her. It felt like home—*she* felt like home.

As he grew in confidence, he thrust his hips deeper against hers and buried his face against her neck. She shuddered beneath him as a sharp cry escaped her lips. It was a beautiful sound of sweet surrender that drove him to the edge. He emptied himself in a wild rush of physical pleasure. He poured every part of himself, even his heart, into Eden. Drums beat inside his body, his heart pounding a wild rhythm he'd never heard before. He'd heard the distant drums of Bwanbale's village once, during a celebration, but these were different. Thorne gasped for breath, his body shaking hard as Eden wrapped her arms around his neck.

He collapsed on top of her. It took him a moment before he realized he might be crushing her. He rolled over, but he held her close so that she rolled with him and lay atop his body like a wonderful blanket of silky palm fronds.

He gazed up at her, the roar of the falls now filling his ears again, and he couldn't believe how blessed he was to have her, to have a *mate* who had gifted him her trust.

"Are you okay?" Eden asked. Her wet hair hung like liquid sunlight down her shoulders to touch his chest, tickling him in the most wonderful way.

"Yes." He was unable to say anything else. He felt complete—he felt *whole*—with his mate in his arms.

Thorne touched her shoulders, then moved his hands down her back, holding her close. He had never imagined being with a mate could be like this. The soft, sweet caresses, the touches that were welcomed rather than snarled at, embraced rather than fought against.

He finally found the words to ask what seemed like a vital question. "Are you okay?"

"It was incredible." Eden rested her chin on his chest, and he saw the waterfall reflected in her green eyes. He couldn't imagine a more beautiful sight.

"So . . . Your first time?"

Thorne smiled and brushed the backs of his knuckles across her cheek. "It was incredible," he echoed. He really liked that word. It was fitting for anything that had to do with Eden.

"Everything you hoped for?"

Thorne nodded. His body was relaxed. Perhaps he would be ready to mate with her again soon, if she wanted him to. But as much as he wanted to keep her in this secret cave forever, they would have to leave eventually.

"I'm honored to have shared this with you." Eden moved up his body to kiss his chin, then his mouth and the top of his nose.

He sighed as she kissed his closed eyelids. Her lips were gentle and soft, and wherever she put her mouth his skin burned in the most enticing way.

"I am honored too." He cupped the back of her head

and held her face to his for a long, deep kiss. He liked this kissing, liked tasting Eden's sweetness—especially after she had eaten mangoes. Kissing was something the animals in his world didn't do. They didn't share such intimacy. Whenever he kissed Eden, he felt his bond with her grow stronger.

"Are you hungry?" he asked.

She kissed him one more time before nodding.

He helped her up from the bed of furs, and they splashed back into the pool. Eden was calmer now, less shy with her body as she swam naked ahead of him. Thorne caught her waist, pulling her back to him. She giggled and wriggled in his arms like a slippery fish, but he held fast as he kissed her neck from behind. Her breasts filled his hands as he held her, and she arched against him, her rounded bottom rubbing against his hardening shaft.

He didn't ask this time. By the way she was moaning and rubbing against him, he knew that she wanted him. He turned her to face him so that they stood chest-deep in the water, and he lifted her up against him. Her skin was flushed, her eyes wide, lips parted, and all he could think about was feeling her, tasting her. Ripe mangoes and crisp waterfalls. For a second they simply stared at each other as his grip on her waist tightened and her nails dug into his biceps in silent invitation.

A growl came from the back of Thorne's throat, a deep sound of domination as he lifted her up against him. Her body opened around his, her legs curling tight around his hips. He gripped his cock, feeding himself into her as she had shown him. She clutched his shoulders, her green eyes dark like the jungle just before twilight. He ignored the sting of the lion's claw marks. The bite of that pain somehow only heightened his pleasure in this moment—as though by protecting her, he'd won the right to mate with her.

Thorne thrust deep, claiming her in slow, measured movements, enjoying how she responded with soft moans that escaped her throat. Wet skin against wet skin, heated friction built between them, quivering and shivering. Breath broke, hearts raced, and fingers clawed at skin. He fisted a hand in her hair, and she raked nails down his back as he took her rough, took her raw. Harsh and beautiful. Her breasts rubbed against his chest as he lifted her up and down over his body. Eden buried her face against his neck, clinging to him as she cried out in his arms. The sweetest pleasure exploded through him as he came a heartbeat later. For the first time, he felt . . . complete. To know the companionship and physical love of a mate, just like this.

His body trembled with the slow, sweet fall into that blissful state that seemed to come when he and Eden mated.

In that moment of joy, he hoped that they had created a new life between them. He longed to have his

EMMA CASTLE

own son or daughter, and now that Eden was his mate, that dream seemed possible.

They lingered in the water, their limbs tangled and breaths shared as they recovered. Her legs stayed wrapped around his body, her fingers were still dug tightly into him as if she too didn't wish to let go. Life was ever a battle of clinging with desperation and letting go with longing. It was a lesson of the jungle, one he'd learned so often, but never so bittersweetly as he did now while holding Eden in his arms. He wanted to mate with her forever, and yet he feared the moment that it was over, because then it would be one second closer to when he would lose what he was beginning to love more than anything else.

Cold water drizzled across their bodies from the nearby falls, chilling their heated skin. Eden finally relaxed; her legs slid down off his hips, and her grip on him eased, but she didn't let go. Sweat still clung to their skin, and he playfully dipped them both beneath the surface of the water. Her trust in him, so instinctive now, made him want to roar with leonine pride.

All around them the jungle was quiet, and a stillness settled over the world as birds sang soft symphonies against the crash of water into the pool. There were no warnings in the air. All was well in the jungle tonight. He could rest easy.

When they finally exited the pool, dripping and smiling, Thorne enjoyed watching Eden put on her strange skins. He memorized everything about her body. She belonged to him now, just as he belonged to her. Yet part of him knew it could not be that easy. The world of men was nothing if not complicated.

"Thorne, how did you learn English? Is it what you remember from your parents?"

"A little." He pulled his deerskin loincloth back onto his body and tied the leather straps in place. "More comes from Bwanbale."

"Bwanbale?" Eden repeated. "What's a Bwanbale?"

"He is human. A male. He is my friend."

Eden's eyes brightened with interest. "A human?"

"Yes. Enemy first, then friend later."

Thorne did his best to explain his first sighting of a human since he'd been rescued by Keza, and how Bwanbale had stayed with him for a time in the jungle before returning to his village, which was half a day away on foot. Many times Bwanbale had come back to visit him, meeting him in the savanna meadow where Thorne had shown Eden Tembo.

"So by the time you met him, you were around twenty years old."

Thorne shrugged. Time didn't seem to matter here in the humid evergreen jungle.

"He taught you English?"

Thorne nodded. "English and Swahili." They began the walk back through the jungle toward the mango trees.

"Wait, you know Swahili? Then why didn't you respond when we first met? I was speaking Swahili then."

His face flooded with heat. "I was scared to speak."

"You've come pretty far in the last couple of days."

Her praise filled him with pride. "I remember more of how my parents used to talk. The more you speak, the more I remember."

"That's a good thing." Eden rested one hand on her bag, which held what she called her camera, the object that took pictures.

"Tell me more about Bwanbale."

"He lives in a village with his mate and a child. I have not seen them, but he's told me many stories of them." He shared with Eden as much as he could remember of the world Bwanbale had described all those years ago. Then it had seemed like Bwanbale's stories were too impossible to be true. He also told her about the way Bwanbale had showed him how to use tools to refine his home, to make cups, and other things.

Eden climbed over a fallen tree with his help. "Are there a lot of poachers here in the jungle?"

"Many, but south. Not here."

"Do you think the men who . . ." Eden's voice trembled, and her hand tightened around his. "The men who killed everyone were poachers?"

"Yes. Or men who look for gold," he added, thinking of the men who had brutally murdered his parents.

Those men had been looking for gold. Eden had explained the value of it to him, how men and women for thousands of years had placed immense value on the shiny hard metal. Thorne thought it was madness to care for such a thing. One could not eat it or use it as a weapon or for shelter. It served no purpose. And yet it called to him as well. He had brought some of it to his home, had copied the symbols he'd seen onto his walls. The past spoke to him, cried out to him sometimes.

He knew that the people who often came to him in his dreams—the ones where he saw other humans, ancient ones, building homes in the trees—were the ones who'd made the gold and who'd found the glittering stones. Diamonds, as Eden had called them. Whatever belonged in the cave belonged to those long-gone spirits who spoke to Thorne. He and Bwanbale had spoken once of the gold and the cave, and Bwanbale had said that it must be kept secret, it must be respected.

Eden was silent a long moment. "Thorne, we have to find the police. Tell them what happened. The people who died, the other tourists like me, they have families who need to know what happened."

Thorne didn't immediately respond. Every time she brought the subject up, it filled him with fear. If she left the jungle, she would leave *him*.

"We can't leave them there." Eden tugged on his hand, and he turned to face her. "It's the right thing to do."

"You will stay . . . if I do this?"

"Stay with you?" Her tone was full of uncertainty.

"Yes. Stay with me. Here."

Her eyes betrayed her as they softened with sorrow. "Thorne, I can't stay here, not forever. I have a life, a family, a job. These last few days have been incredible, but this world, it isn't *mine*."

Thorne raised her chin up so their gazes locked. "I want you to stay, be mine. *Always*." How could he tell her the truth? That there was no Thorne without Eden. They were two halves of a whole. Why couldn't she see that? But he didn't have the words.

"You have no idea how much that tempts me. It's beautiful here. But this, it's a fantasy, a dream. I couldn't survive here, even with you protecting me." She leaned into him, pressing her cheek to his chest. "You don't have to stay here—you can come to *my* world. It belongs to you too."

He wished he could believe her, but he'd spent too many years in the jungle. Too many nights sleeping beneath the stars and hunting in the wild. Bwanbale's world was strange enough to him, and that was just a small village, seen from a distance. The stories Bwanbale had shared of the larger world had terrified him.

He would not know how to fit into her world, but if he never left the forest, he would never let her down. The time they had together would remain a beautiful memory, a dream that for a time was real. It would have to be enough for him.

A memory crept into his mind, one of a vast world of flowers shadowed by twilight.

His small hands were cupped together, holding something trapped within his palms. Something that glowed. Something he wanted. His mother was there, kneeling in front of him.

"You should set the lightning bug free, Thorne," she said.

"Don't want to!" he argued. "Mine!"

His mother smiled sadly at him, and his tiny heart quivered. He didn't like it when he made her sad.

"When we love something with all our heart, sometimes we have to let it go. Creatures big and small deserve to be free." She gently cupped his palms. Her hands were warm. He felt safe and loved whenever she touched him.

"Set it free?" he asked. He could feel the lightning bug crawling on the insides of his hands. "I don't want it to go."

"But it will be happy if you do. It's not happy there. See? It's stopped flashing." His mother was right—the glowing that peeked out from his fingers had stopped. Thorne spread his palms wide, and the lightning bug on his palm glowed. It buzzed and took flight, vanishing into the night to join the distant winking flashes of the other bugs.

"See? It's making happy flashes."

Thorne's heart was burdened with the loss, but he was glad that the lightning bug was happy again.

Thorne closed his eyes. The memory had been so vivid in his mind. He held on to the image, breathing deeply before he faced Eden again. If he took her to the other humans she would be happy again, and that was all that mattered to him.

"I will take you to Bwanbale tomorrow. He will help you."

Eden bit her bottom lip. "Will you come with me?"

He placed one of his palms on the soft mossy trunk of the nearest tree and shook his head. "My family is here. I must protect them."

Eden was silent a long moment, then nodded. "I understand."

Thorne took Eden to the mango grove, where he climbed high into the trees so he could pluck the ripe fruit, and then he dropped them down to her. When he leapt back to the ground, they carried their mangoes to his tree house, where they ate in a quiet but pleasant silence.

Eden lay back in his arms. Her weight against his chest was a comfort he would miss now that he'd tasted the joy a mate could bring. As the light began to fade outside, Eden turned in his arms, her mouth seeking his.

He could deny her nothing, this spinner of beloved dreams, this creator of wondrous memories. She removed her skins slowly, letting him take in the sight of her before she lay back on the palm frond and grass nest. He kissed her lips, her chin, the hollow of her throat, and further down. Each time he touched her, he was stunned by the beauty of her feminine form. He caressed her breasts before sucking one nipple into his mouth. She arched her back, pressing herself closer to his exploring mouth. Thorne savored her every sigh and moan as he explored her body. She giggled as he kissed the inside of her thighs and her smooth belly.

As their bodies joined, he struggled to hold back, to go slow. He wanted to remember everything about her. He took his time, mating with her with exquisite slowness. If this was to be his final time with her, he didn't want to rush it. As Eden writhed with pleasure in his arms, he followed her, and then they lay quiet a long while after, their bodies still connected.

Just outside the tree house, the sounds of the wild came to them. Birds, monkeys, insects, even the deep trumpets of elephants and the mating calls of the jaguars.

He waited for Eden to fall asleep, but she stayed awake, holding on to him. Perhaps she dreaded the goodbye that tomorrow's sunrise would bring as much as he did.

"Eden, tell me of your home again." He wanted to see in his mind's eye the world that she would be returning to so he might picture her there when he lay awake in the dark jungle, all alone and missing her.

"Well, in Little Rock the summer heat is almost as hot as this jungle. The cicadas—those are insects—they buzz so loud that you can't hear anything else in the late summer evenings. Mom is usually on the swing on the front porch, a drink in one hand and a book in the other." She paused to cuddle closer to him. "Dad is usually out in the shed—sort of a small home to store things in—and he'd be fussing over his newest tools." She sighed. "I miss them."

It was true. He could hear it in her voice, and he knew that letting her go was the right thing to do, even if it broke his heart. She would be happy.

"Tell me about the jungle," she said. "About your adventures with Akika and Tembo."

Thorne held her close, taking in the scent of her, imprinting it upon his soul. "Every animal has its place, from the mighty Tembo to the smallest insect. I grew up in the trees, swinging among the vines and facing down the dangers of the jungle."

She yawned, and he could feel her slip slowly into sleep as he spoke. Eden was asleep before he finished, but he continued to talk, speaking to her of his new hopes and dreams, that perhaps one day she would return to him. But only the creatures of the twilight jungle were witness to his confession of love and hope.

9

Eden followed Thorne, careful to step only where he stepped. He had warned her after breakfast that they would be walking toward an area of the jungle that held more danger—which, given what she'd already experienced, was saying something. He'd been insistent that she stay close, step where he stepped, and not touch anything thin and green, referring to the black mamba snakes of the area, which were actually grayish brown, and whose bite was fatal.

They hiked down the sloping mountain and left the canopy of hagenia trees behind them before they journeyed into the bamboo forests. They reached the village by early evening, but Thorne remained at the edge of the woods. He would not go farther.

She saw him studying the structures with intense focus, and Eden followed his gaze. He was watching the people who were interacting in the street. She knew he'd never been into the village before.

He nodded toward the village. "Bwanbale lives there." None of the villagers could see them, hidden as they were in the foliage.

"Aren't you coming with me?" Eden took hold of Thorne's hand.

"No. I stay in my world." He looked back at the dense jungle behind him. "You can go home now." He stood so still, a tall, breathing wall of muscle. She could feel his heart beating as she placed her other hand on his chest. His blue eyes, with a color so pure and reflective whenever he looked at her, were dark with mystery and pain now. Agony because they had to say goodbye.

Eden found it hard to breathe. The thought of leaving him, of never seeing him again—it wasn't right. It wasn't fair. Eden threw her arms around him, hugging him tight.

"Come with me. *Please*, Thorne." She would have begged on her knees if she thought it would have made a difference. Thorne raised her chin, and she saw a deepening pain glinting in their gentle depths.

"You must go. Tell Bwanbale you belong to me. The mate of Thorne will be protected."

His mate. Eden couldn't deny that claim. It was primitive. But it was also true. In a few short days, she truly felt as though she had become his mate, *his* woman in a way she never would be with any other man.

"Thorne." She choked on his name, the pain so deep within her that she wasn't sure she would ever feel joy again.

He lowered his head to hers and pressed a kiss to her lips. She felt that kiss deep within her soul. It was a kiss of goodbye, a kiss of infinite longing, heartache, and love.

"Be free, Eden. Go home."

He *loved* her. She could taste its bittersweetness upon her own lips.

"You gave me great joy," Thorne said. "I belong to you. *Always.*"

Eden's eyes blurred with tears. She shut them and looked away, trying not to let him see her cry. She felt his hands drop from her body, and by the time she turned back to him, the lost Earl of Somerset and Lord of the Wild was gone.

She covered her mouth with one hand, desperate to hold back the sobs that came next. Part of her wondered if it hadn't been some insane dream. But the gold ginkgo leaf necklace lay warm against her neck, a reminder that it had been real.

It only made the pain of their parting that much worse.

Eden did not venture into the village right away. Part of her hoped some other option would miraculously present itself. She stayed at the edge of the village until evening came. Only then did the dark jungle lose its comforting presence, and she longed to be surrounded by people again.

The village was a loose grouping of small family farms known as *shambas*. They bled into the rolling green hills in the distance that led toward the papyrus-lined shores of a small lake. As Eden came out of the woods, some of the children noticed her and came running. Many wore green-and-blue school uniforms. Several laughed and called out to her in Swahili, but she couldn't understand most of what they were saying because they were speaking too fast. One girl dashed right up to Eden and clasped her hand, chatting excitedly in Swahili, a bright, beautiful smile on her adorable face.

"Bwanbale," Eden said, hoping one of the children would know him. Eden looked to the girl still holding her hand. "Can you take me to Bwanbale?"

The girl nodded, tugging her ahead of the others, who still clambered around her. They all seemed excited by her intrusion upon their peaceful village, which put her a little more at ease.

A pair of brown parrots flew overhead and landed on the roof of a nearby home. Some of the children pointed to the parrots and ran off to play. Several adults from the village came out of their houses to see what was going on. So many people had the wrong perception about African communities. They assumed everyone lived in grass huts and beat drums while wearing no clothes. There were still some very tribal

LOVE IN THE WILD

communities existing in Africa like that, but much of
Africa was advanced, and the villages and cities were
perfectly comfortable. Bwanbale's village was a lovely
grouping of well-built homes, small gardens, and farms.
The villagers were well dressed, and they had modern
cars, trucks, and tools. She understood now how
Thorne would have been confused by Bwanbale's very
modern world when the two talked during their times
together.

The air smelled of earth and blossoms, with a hint of
woodsmoke from cooking fires. A faint drumbeat and
some singing drifted from the direction of the lake
where some men and women were gathered. The lake
was a deep purple beneath the setting sun, and though
the sight was breathtaking, she had a mission and could
delay no longer.

"Papa!" the girl shouted. A door opened from the
small home they were now in front of. A tall man in
cargo shorts and a faded polo shirt approached them. He
was a handsome man in his late forties with kind brown
eyes.

The child giggled and pointed at the man.
"Bwanbale!"

"Are you Mr. Bwanbale?" Eden asked.

"Mister?" The man chuckled. "I am Bwanbale Apio."

"Oh, I'm so sorry. I wasn't sure if it was your first or
last name." Eden's face heated with embarrassment.

"Do not apologize." Bwanbale looked her over, and

Eden knew her appearance must be a dreadful sight. Her clothes were torn and covered with dried blood.

"I'm so sorry to intrude, but a mutual friend said you could help me." Eden felt a sudden urge to cry. God, she was so not a crier, but the memory of watching everyone die around her was catching up with her again. It had been easy to bury those memories while she was with Thorne, but now that she was in civilization again, it all came screaming back to her.

"A mutual friend?" Bwanbale asked.

The girl still held Eden's hand as she watched this exchange, and she squeezed Eden's hand in silent support.

"Yes. Thorne." She said his name quietly, and Bwanbale's eyes widened.

"Please, come inside." He gestured to the house he'd just exited. "Dembe, come." The girl grinned at Eden, let go of her hand, and rushed on ahead of them.

Eden followed Bwanbale inside his home. A woman who appeared to be a little older than Eden was in a small kitchen area cooking over a pot. It smelled good, and Eden covered the rumble from her stomach with an embarrassed smile. Bwanbale smiled at her.

"Afiya, we have a guest. This is . . ." He waited for her answer.

"Eden Matthews."

"Welcome, Eden. This is my wife, Afiya, and this one

is Dembe, our daughter." He nodded at the child, who Eden had guessed was six or seven.

"It's lovely to meet you," she said to Afiya. Dembe was almost bouncing with the excitement and energy that all children seemed to be blessed with at that age.

"Please sit. We will eat soon." Bwanbale pointed to a pair of chairs on a red-and-white patterned rug with a small coffee table between them.

Eden chose the closest chair, and Bwanbale sat across from her. Dembe climbed onto her father's lap, and he held the girl with a gentleness that made Eden's heart swell. She could see why Thorne liked this man.

"I see from your appearance that you have been through much. Please, tell me what happened." Bwanbale set his daughter down and spoke to her softly in Swahili. She nodded and went to join her mother in the kitchen. Then Bwanbale leaned forward. He seemed to hold a universe of patience within him that gave her some of her own serenity back, and the courage to relive what she wished she could bury away forever. She could see why Thorne had such trust and affection for this man.

She told him everything. When she was done, he asked, "These men who killed the guides and tourists, what did they look like?"

"Some were men with English accents—from England, I mean, not America. The others were Ugandan, I believe." She did her best to describe them in detail. So much of what had happened was still locked in her memory and only emerged as wild flashes.

"And Thorne killed them all?"

"Yes, I think so. It's all still a blur." Eden's head was aching now as the panic and fear of those moments came back with the retelling of her story.

"We must get you to Kampala tomorrow. I can take you. The police must be informed. I can also take you to the embassy there."

Eden sagged in relief. "Thank you." She'd been tense ever since Thorne had left her, and now she felt she could finally relax.

Afiya came over with two plates in her hands. She gave the first to Eden and the second to Bwanbale. Then she and Dembe gathered their own plates. Dembe sat down on a cushion on the floor, and Afiya collected a third chair from the kitchen to join them.

"I made *muchoma*, which is roasted chicken, and *matoke*, a green plantain," Afiya explained.

"Thank you, Afiya." Eden was never so glad in her life to see meat and cooked food. She had enjoyed eating the celery, nuts, and mangoes Thorne had provided, but she'd had too much of that in the last few days.

Bwanbale explained Eden's situation to his wife, and Afiya put a protective arm around Dembe as she gaped at her husband.

"The jungle is dangerous," Afiya said solemnly. "And not usually because of the animals."

"My wife is right. For the last two decades, the forest has been full of men with hearts of greed. Between the deforestation and men hunting gorillas for bushmeat, there has been so much destruction." He hesitated, and Eden sensed he wanted to mention something else, but perhaps he didn't know if he could trust her.

"It's the gold and diamonds in the cave, isn't it?" Eden asked after she finished cleaning the plate. She had been starving, and Afiya was an amazing cook. "What do you know about that?"

"An ancient people once lived deep in the jungle, so long ago that most memory of them has faded away and exists now only in myths and legends. When I met Thorne, I saw the crown upon his brow, and I knew that he had found the old-world treasures. I asked him about the gold and the diamonds, and he told me he had found a cave, a cave that called to him, a cave that held the stars themselves. I never believed in those myths myself—until I saw that crown. Most men would have been tempted to ask where the treasure is, to make Thorne show them, but that day, I saw him and I knew that he was there for a reason. The jungle protects itself, often in the most mysterious of ways. I believe he was chosen by the forest, so I keep the secret of Thorne. The legends of the gold and diamonds have always been here, but the forest has kept most men away. If Thorne found this cave, it's possible others have as well. Most poachers would not have killed the tourists and the guides—they would have simply fled. I think whoever attacked you were not poachers."

"Bwanbale, how did you meet Thorne? He told me only a little about you, but I'm learning that his way of telling stories is very different than what I'm used to." This was something she'd been desperate to know. Thorne had explained what he knew of Bwanbale, but as a journalist, she knew there were two sides to every story, if not more. Bwanbale glanced at his wife, his embarrassment apparent on his face.

Afiya gently patted his shoulder. "Tell her. I will not be angry."

He sighed. "It was five years ago. Dembe was only a year old. Our crops were failing, and I could not feed my family. I joined a group of men from Bunagana who planned to sneak into the Impenetrable Forest to hunt gorillas. In the old days it was common for men to hunt them as food for their families, but now the bushmeat trade puts a high price on eating gorillas. The wealthy believe it's prestigious to dine on them, and there are those who believe that some parts of a gorilla's body can be medicinal or hold some magical charm. Then there are the collectors who wish to have the hands, heads, or feet as prizes. There are the poachers who kill a few gorillas at a time, but there are others who abduct infants for researchers or zoos or the pet trade. When those men take the infants, they almost always kill every single adult in the band, as they try to protect their young."

Eden had heard of such horrors before, but now that she had seen them in their natural habitat, it was even more gut-wrenching to know how thoughtlessly they were being slaughtered.

She thought of Akika, Thorne's brother, and his infant son. This was the reason she had come here, to write and take photos. She wanted to remind people that it wasn't just the gorillas at risk, but all life in the jungle, due to deforestation and poaching.

Sometimes people needed to be reminded of how they were connected to the world. In this modern age, it was easy to feel like a person was set worlds apart from the animals, and that the vanishing forests didn't matter. But when a person actually saw the face of a gorilla, saw those soulful eyes that at times seemed so human, it reminded people what was at stake. Reminded them that what was being lost in the world existed outside their smartphones.

All her life, Eden had wanted to make a difference, to protect what deserved protection. Thorne had shown her the jungle and the life within it in such a way that she was forever tied to the ancient forests and the mountain gorillas.

"To my shame," Bwanbale continued, "I went with those men, intending to find gorillas and kill them. But Thorne startled us. I fell and hit my head and lost consciousness. When I came to, I was alone, and there was a wild young man with dark hair staring down at me. I had never seen anything like this man. He wore no clothes, save a deerskin cloth around his loins. His hair was long and dark, his skin deeply tanned. I thought that maybe he was a vision, or perhaps my fevered imagination's creation of a strange dream. He bore markings here." Bwanbale touched his shoulders. "Symbols that I thought looked familiar, but they were too ancient for me to know. I had the strangest sense that when I gazed up at him, I knew my life had been changed forever by this jungle man."

Eden knew that feeling all too well. She was still certain that there was something dreamlike about Thorne.

"I was injured, my head." Bwanbale touched a pale thin scar on his scalp "Thorne was as well. One of the men I was with had shot him. He had only been grazed by the bullet. He hadn't even known what guns were. We tended to each other's wounds, and I stayed with him for a full month, letting my head heal, before I felt I could make the journey home. He shared his world with me, and I realized the error of my ways. I left my life of poaching behind and made amends by seeking to protect the jungle. I work with conservation groups now and meet once a month in Kampala to lobby for change. We have protected much of the land here, and the Bwindi Impenetrable Forest has much more protection now, as do the gorillas. Ugandans care about our land, and I am finding more and more people are rallying behind the cause with me. Thorne reminded me what it means to be Ugandan, to be a part of this beautiful country. I am proud of what we have done, and I am thankful to him for reminding me of that."

Eden smiled sadly. "Thorne definitely has a way of changing your life. He just swoops in like a big wrecking ball and destroys all your assumptions about life and leads you on the most amazing adventures instead."

Bwanbale smiled. "You see him as I do. A man with a pure heart. Thorne knows no evil and knows no greed. He uses violence only to protect and survive."

"Yes," Eden agreed. "That is exactly how I see him." And she'd seen so much more of him. He was passionate, playful, tender, and fierce all at once. "I admit, it all seems a bit fantastical at times, the way he seems so attuned to the jungle, how he understands the animals when they interact with him."

Bwanbale offered a secretive, affectionate smile. "Thorne is no mere man. No man knows the language of the animals as he does. It is not natural, and it cannot be taught. I believe he was chosen. There is a deep magic in the jungle, older than the history in our books. The ancients of the old lost civilization were like Thorne, attuned to that magic. I believe that the cave he discovered is a resting place for their spirits. If what you say about Thorne's parents is true, then I believe their resting place was disturbed by the men hunting for gold, and the spirits reached out and chose Thorne."

"Why?" Eden asked, her skin breaking out in goose bumps.

"To avenge a wrong, perhaps. Or maybe to find peace. Perhaps so that their past isn't lost forever. You saw the homes he built in the trees—he spoke to me of visions, of seeing men and women build them in his head. I helped him, gave him tools, but the ideas were his. The symbols on his shoulders—those too came from the cave. Thorne is part man, part dream."

Bwanbale was quiet a long moment, and Eden let the weight of this new knowledge about Thorne sink in. Chosen by the jungle, by ancient spirits. Did she believe it? It was becoming harder and harder *not* to believe that something mystical was connected to Thorne.

"He speaks of you fondly," she told Bwanbale. "You are his dearest and only friend in the world of men."

Bwanbale looked bashful, and Afiya chuckled at her husband's response. She flashed a smile at Eden before she collected the empty plates. Bwanbale's gaze turned distant, as though the past were playing before his eyes. "To know Thorne is to love him. To love him makes one a better person."

Bwanbale's reply was so full of honest emotion that it made Eden's heart ache. She tried not to think of that moment when she and Thorne had parted ways.

"Come, you must be tired." Bwanbale stood and

looked toward Dembe. "You will sleep in my daughter's room. Dembe, show our guest your room."

Dembe bounced with renewed excitement as she followed her father and Eden toward the small room. A narrow cot sat in the corner of the room, and a tiny bookshelf held a stack of children's books, along with a bin of some toys and dolls. The plaster walls were painted a soft orange and decorated with sketches of colorful birds and other drawings, clearly done by Dembe. The room's cheeriness was like a mirror of the girl who lived here.

"Thank you for letting me have your room tonight, Dembe." Eden hugged the little girl, who smiled brightly.

"We will leave tomorrow morning for Kampala once you are ready." Bwanbale kissed his daughter's head, and then they left.

Eden put her camera bag and backpack down on the floor and sank onto the small cot. Fortunately, she was just short enough to fit. Her limbs grew as heavy as her heart now that she was alone again. It was too humid for her to get comfortable.

She sighed after a long moment and reached for her camera, flipping through the hundreds of photos she had taken. She paused as she reached pictures of Maggie and Harold, smiling as they ate lunch in the mountains, along with the other tourists. Then she found the photos of their two guides, posing by the entrance to the national park with bright smiles. Eden's heart squeezed in pain.

All of them were gone. So many lives taken. All in the name of greed.

When she got to the portion of pictures showing Thorne and his family, she paused again. There was sweet Keza, watching with a mother's love as her adopted son interacted with them. And Akika, the playful brother who saw no difference between Thorne and himself.

We could learn a lot from them.

It was true that the jungle could be merciless, that everything was divided between predators and prey, but there were no wars between these creatures over differences that were skin-deep, differences that were so minor they didn't matter.

Eden saw Thorne's face on the camera screen. She fought the pain she felt thinking these photos would be all she would ever have of him, along with the memories of making love with him in the deep wondrous jungle. Everything that had stopped her from maintaining a relationship with a man hadn't been there with Thorne. Being with him, caring about him—it had all been so *simple*.

The worries and concerns of modern life didn't exist with him. She had no deadlines to meet, no appointments to keep, and no bosses to satisfy. She had felt free for the first time in her life. But as much as she'd longed to stay with him, she couldn't. She owed the other tourists justice for their deaths, and her parents couldn't be left to worry about her. She couldn't just run off into the jungle with a wild man, no matter how much she was tempted.

Eden finally put her camera away, but as she did, she saw something glint in the corner of her front mesh pocket, where she kept the lens cleaner packets. She pulled the object out from the front pocket and gasped. It was Thorne's father's ring. He must have slipped it in there. She stroked her thumb over the carved setting sun on the signet ring's surface, and then she brought it to her lips and kissed it. The tears came swiftly, blurring her vision as she wrapped her arms around her body and wept. A long while later she lay exhausted, body aching with grief, the ring still in her hand, she gazed up at the ceiling of the small *shamba* and wondered where Thorne was and if he was all right.

THORNE WATCHED THE MOONLIGHT POUR OVER THE pool at the base of the waterfall. Bright ripples rolled along the dark surface of the water until they came to a stop by the shore. This beautiful sight normally would have captivated him for hours, but not tonight.

Thorne was numb. It was as though everything inside him had been ripped out and left open. In just a few days, Eden had become his life, and now he was lost without her.

I did the right thing. I let her go. She can be happy.

Then why did it feel so wrong? Why did it feel like a huge mistake?

Thorne touched his right hand where his father's ring had been. He'd only worn it a couple of days, yet he felt its absence acutely. He did not regret giving it to Eden, though. The ring and the necklace belonged together. It felt right that they should not be separated, and Eden would care for them both.

He removed his loincloth and waded into the dark water until it was too deep to walk. Then he swam toward the falls and climbed the ledge to reach the cave.

Once enveloped in the blackness, he sought out his bed of furs and lay down upon them. Eden's scent still clung to the soft furs, and he breathed it in. It would be a long while before he could fall asleep, but he knew he would dream of her.

His Eden. *His mate.*

Thorne roared with rage and sorrow, until the cave walls echoed with his heartbreak.

❦ 10 ❦

Eden gazed at the vast city of Kampala, Uganda's capital city. For a few minutes when she'd been on her knees with a gun to her head, she'd thought she'd never see a city again. It felt good to be back in civilization, but there was an emptiness inside her too, a longing for the deep sable jungle—and for Thorne. She pushed thoughts of him away tried to focus on where she was now and moving forward.

When she'd first come to Uganda, she had flown into the city of Entebbe before catching a bus to Mbarara, where she'd stayed at a hotel before traveling to Bwindi Impenetrable Forest.

Kampala, however, was an urban sprawl, with a mix of ancient and modern art and architecture. This city, as Bwanbale had told her, was the heart of the Bugandan kingdom and was rich with a colorful history.

Bwanbale parked his car in front of the US Embassy and helped Eden collect her gear. Before she headed toward the gate, she turned to the man she now saw as a friend.

"You have my number," he reminded her. She nodded. Bwanbale and his wife shared a cell phone, and he'd given her the number that morning before they left his village.

"Text me where you will stay so Afiya and I don't worry."

"Thank you, Bwanbale, for everything." She hugged him, and he returned her embrace with a soft, warm laugh. Saying goodbye to him was like saying goodbye to Thorne all over again. Bwanbale knew what lay in her heart, how she had said goodbye to the mysterious Lord of the Jungle and would be forever haunted by losing him. They both shared that unbreakable connection to Thorne. She trembled in Bwanbale's arms.

"Do not cry, Eden," he murmured. "Someday you will come back. You will see him again."

Despite his confident words, Eden heard the note of sorrow in his voice. They both knew she would likely never return. Saying goodbye once was agony. A second time of parting ways would be the end of her heart.

"Why do I miss him so much?" she asked. "I only knew him a few days. That's crazy, isn't it?"

Bwanbale smiled. "In many ways, Thorne is the last

vessel of the old gods and the people who worshipped them. He is alone, without a family or a place to belong. His heart belongs to the wild, yet it hungers for more. You gave him a glimpse into the life that should have been his, and he will mourn losing you as no other man will.

"But I think, perhaps, there is more to your bond with him than you have told me. Such a bond doesn't need more than a few days to become real to the both of you. It is right you should grieve being parted from him."

Bwanbale was right. Some part of her had been left behind, lost forever deep in the heart of the Impenetrable Forest. It belonged to *him* now, *always*.

Eden wiped at her eyes and tried to smile. "Thank you."

Bwanbale smiled back and gave her another hug before they parted ways. "Take care, Eden."

A US marine met her at the gates. Eden showed him her passport, which had been kept in a pouch in her camera bag. Once inside, Eden was escorted into the office of one of the embassy officials, a woman who looked to be a few years older than her. The woman was dressed in khaki pants and a colorful blouse.

"Have a seat, Ms. Matthews. My name is Cara Tucker. I'm one of the civilian liaison officers."

Eden sank into a chair opposite Cara's desk.

"I'm told that you were attacked?" Cara focused

briefly on her computer as she typed something before she turned to look at Eden.

With a heavy sigh, Eden told Cara about the murders in the forest and her rescue by Thorne. That part was much harder for her, because she couldn't talk about him without sounding like she had lost her mind.

By the time she was done, Cara was staring at her, mouth parted in shock. Then she seemed to recover herself, and she picked up the phone on her desk and hit the red button. She waited a few seconds before she spoke.

"We have a serious incident. You need to talk to Ms. Matthews. Yes, that's correct. I've just emailed you her information." She hung up and cleared her throat.

"Right, so one of the other officers will want to talk with you. Until then, can I take you to the residential area in the building? We have hot showers, beds, clean clothes, and food. Oh, and here." She opened a drawer and pulled out a slender flip phone. "It's not much, but it's yours. You can make any international calls you need to through it. Let people know you're okay."

"Thanks." Eden followed Cara as the woman led her through the maze of halls. They soon stopped next to a room with a number on it.

"This is residence number eighteen, in case you get lost. Any embassy employee will know how to get you back here if you tell them the number. You have a fully stocked fridge with food, a bed, a shower. I'll have some clothes brought down for you while we have someone drive to Mbarara to retrieve your luggage from your hotel there. Just tell me your size."

"Uh, ten. And for shoes I'm an eight," Eden said.

"Thanks." Cara smiled. "Go shower and get some rest. I'll check on you later."

Eden entered the small residence and stared at the twin-size bed. She sat down on the edge and pulled out the basic cell phone Cara had given her. She dialed her parents back in the US. It was late afternoon here in Kampala, which meant it was early morning in Arkansas.

Her mother answered after a few rings. "Hello?"

"Mom, it's me."

"Eden? Oh, I didn't recognize the number you're calling from."

"I got a temporary cell phone from the US Embassy."

"The *embassy*? What happened? Are you okay?"

"I'm okay." Just getting those words out was a huge relief, and she felt a weight lifted off her shoulders. But now came the hard part. Eden shut her eyes and fell back on the bed as she rubbed at her closed lids with her thumb and forefinger. "Mom, I need you to sit down, okay?"

"I'm sitting," her mother assured her, though her clipped tone hinted at her growing anxiety.

"Our tour group was attacked by some armed men in the jungle. They killed everyone but me, Mom."

"Oh my God! Oh God!" There was a harsh intake of breath. Then another. "Okay . . . okay. Oh honey, thank God you're all right. What happened? Who were the men who attacked you? Why?"

She was so tired of telling everyone the same story, but she related the details again and listened to the silence on the other end of the phone.

"Mom?"

"Oh God, honey." Her mother's usual tough-love approach would have been to tell her to shake it off, but this wasn't like losing a job or having your laptop stolen at a Starbucks. She sounded terrified. "I want you to come home *right now.*"

"I'm not sure I can just yet. I'm at the embassy, and they still have some questions."

"Eden, how did you get away?" her mother suddenly asked.

"I was rescued." She wasn't sure how much she wanted to tell her mother. She'd told Cara everything to help them with their investigation of the murdered tourists, but her mother?

"By who? The police?"

Eden bit her lip. "By . . . You're going to think I'm crazy."

"Honey, please. I have to know. What happened? Who rescued you?"

She took a deep breath. "By a man who lives in the jungle, like a hermit."

"A hermit?" her mother echoed, unconvinced.

"Yeah. He's a conservationist. He stays away from the villages, preferring to be close to the animals. He saved me and helped me get to a village." She had to admit, describing him this way sounded almost plausible.

"I need to find your father. He'll want to hear this."

"Just tell him that I'm okay. I'll call you back as soon as I know when they'll let me leave for home."

"But, honey—"

"Please, Mom. I need to shower and get some food. I've been through a lot."

"Okay. But call me tomorrow, no matter what," her mother ordered.

"Fine. I will." Eden sighed. "Love you, Mom."

"Love you too."

Eden hung up and tossed the phone on the bed, then dragged herself back to her feet and into the shower.

Drenching herself in the hot spray, all she could think about was the cold water from the waterfall and how she missed standing in the rippling pool as Thorne held her in his arms. She missed him so much already. She wiped away tears as she chastised herself for being so foolish as to fall for Thorne in just a few days. Despite Bwanbale's romantic take, this wasn't some romance novel, and she wasn't some barely out of high school girl who let her hormones control her. Yet everything that had to do with Thorne made her emotional.

Focusing on the shower took some effort, but Eden

cleaned herself off, wincing each time she discovered a new cut or scrape. She hadn't been aware of her injuries while in the jungle, but she'd apparently gotten quite bruised and busted up. Now her body seemed fully depleted of adrenaline, and her legs shook as she tried to use the cheap plastic razor in the shower kit that had been left in the bathroom.

By the time she was done, she had only enough energy to braid her hair, crawl into the clothes someone had left on her bed, and fall asleep.

Her sleep was dreamless and dark. When she finally awoke a short while later, a note had been slipped under her door stating that Cara's boss wanted to speak to her. She checked the digital clock and groaned. She had half an hour. Not enough time to go back to sleep, but she could get another phone call out of the way. She sat up and dialed her editor at *National Park* magazine.

"Paul Lester speaking," her boss answered.

"Hey, Paul. It's me, Eden."

"Eden! Hey, how's the gorilla piece coming?"

Eden drew in a breath. "You won't believe what I'm about to tell you." She reached for her bag and pulled out Thorne's ring. "But first, I need a huge favor."

THORNE RACED ALONG THE THICK BRANCHES OF THE hagenia trees and dropped to the ground with barely a sound. Before him lay the white tomb that held the bones of his parents. The airplane that had once carried him in the sky.

All night and much of the day he had debated coming back here. But something compelled him to return. Perhaps it was how much he missed Eden, or how much he longed for the company of another human. But this quiet tomb was all he could manage. Whatever it was that drove him, he walked slowly toward the plane, his heart fracturing inside his chest.

The dark cabin was unchanged from his visit a few days ago. The two skeletons sat in their chairs. These silent watchers filled him with a bittersweet longing to remember more about them.

Amelia and Jacob. The names were now known to him, carved into his heart forever, and yet they were strangers. He knelt first by the bones of his mother and bowed his head. Then he moved to kneel before his father.

"I wish to honor you, as I have done my best to honor Keza. But I am full of fear. What if I cannot live in Eden's world?" He spoke his questions knowing they would not answer him, but it felt good to at least voice his worries aloud. He'd been debating whether to stay in the jungle or to try to embrace Eden's world so he could be with her.

He gazed upon the bones of his parents. They still felt like gods to him, silently resting, their lives and memories out of his reach, yet their presence was soothing in a way he couldn't fully explain.

Thorne lowered his head, bowing in respect as he listened to the distant jungle symphony outside. The parrots in the trees, the throaty calls of leopards, the distant trumpet of Tembo and his herd. All the sounds seemed in that infinite moment to blend together to form one word.

Eden.

He knew what he was meant to do. The jungle was speaking the name of his mate. He had to obey. It was time, whether he succeeded or failed, to find Eden and try to fit into her world.

Thorne rose, and with one final goodbye to his parents' resting place, he returned to the jungle. Within minutes he was swinging on the thick vines and landing on crisscrossing branches until he reached the path that would lead him to Bwanbale's village.

As he reached the forest's edge, he stood in the same spot where he had let Eden go. His heart hammered at the memory that had once hurt him, yet now held hope. He saw the small brightly colored *shamba* houses, their grounds, according to Bwanbale, thick with fruit and vegetables, many of which Thorne had never seen before.

At the time, Thorne could not fathom what else he would ever wish to eat besides nuts and mangoes, other than the occasional deer he hunted. But now he wondered—wondered about all the things Bwanbale had spoken of.

The sun was cresting the tops of the trees as Thorne stepped out of the jungle. He would show no fear, even if his heart felt it. A few humans nearby noticed him and froze. One human child was brave enough to approach him. She stopped a few feet away, her beautiful brown eyes warm with innocence and curiosity.

"I am Dembe Apio. You are the jungle man?" she asked in Swahili.

"I am." He crouched to put himself level with the child. He had never seen a human child up close before. He saw Dembe and thought she was beautiful.

She held out a tiny hand. "Come this way." He took her small fingers gently as she led him through the village. He didn't shy away from the stares of the others, but he was very conscious of them. He wore nothing but his loincloth, while those around him wore far more coverings, like Eden. He now regretted not asking Bwanbale to explain more about this world to him. He had much to learn if he was to find his mate and win her back.

Dembe brought him to a dwelling and called out in Swahili, "Mother, come! Look what I found!"

A beautiful woman in a blue sundress emerged from the home and gasped when she saw Thorne.

"Dembe! Who is this?" The woman gestured for Dembe to release his hand and come toward her.

"Father's jungle man!" Dembe announced proudly and shot Thorne a grin.

"This is Bwanbale's friend?" The woman met Thorne's steady gaze. "You are the man from the forest?"

Thorne bowed his head respectfully as he realized he was in the presence of Bwanbale's mate and offspring.

"Would you like to come in?" the woman asked him. Thorne nodded and followed her into the dwelling. It was so solid, so smooth, so colorful.

"Bwanbale is not here, but he will be soon. He took Eden to Kampala this morning."

The mention of his mate diverted Thorne's focus from examining this human dwelling.

"Eden is safe?"

"Yes, she's safe." The woman smiled a little nervously. "My name is Afiya, and this is Dembe." She placed protective hands on the child's shoulders.

"I am Thorne . . . Haywood." It was the first time he'd claimed that name, but it felt right to do so now. He did not wish to deny the parents who had died protecting him. Even though he could not fully remember them or their world, he was feeling more and more bound to it.

"Would you care to sit?" Afiya gestured to the two funny looking objects. Dembe rushed toward one of them and sat down.

"This is a chair!" Dembe said.

Chair. Yes, he knew that word, and others that came

to him as he looked around the room: *table, kitchen, stove,* and so many others.

"Where are your clothes?" Dembe asked him with an innocent seriousness that made Thorne want to smile.

"Clothes?"

Dembe flared her small hands over her animal skin. "Clothes." It was dark blue and green. "This is my dress."

Dress. The word brought back flashes of his mother in a long gold dress, twirling around in a room. His father had held her close, whispering and smiling before his mother had noticed him watching. She'd held out a hand, and he'd run to them. The memory faded.

"I have only this." He waved to the deerskin loincloth.

"Thorne, would you like to try some of Bwanbale's clothes?" Afiya asked. "I'm sure he wouldn't mind."

Thorne hesitated, but agreed. The people in the village had stared at him strangely, and he didn't want to be dressed improperly.

"Yes, thank you."

"Come. Dembe, stay there." She waved for Thorne to follow her, and she led him into another space within the dwelling. This one had a large piece of carved wood. A *dresser.* Yes, he recognized that too. She opened a drawer and pulled out some clothes.

"Let's see if some of these fit. You are bigger than my husband, but these might work."

Thorne held up the strange clothes, and Afiya chuckled. "I guess I'll have to demonstrate." She showed him all the clothes and how to put them on while she told him their various names: *boxers*, *cargo shorts*, *T-shirt*, *socks*, *boots*. When he was done putting them on, Afiya turned to look at him and smiled.

"Yes, they fit. Barely."

Thorne stared down at his body, now covered in the strange clothes. He wasn't sure he liked the restrictive feel of these clothes, but if it was what he must do to be with his mate, he would do it.

"Father's home!" Dembe's voice came from the other room.

"Bwanbale is here?" Thorne said with breathless excitement, or perhaps that was the shirt constricting him like a great snake. He and Afiya rushed into the other room in time to see his old friend step inside. Bwanbale's jaw dropped.

"Thorne!" He laughed as he crossed the room to embrace Thorne. He clapped his back and squeezed him hard in friendship. "But how did this happen? You would never come home with me before, and now I find you dressed in my clothes! Look at you, my friend, you look almost normal."

Almost? Thorne wondered what was wrong with him. His friend touched his hair and the gold crown on his head. He had forgotten to leave the crown in his tree house.

"But most of us do not wear crowns, you might have noticed."

Thorne nodded his understanding.

"So why have you left the jungle after all these years?"

"For Eden."

Bwanbale's eyes softened with understanding. "As I expected. A man will do a great many things for a woman he loves. But I'm afraid she's not here. I took her to Kampala to the US Embassy."

Thorne hadn't a clue what those words meant. "What is *the US Embassy*?"

"It's where her people are. She is not from Uganda. She lives very far away."

"Little Rock," Thorne added, hoping he understood. "How many villages away?"

"Far more than you can run." Bwanbale patted Dembe's back. "Go fetch your geography book." He pushed the child toward her room. She returned with something that looked like his father's journal, only much larger, and Bwanbale opened it up. It was filled with colorful pictures, but there were shapes he didn't recognize.

"Come, let me show you. This shows all of the land around the entire world. Great oceans, bigger than any lake or river you've seen—these colorful shapes here are separate lands called continents."

Bwanbale explained geography to him, and Thorne stared in open wonder at the maps. Bits and pieces of old memories of his mother teaching him came back to him.

"You are from England, here." Bwanbale pointed to a small piece of land that was completely separated from other land by oceans. Well, it was small compared to the land next to it. He then pointed to a large mass across the ocean.

"And this is America. Inside America is Arkansas, and the city of Little Rock is inside that. America is far away from Africa, but they have a building in Kampala where people from her country can find help if they need it. It's called an embassy. That is where I took her."

Thorne's thoughts drifted to the things Eden had told him about her home. He wished he could see it, but now he had some understanding of how far away her home was. These distances were too great to truly grasp, let alone travel to by foot. Thorne's stomach pitched as he realized that he could never get to Eden, not on his own.

"Will you take me to this embassy?" he asked his friend.

"Yes, but you are not from America. They may not let you inside."

Thorne had to try. He had to show Eden that he wanted to be with her.

"First, we need to cut your hair."

Afiya came in from the kitchen, wielding two small knives that were somehow cinched together. The woman smiled deviously at Bwanbale and Thorne. Little Dembe giggled.

"Did someone say haircut?"

Thorne removed the gold leaves from his head and passed the circlet to Dembe. "Will you keep this safe for me?"

The child nodded and accepted the crown. "I will hide it in my memory box, under my bed." She rushed away to her room.

Thorne then faced Afiya and the two small knives. "I am ready."

EDEN WALKED OUT OF HER SECOND INTERVIEW WITH embassy officials and met Cara in the hall.

"Hey, how'd it go?" Cara asked.

"We all agree that my story sounds crazy, but I think they believe me. They're sending people now to look for the bodies." She had told the officials about how Thorne had killed the poachers, and how she'd discovered his true identity. One of the officials had immediately left the room to put in a call to the UK Embassy to see if they could contact the Haywoods in London.

"I've heard that a few of the older officials here remember when the Haywoods went missing. It was such a tragedy. Are you certain it's their son?" Cara asked.

Eden nodded. "I have Jacob Haywood's journal in my room, plus a family photo that I found on the wrecked plane." She didn't mention the signet ring or the necklace she wore. Those belonged to Thorne's family by right, and she didn't want them getting confiscated, not when she could deliver them to Cameron Haywood herself, assuming he believed her.

"Cara, can I get access to a computer for an hour?"

"Of course, we have a few laptops for guest use. I could sign one of those out for you. They're fairly basic, though."

"That's fine." All she needed was access to her email and a way to upload the photos from her camera to her Dropbox.

Cara left to get the laptop, and Eden settled in to wait. She hadn't texted Bwanbale yet, so she grabbed her loaner phone and texted him an update. She'd decided to move into a hotel once everything was settled here. Kampala was a safe city, and her boss had already booked her a suite and covered her expenses, including a new laptop and smartphone to be delivered there.

Eden texted Bwanbale the address of the hotel where she'd be for the next few days. Paul had offered her a first-class flight to come straight home, but the thought of leaving, of never seeing Thorne again, felt wrong— worse than wrong. So for the time being, she would stay in Uganda until she could sort things out.

Besides, the more she thought about it, the more the

story of the treasure thieves and the murder of the tourists could be a powerful call to action. She was not the sort of journalist to sensationalize stories like these for the sake of shock value or publicity. But she was the sort of person to use this tragedy as a way to get people to wake up to the problems the world was facing when it came to deforestation, the theft of a country's natural resources, and the murder of innocent animals and humans. If she could write an article about that and expose whoever had hired those men in the jungle, maybe she could change the world too, as Bwanbale was doing.

Be the change in the world that you want to see. It was something her mother had always said to her, and now she truly felt she had a chance of doing that.

Cara knocked ten minutes later and handed Eden a laptop. She sat down on the bed and plugged in the camera memory card. She uploaded the pictures to her cloud storage while she checked her emails, and she soon found the one she was looking for. Her boss had called in every favor he had, but he had done it. He'd gotten Cameron Haywood's private cell phone number.

She dialed the international number and waited. Her body vibrated with nerves and excitement as he she counted the rings.

After five rings she feared he wouldn't answer, but suddenly he picked up, and she heard a cultured British baritone.

"Hello?"

"Lord Somerset?"

"Yes, who is this? The caller ID says the number is from Uganda." Cameron sounded irritated.

"Yes, it is. Lord Somerset, my name is Eden Matthews. I have to speak with you about something very important."

"Ms. Matthews, I do not know how you came by my number, but—"

"I found the plane," she cut in quickly. "Your brother's plane."

There was a long moment of silence, and then he replied coldly, "Is this about the reward? That ended a long time ago."

"Reward? What? No, I didn't know about that. I don't want money. You must listen to me, Lord Somerset."

"Ms. Matthews, I have faced almost a decade of charlatans and con artists who've tried to convince me they found the plane and the bodies. None of it was true."

Eden's heart was racing as she struggled for the right words to make this man believe her.

"I have the ginkgo leaf necklace. The one Amelia wore." She unclasped it from her neck. "I can send you a picture. Her initials are engraved on the back."

"Quite a few people knew about that necklace. She

wore it every day. You could have faked a necklace just like that." His tone was dismissive.

"And the signet ring, the one that belonged to your brother—"

"*Another* easy replication. The ring is a family heirloom, one well recorded. Many people knew what it looked like." Cameron's tone was hardening, more than two decades of anger and pain building behind his voice. But until he believed her about the plane, he would not believe the news about Thorne. That gave her a sudden idea.

"I have *The Jungle Alphabet*, the book Thorne had with him, along with a photo that was tucked inside." She took the weathered book from her bag, having managed to clean it early that morning at Bwanbale's house. "And I have Jacob's journal from the cockpit. Please, let me text you a few pictures. Then call me back at this number. I have so much to share with you. I have the answers you need."

"Very well, but don't expect a call back. If you contact me again without permission, I will find out exactly who you are and you will face the consequences."

"I understand, Lord Somerset."

Cameron hung up, and Eden retrieved the alphabet book, the necklace, the ring, and the journal, as well as the family photo of Thorne with his parents. She took close-up pictures of each of the items, then sent the pictures to Cameron's cell number. She anxiously waited.

After a few minutes, her phone rang.

"Hello?"

She heard nothing for a moment, then a world-weary sigh, as if he expected to be disappointed once again but had just enough hope left in him to try one more time.

"I'm listening, Ms. Matthews. Tell me everything."

11

The moment Eden's phone rang, she'd felt like a plucked string on a violin, vibrating with tension. But when he'd asked for her to tell him everything, that tension had ebbed away. He *believed* her.

"First of all, you should know that you can contact the US Embassy in Kampala to confirm my story. They're following up on everything I'm about to tell you."

"Very well, I'm sure I will. Proceed."

"I was hiking in the Bwindi Impenetrable Forest with a group of tourists to see the gorillas. Our group went deep into the jungle and found the gorillas. But shortly after that . . ." She took a deep breath and once again relived that horrible day. A lump formed in her throat as she struggled to retell these memories.

EMMA CASTLE

"Ms. Matthews, you need not share the details if it pains you," Cameron said in a gentlemanly tone that reminded her of Thorne.

"No, I'm afraid I have to." She cleared her throat and wiped her eyes before she continued. "I was about to be shot, but a man rescued me. He literally came out of the jungle and killed the poachers with his bare hands. I thought he might kill me too, but he helped me instead. He took me to his home in the jungle." She had to avoid some of the details; otherwise, her story would sound too fantastic to be believed. "When I had recovered, he took me to what he called *the white rock*. But it wasn't a rock—it was a plane. The door was open, and when I went inside I found two sets of remains. One bore a signet ring and the other a ginkgo leaf necklace. I found the alphabet book on the floor, with the photo of your brother and his family tucked inside." She paused, trying to decide how best to continue.

"And the journal?" Cameron questioned.

"That was in the cockpit."

"You mentioned two bodies. There should have been a third, the pilot. And a small toddler's body. Did you see either of those?" His tone was quiet, and Eden could hear his heartbreak.

"No. The pilot died in the crash. Your brother buried him. According to the journal, Jacob and Amelia lived for a couple of weeks in the wreck, waiting for rescue. As for the child . . ." Eden closed her eyes. "Lord Somer-

202

set, the man who rescued me, the man who showed me the plane . . . is your nephew. He survived."

"Thorne!" Cameron uttered the name hoarsely, as if he suddenly was disgusted. "Ms. Matthews, now I know you're lying. A toddler could not survive alone in the jungle."

"He wasn't alone. He was taken in by a family of gorillas."

"A family of gorillas? You must think me mad to think I'll believe *that*."

"I have pictures of him." From the laptop, she forwarded him one of Thorne facing her, smiling at the camera, but the line had already disconnected. Cameron Haywood hadn't believed her—at least not about the most important part of all of this.

Eden had hoped to put these two broken family members back together, and she had failed. She had silently vowed that she would repay Thorne for saving her life, and the most important way would have been reuniting him with his family. That was the part that hurt most. The taste of defeat left her empty and cold inside. She'd been so hopeful, so sure that if he just looked at that picture of Thorne, he would have to believe her.

Eden closed the laptop and started to pack. Cara had texted her to let her know that her luggage had been picked up from the hotel in Mbarara and was now at her new room in Kampala. She would leave for the hotel straightaway and take a few more days to figure things out. She needed time to think about Thorne and what she should do next.

CAMERON HAYWOOD DROPPED HIS MOBILE ONTO HIS desk and buried his face in his hands. How dangerous a thing it was to hope. For a brief moment he had been full of it, hope of knowing the truth of Jacob, Amelia, and Thorne. But the young woman was just another charlatan. She'd lied with an exquisite perfection that had tricked him, until she grew too greedy.

Thorne, alive? Preposterous. It had to be some ploy, like Anna Anderson claiming to be the lost Princess Anastasia in the early twentieth century.

His phone vibrated, and he dragged his hands through his dark hair, pulling at the strands. Reluctantly, he looked at his phone. It was another text from Ms. Matthews, with an attachment. He knew better than to look, but damnation, hope was a hard thing to crush. He opened the text and saw a photograph.

For a second he simply stared at the picture's subject. Then he reached for his glass of brandy on the desk. A good stiff drink would do him some good. But the second he lifted the glass up, his hand began to tremble so badly that he dropped the glass. It hit the hardwood floor and shattered.

His wife rushed into his study a few seconds later. "Darling?"

Cameron looked up from his phone. His wife joined him at his desk and bent to pick up the broken glass. Her gaze strayed to his phone.

"Is that a photo of Jacob? I haven't seen that one before." Isabelle smiled and then chuckled. "That hair . . . I bet when he met Amelia he had to cut it. He looks like he would have been at Woodstock."

Cameron's eyes drifted back to the phone and the face of the young man who looked exactly like Jacob except for his smile. It was softer, less rakish than Jacob's, though it was no less charming. But it held a boyish innocence. It was a smile that reminded Cameron more of Amelia.

"No, it isn't Jacob. You think it looks like him?" he asked Isabelle.

"Of course. You're sure it isn't him?" His wife picked up his phone and examined it closely. "I suppose it's not, but look at that cleft chin, those blue eyes." She placed a loving hand on his shoulder. Then she bit her lip. "If it's not Jacob, then who is it?"

He took a long, slow breath. "It just might be his son."

Isabelle gasped. "Cam, what on earth . . . ?"

Cameron pulled his wife down on his lap, suddenly desperate to hold her, as he told her about the call from Eden Matthews. He showed her the photos of the artifacts and admitted how he'd hung up when Ms. Matthews had said Thorne was alive.

"I didn't believe her. How could I? Wouldn't we have found him by now? How could he have survived all these years if he was alone?"

"But he wasn't—the woman said he was raised by gorillas."

"Isabelle, you can't believe that, surely. Wild animals don't just raise human foundlings. Thorne did not grow up like Mowgli from Kipling's *The Jungle Book*."

"Mowgli was raised by wolves," Isabelle noted. "But I see your point. It's difficult to believe. And yet . . ." His wife stared at the photo of the young man with long hair and was silent for a moment. Then she tapped the screen. "As impossible as this may seem, darling, I think we need to call Ms. Matthews back and arrange for a DNA test with this man. It would tell us straightaway what we have. If it's a confidence game they're playing at, they will look for some excuse not to allow it, and no doubt will miraculously forget how to find the plane."

Isabelle was right. And if this was an elaborate ruse, by God they would feel his wrath and see the next years of their lives in prison. But if it wasn't . . .

"Very well." Cameron dialed the number, but it went to voice mail. "Ms. Matthews, this is Cameron Haywood. I've seen the picture you sent of the man. I would like to arrange for a DNA test to be run at your earliest convenience. I would also like a team to be sent to the plane crash site to verify the wreck. Please call me back." After he hung up, he placed the mobile on the desk and wrapped his arms around his wife, holding her close.

Was it possible that Thorne might be alive, after all these years? Cameron's heart quivered at the thought. Jacob's little boy might come home. He would be the Earl of Somerset, and Cameron could, over time, release some of the duties of the title to the boy, until he was ready and able to fully assume his position as the earl. Cameron had never wanted the title, nor had his wife. All he'd wanted was for his family to be alive. Jacob and Amelia were gone, but Thorne? Thorne could come home.

Hope could be a dangerous thing, like tinder beneath dry logs. Once a spark was lit, it caught fire, burning brightly into the night.

JEAN CARILLET FOLLOWED ARCHIBALD HOLT THROUGH the jungle, toward the site of the killings. Even though Holt hadn't been there with him, he seemed to know where to go better than Jean did, even without the expensive GPS devices they both held, but that shouldn't have surprised him. Holt had lived in Uganda for more than twenty years. Holt had a fancy manor house in England, but he spent nearly all his time here in

Uganda. He'd been only twenty when he'd first come here to hunt for gold and diamonds.

"Up there!" Jean recognized a peculiar growth hugging a tree that was shaped like a fork. Holt pressed on, and in another dozen feet, a rotting smell overwhelmed them as the hum of hundreds of flies grew so loud that Jean nearly emptied the contents of his stomach.

The bodies of the tourists mixed with those of Holt's men lay strewn everywhere. Decay and the environment had set in, bloating the bodies, though no large animals had scavenged them as of yet.

Holt examined the surroundings, unmoved by the sight of so many corpses.

"You bloody fool," Holt growled as he kicked Cash's leg.

Jean flinched at Holt's impotent anger, which was unmarred by any other emotions than frustration and disappointment.

"We need to move Cash's body. He's the only one who could be tied to my company." Holt nodded at Cash's body. "Leave the rest where they lie."

Despite the corpse's bloating, it was clear that Cash's neck had been snapped. Holt seemed to notice the same thing.

"You're right, Carillet. No animal would do this." He pointed down at a very human-looking footprint, made by a bare foot. "Someone hunted them down, someone human. Are you sure it wasn't someone from the Batwa tribe? I know they were pushed out of the forests and national parks, but I wouldn't be surprised if a few still hid out here."

Jean remembered hearing how the ancient hunter-gatherer Batwa tribes had been displaced all over Rwanda, Uganda, and Burundi, all for the sake of park development, but he personally hadn't seen any evidence of the tribes during the six months he'd been here.

"I'm quite positive it wasn't the Batwa."

"Then we face a much bigger problem, don't we?" Holt said, his tone hard-edged.

Jean didn't know if Holt told him this to reassure him that he wasn't going mad, or if he wanted to scare Jean with the idea of some madman running about the forest.

"Grab his legs," Holt ordered as he reached for Cash's arms. "We'll carry him to the river."

Jean grabbed Cash's booted feet, and they began to drag the body between them. They were about a hundred yards away when they heard voices shouting in the woods.

"Drop him behind this thicket and get down." Holt shoved Jean down to a low crouch as they hid.

Through the tangle of branches, Jean made out a group of ten people approaching the clearing where the other bodies were.

"Here they are! Just like she said!" one man shouted.

Then he got on his radio. Holt reached for a radio on his belt and turned it on, keeping the volume low as he scanned the channels until he found the one the man was speaking on.

"This is Landry. We found the site where Ms. Matthews said the massacre took place. Stand by for details . . ." There was a pause, and then he continued. "I see seven tourists and two guides, but there's at least three other bodies here, all armed. They must be the poachers. No signs of bullet wounds, though. The guy killed the bastards with his bare hands. Jesus . . ."

"Landry, send in your GPS coordinates, and we'll get a recovery team out to you as soon as possible," the man over the radio ordered.

"Copy that." Landry clicked the radio back on his belt and pulled out his GPS device.

Holt turned his radio off so no one would hear it if it picked up any chatter. "Come on, we need to move." Jean helped him resume dragging Cash's body toward the river.

"You didn't tell me that bitch Cash was going to kill survived," Holt said once they were far enough away to not be seen or heard.

Jean hoisted Cash's legs even higher to step over a fallen log. "I didn't know. I assumed that whatever creature had killed Cash and the others would have killed her too."

Holt's cold blue eyes met Jean's for a long moment,

until Jean wondered with dread if Holt might shoot him and toss him into the river too.

"You will help me find this Matthews woman, and she's going to have a little accident, understood? She might have heard something that ties back to me, and we need to make sure that any details she might remember die with her."

"*Oui*, Monsieur Holt," Jean murmured, his stomach knotted as they carried Cash's corpse deeper into the dark jungle.

THORNE COULDN'T STOP STARING AT HIS REFLECTION in the mirror Afiya held up. He looked strange. His long dark hair had only ever been shorn with sharp bits of shale until Bwanbale had given him a knife. Even then, the task had not been all that much easier.

Afiya and her scissors, as he learned the blades were called, had effortlessly created a great change in his appearance. Now his hair was just barely above his ears in places, though it still fell in his eyes. When he had questioned Afiya about why she had left it long enough to cover his eyes, she laughed and told him that Eden would prefer it this way, that it made him very attractive to women. Thorne didn't care about *women*—he only cared about what Eden thought.

EMMA CASTLE

"There. You look good." Afiya chuckled and headed back to the kitchen to put her scissors away.

Thorne turned to Bwanbale. "You agree? This is good?"

"It is." He flashed Thorne a mischievous smile. "Eden will definitely approve." Bwanbale suddenly tensed as something in his pocket buzzed. He pulled it out. Thorne recognized it as something called a cell phone. Bwanbale had explained it to him, along with some other devices like the TV, something Thorne vaguely remembered having watched as a child. He also remembered phones, but he thought you were supposed to talk to them. This Bwanbale seemed to read instead.

"It's Eden," Bwanbale said. "She says she is moving out of the embassy to a hotel."

"A hotel?" The new word made him restless. Was this yet another obstacle he would face in order to get to his mate?

"This is good news, old friend. You will not have as hard a time reaching her. Come, we'll leave now and be there in a few hours if I drive fast."

"Shouldn't you tell Eden he is coming?" Afiya asked.

Bwanbale flashed a grin at her, then Thorne. "My heart, you forget young love. Surprises are best for romance."

"What is romance?" Thorne asked suspiciously.

His friend chuckled. "*Mating* is what I believe you call it. We will surprise Eden."

Afiya rolled her eyes. "I hope you do not make her angry. A heartbroken woman doesn't always like surprises."

"Not even good ones?" Bwanbale challenged with a teasing chuckle at her before he kissed her and Dembe goodbye.

Then Bwanbale took Thorne to a massive strange object outside that made Thorne grin as he recognized it.

"Truck!" he exclaimed. Memories of holding a tiny truck as big as a child's hand came back to him. He remembered he used to play with the toy truck.

"It's good to see you remember more words, but you have many more to learn if you wish to be out in the world."

Thorne nodded solemnly. He needed to leave the language of the birds behind and speak the language of men and women.

As Bwanbale drove, Thorne listened to all the advice his friend could give him. It was a little hard to focus on what Bwanbale said at times, because Thorne was distracted by being inside a moving vehicle for the first time since he was three. The roads were bumpy, and the old leather of the seat squeaked as he shifted on it, but there was something intrinsically fun about the experience that had him grinning the entire time.

"Are you listening, Thorne?" Bwanbale's laughing question pulled Thorne away from staring out the window as they flew past faster than he could ever move on foot.

"Yes," he replied, and once again he pushed himself to focus on his friend.

Two hours later, his head had begun to ache, and he wasn't sure if it was because he was trying to learn too much too fast, or because he wasn't used to riding in a car. He was relieved when they finally reached Kampala. The towering buildings were brightly lit, and the city was noisy. Despite the rain that started to fall, he could hear the hum of the city, not unlike a great hive of bees. The sound made him restless.

"I will park here, and we can go to the front desk to find her room." Bwanbale parked in front of a reddish-brown building. A clear pool in front of the building was dark with the stormy night sky as Bwanbale stopped the car and turned off the engine. Bwanbale cursed the rain, but it didn't bother Thorne. Rain brought life—he would never curse it. He started toward the pool, ignoring Bwanbale calling his name.

There was a wall of roughhewn rocks, like the back side of the waterfall, and palm fronds banked it, making it look like the jungle, but it wasn't real. Thorne knelt by the pool and cupped the water in one hand and raised it to his lips, tasting it. He spat it right back out. There was an unnatural taste to it—it was wrong somehow.

"What is wrong with the water?" he asked.

Bwanbale shook his head. "That is pool water. There

are chemicals in it."

Thorne's eyes widened. "It is poison?"

Bwanbale sighed. "Not exactly. Just don't drink it. We can get water inside."

Thorne let the falling rain wash his hand of the tainted water, and he straightened.

"Thorne, follow me. We must use the entrance." Bwanbale pointed to an entrance glowing with artificial lights.

Thorne was about to follow when he caught sight of someone standing on a ledge above the pool. It was a strange small opening in the building, like the entrance to a cave, but filled with light. Cloth billowed out around the opening. But despite the rain, Thorne recognized the figure standing there.

"Eden," he gasped. He looked to Bwanbale. "She is there. I will go to her."

"Thorne, wait!"

But Thorne had already waited too long. Eden's figure disappeared from the ledge. He raced toward the building. She was perhaps as high up as his favorite waterfall. He could easily climb that.

Thorne paused at the wall. This was not like a tree; it was more like the cliffs by the falls. Thorne's hands searched the stones for tiny gaps to find a grip. He felt certain he could climb it. The boots on his feet made things more difficult, but he would not give up. He would get to his mate at long last.

❧ 12 ❧

Eden left the balcony door of her room open as she listened to the staccato sounds of rain pounding the hotel and the pool deck below. She had always loved the storms in Arkansas. She had grown up in storm country, so normal rainstorms were actually soothing. The rumbling sound of the thunder and the ephemeral striations of lightning across the sky made her miss home.

She lingered at the edge of the pale-blue curtains of her hotel suite, embracing the static charge in the air that sent a strange ripple of excitement through her. It was as though something was coming through the storm, something coming for *her*. There was a good chance she was simply on edge because of everything she'd been through, but the longer she stood there, listening to the rain, the more she could have sworn she could hear a voice beneath the pattering rhythm of the raindrops. Straining, she thought she heard a word that was more a whisper than anything else.

"Thorne . . ."

Eden closed her eyes. *I'm just missing him, that's all. I need to focus on moving forward.*

After her ordeal, her boss had sprung for the nicest available room while she stayed in Kampala a few more days. There was still unfinished business to attend to.

She rubbed her stiff neck and yawned. It had been a hell of a day, between the embassy interviews and Cameron Haywood. Thorne's uncle had left her a voice mail after seeing the picture, wanting a DNA test. She'd returned his call and told him that Thorne had refused to leave the jungle, but that she believed she could lead a recovery team to where the airplane was.

Cameron had been suspicious at the mention of Thorne not being available, but he'd offered to fly to Kampala to try to find him. Eden cautioned against it, not without support. She was convinced that the poachers Thorne had killed were part of a bigger problem, if what Thorne had said about the treasure cave was true. But she couldn't warn him about that. Her story was hard enough to believe as it was. She needed to crash and sleep for days before she would feel normal again, or at least close to it.

Eden wore the pajamas she'd gotten from her suitcase, a small cotton button-up top and matching shorts.

It felt good to be clean again. She'd taken a shower and allowed her hair to dry in loose waves before she ran a comb through it. Then she pulled back the covers on the king-size bed and crawled under them. The sheets were cool against her skin despite the humidity. As she reached for the light on the bedside table, the fine hairs on her neck began to rise. She wasn't alone. She turned to face the window and balcony.

A dark shadow was visible through the pale-blue translucent curtains.

A large, masculine, yet elegant hand, dripping with rain, pushed the curtain back. Eden opened her mouth to scream, but the shadow stepped into the light. Eden stared at the intruder's face, not quite sure she believed who she was seeing. It was as though she was supposed to recognize him. Yet he was so different than what he'd been a day ago.

"Th-Thorne?" She gasped and scrambled out of bed to run toward him.

He opened his arms, and she flung herself at the dripping jungle god. He was wet, but he was warm to the touch.

"Come inside." She dragged him away from the rain and into the dim gold light of the bedroom. She was lost for words as she saw the transformation he'd made. Gone was the dark leather loincloth and the crown of gold leaves. He wore cargo shorts and a black T-shirt that clung wetly to his chest. But his hair . . . The long, dark locks that had once draped down over his shoulders were gone. His hair was cropped short, yet it was still long enough for her to comb her fingers through. The ends at the base of his neck curled slightly with the rain.

As he held her, he sighed softly, and a lock of his newly shorn hair fell over his eyes. Eden brushed it away, her fingertips lingering over his cheek. His blue eyes, so deep and penetrating, remained fixed on her.

"Eden." He whispered her name reverently. "I found you."

The way he said it told her a world of things. He'd walked away from all that was familiar and comfortable to him in order to find *her*. It stole her breath, and for a moment she couldn't speak.

When she finally found her tongue again, she had nothing but questions. "How did you get here? Who cut your hair? Whose clothes are these?"

Thorne nuzzled her cheek. A low, almost purring sound escaped him as he held her flesh to his body. "You have many questions, little mate," he said with a chuckle. The rich timbre of that sound rippled through her.

"Little mate?" She tilted her head.

He brushed his fingers over her cheek, smiling. "You're so little—and you're my mate."

"Ah!" She almost laughed. He wasn't wrong—on either count—so how could she deny him that nickname? "I think I'm going to have to teach you about nicknames."

"What is nicknames?"

"Nicknames are names you give to people you love —*sweetheart, darling, my love, my heart, honey pie* . . ."

"Darling," he whispered softly, his deep voice rumbling over that one word so deliciously that she trembled.

"Yeah, like that one."

She laughed a little giddily, so relieved and overjoyed that he was here with her. The puddle of water growing at his feet called her attention to the fact that he had to be freezing.

"You're wet. Let me get a towel." She tried to pull away, but he wouldn't let go of her. "Come on. Trust me." She pulled him into the large bathroom with her, and she pulled a fluffy bath towel off the rack and tossed it over his head. He peered at her as he lifted the towel up, his fingers fisting in the cloth's soft surface as he began to rub it over his body.

"Okay, so let's start again." Eden helped him dry off, but she knew that he eventually would have to get out of his clothes. "Why did you leave the jungle? I thought you wouldn't."

"When you left, I felt sick." Thorne touched his chest. "Here." He looked down at her, and she could see his soul in his eyes.

Eden had spent so much time trying to convince

herself that what she'd felt for Thorne was not as intense as she remembered, that it was driven by adrenaline and survivor's guilt, that she'd overreacted. But the truth was that what she felt for him was all too real, and even deeper than she could ever imagine.

"I went to Bwanbale's village. He gave me clothes, and his mate cut my hair. He drove me here to find you."

Eden slipped out of the bathroom to grab her phone. She pulled up her text message thread with Bwanbale and typed a new message to let him know that Thorne was with her. A second later, Bwanbale responded.

Take care of him. Call if you need me.

"He knows you're here and that you're safe," Eden explained.

Thorne smiled. "That is good." Then he tossed the damp towel on the bathroom counter.

"So, you're here." She still couldn't believe it. A strange shyness overcame her as she realized that he was here in her hotel room, wet with rain, a hungry look in his eyes that belied his now somewhat civilized appearance.

"I am. *With you.*"

The muscles of his body were molded by his black shirt, and he lifted it off himself, moving slowly and purposely toward her. Eden backed away, but the backs of her knees hit the bed and she fell onto it. He stopped in front of her, his chest bare, his breathing slow and measured, unlike her own quick breaths and pounding heart.

She knew what was coming, knew what he wanted. She wanted it too, but he needed to know that his uncle and aunt knew he was alive and that they wanted to see him for themselves. Eden put a hand on his bare stomach, which was level with her face as he reached up to undo his cargo shorts. His hard, chiseled abs were beneath her fingertips, teasing her with all the wicked things she wanted from this beautiful man.

"Wait. We have to talk," she said, but even she didn't sound convinced.

Thorne cupped her chin and gazed down at her. "We can talk after we mate," he murmured softly. He leaned down and kissed her soundly, his lips conquering hers in a way that made her dizzy. How he had gotten better at kissing in just a day she had no idea.

"Mate," she said, echoing that wonderfully primitive word. "Have sex, you mean," she corrected.

"Have sex," he said with a slow smile.

"We also say we *make love*." She knew she was starting to ramble a bit, but she felt oddly shy with him here in this modern world. Before he'd fit right into the dark-green leafy expanse of the jungle, but here he was almost too dominant, too big and real.

"I like *make love*. I wish to make love with you, always." His words melted her heart and made it race wildly all at once. Despite the sensuality coming off him in raw waves, there was a tender vulnerability in his blue eyes that shook her. That same vulnerability echoed deep within her too. Was this what it meant to fall in love with someone? To crave him so madly, to long for him with all her heart and feel laid bare like this? If so, she wasn't just falling—she was tumbling, crashing, cartwheeling down the cliff that led to love.

"How did you get up to my room? I'm on the second story." She tried to distract him as he removed his shorts. He wore black boxers that were a tad too small, and his erect shaft was far too obvious in them. "You didn't climb, did you?"

"I did." Thorne removed his boots and socks, chucking them away, completely uncaring about them as he leaned over her.

Eden scooted back on the bed, trying to put some distance between them, even though she knew sex with him was inevitable. They both wanted it too much.

"Climbed? Thorne, don't do that again. You could have been seriously hurt."

He raised a brow, his sensual mouth hardening into a hard line. "I did not fall." He looked insulted by the suggestion that he could have gotten injured.

"This isn't the jungle. You aren't familiar with the buildings or the materials they're made of. You could get hurt."

"You worry about me?" he asked. His gaze softened

as he got on his hands and knees on the bed and slowly crawled over her prone body.

"Of course I worry," she replied before he silenced her with a kiss.

His body lowered over hers, and she spread her thighs, welcoming him between them. She was still dressed in her pajamas, but it didn't stop her from feeling his cock rub against her core as he slid against her, torturing them both with a hint of what was to come. She wrapped her arms around him, surrendering to the moment and to him. They could talk after.

Eden abandoned herself to his hard, scorching kisses and tumbled through spirals of ecstasy. He instinctively knew what to do when he kissed her, which made her forget everything else. She responded eagerly, her body set aflame by his. Deep down she knew it would *always* be like this for them, they were an inferno together. Her heart thundered as he gripped the button-up top she wore and ripped it open.

Buttons scattered everywhere, plinking on the floor, and she began to laugh, but his mouth covered one sensitive breast, sucking on her nipple, while his hand gently explored the other. She could barely breathe. He was so tender yet urgent as he explored her body. When he tugged her shorts and panties off, he kissed his way down to her mound and knelt between her parted thighs, gazing at her body with wonder and appreciation.

"You are incredible," he murmured before he lowered

his mouth to her sensitive folds.

It was just as she'd thought—he was a masterful lover, licking her wet slit, laving at the taut bud of nerves until she was writhing desperately beneath him. If he didn't stop, she would die. If he did stop, she would die. There was just pleasure, wild, mind-blowing pleasure as he made love to her with his mouth. His tongue sank deep into her channel, and she groaned as he licked deeply at her. She clawed at the sheets, near animalistic in her aroused excitement.

"Oh God. Oh my Gawwwwd! Where the hell did you learn that?" She couldn't think. When the climax exploded through her, she had only a second to cover her own mouth with one hand.

"You are beautiful when you feel pleasure," he said as he slid back up her body and kissed her lips. "And Bwanbale told me some ways to take care of you. He knows much about pleasing a woman."

Eden tried not to laugh, despite the fact that she was incredibly aroused. "You and Bwanbale had the birds and bees talk?"

He tilted his head. "There were no birds or bees."

"Oh, never mind—that's a discussion for another day." She curled her arms around his neck.

She shivered as her heart quickened with other, deeper emotions that would worry her later. She drank in his sweetness. He moved above her, shifting, and she felt his cock free of his boxers, pushing deep into her.

She groaned at the sudden fullness thrusting inside her, and his tormented groan was a heady invitation to her.

"You can go faster, *harder*," she whispered in his ear. He was holding back, she was sure, and she wanted him to let go of his control.

He growled softly, the animal inside him clawing its way to the surface. He pinned her hands to either side of her face as he rose above her, and then he showed her what he could really do.

Eden gasped as he fucked her hard and raw. It was glorious. She'd always enjoyed a bit of roughness, but this was primal, instinctive, animalistic, and she couldn't get enough. He knew just how to dominate her, how to claim her as his own. Thorne didn't give her a chance to catch her breath. The bed frame smacked against the wall hard enough to leave marks and probably wake up the neighbors. Each pump of Thorne's hips mixed with his gentle but strong hold on her trapped hands, and it completely undid Eden.

Their breaths mingled and the bed creaked in protest as they made love, frantic and intense. It was as though they were back in the jungle, surrounded by the roar of the falls and the call of the birds. They were joined, man and woman, two hearts racing wildly over the same cliff.

She came a second time and cried out his name, and he was there with her in that beautiful perfect moment. He nuzzled her neck, his lips exploring her skin as he caught his breath. He still held her pinned to the bed, and Eden quivered with aftershocks from the excitement of still being trapped beneath him. Being so thoroughly owned by him, as though he'd invisibly marked her, was the most amazing thing she'd ever felt. She was fully and truly his.

After a long moment, he rolled off her and pulled her into his arms, holding her close. His reverence for lovemaking, for *her*, left her reeling, like she'd stumbled into a wide world of amazing wonders. Every time he touched her, it felt like magic. It was the one thing she'd always craved in a relationship yet had never found, until him. How could she feel this way for a stranger? Emotion choked her words deep into her throat when she would have spoken to him.

"Are you okay?" he asked, his deep voice almost rumbling like a jaguar's growl.

She finally managed to find her tongue. "Yes. Being with you, it's just so different." She flushed and hid her face in his shoulder.

"Is that bad?"

She sensed a hint of worry in his tone. She raised her head to stare at him. "No, no. It's a good thing. I'm just not used to it. But . . . it's what I've always wanted with a man." Growing up in the wild the jungle made him see *her* in a way that others did not. It was freeing, to know she could open up to him like this.

Thorne threaded his fingers through her hair, smiling. His sweet yet seductive expression melted her heart, and she cuddled closer. He tightened his arm around her body and pressed a kiss to her forehead, the touch both warm and tender. Eden closed her eyes, taking in the scent of the jungle, rain, and man, burning it into her mind forever. Now was the time to tell him about his uncle and the new life that awaited him.

She kissed his chest. "Thorne, please don't be angry, but I spoke to your uncle today. Cameron Haywood."

His chest grew still beneath her hand.

"He wants to meet you. I told him how we met. He is so excited to find you alive. He's your family, Thorne. You really should meet him."

Thorne drew in a breath. "If I meet him, you will leave me?" he asked.

She hadn't expected that reaction. "Leave you? I . . . No, no, I won't leave you. I would be happy to go wherever you go if you want me to."

He suddenly relaxed, the tension in his body releasing beneath her.

"If you are with me, I will meet this *uncle*," he said the word with a childish suspicion that made her smile. She tapped his chest with a finger.

"Remember, you are an uncle to Akika's son. Remember how much you love Akika and his child? That is how Cameron feels about you."

He arched one dark brow. "How do you know this?"

"I know, because I could hear it in his voice. He

spent a decade looking for you, ten years. I know you don't know what that means, but it's almost half the time you've been alive, Thorne. That's how long he looked for you. He didn't believe that I'd found you at first, but I sent him pictures of your father's ring and your mother's necklace."

Thorne brushed the backs of his fingers over her throat. "You are not wearing it."

"I didn't want to break that delicate chain while I slept. It's in a special pouch, along with your father's ring."

Thorne seemed satisfied with that answer. "He believes you now? About me?"

"Mostly. Many people have pretended to have found you and your parents over the years for money."

He growled darkly. "You mean gold?"

"Something like that. People can be greedy, and they can be cruel to get what they want." She cleared her throat. "But people can also show compassion and love without end to one another. Most people believe in the goodness of humankind, and they are the ones you should put your faith in. I believe your uncle is a good man, as well as his wife, your aunt. Will you trust them?"

He was silent a long moment. "I trust *you*. You have a pure heart. I will always trust you."

His words shook her. How could he have such faith in her in so short a time? She hadn't done anything to deserve such loyalty from him.

"Will you trust me then if I trust your uncle?"

Thorne spooled a lock of her hair around his finger. After a long moment, he nodded. His vivid blue eyes seemed to glow in the lamplight.

Eden hugged him tight and then reached for her new phone on the nightstand and sent Cameron a text that she had found Thorne and he'd agreed to a DNA test. She almost immediately received a response.

I will have a private flight to London arranged tomorrow. I want you to bring him to England. Bring him home.

Eden stared at the words *Bring him home.* Then she turned to Thorne.

"Your uncle wants you to come to England to meet him. To see where you were born." She licked her lips nervously. "Will you come with me?" Then she tried saying it another way. "Will you let me bring you home?"

She saw flashes of uncertainty shadowing his eyes, but he nodded again.

"If you are with me, I will go."

Thorne rolled her beneath him on the bed, his mouth capturing hers, and all thoughts of London were forgotten.

Archibald sat in his office in Fort Portal as night closed in. The French gemologist Jean Carillet was asleep in a hotel room across the street, paid well for his silence and for helping Archibald dispose of Cash's body.

The flat-screen TV in his office was on, but muted. The BBC was covering the discovery of the murdered tourists in Bwindi Impenetrable Forest. A reporter stood in front of the dark park entrance, speaking to the camera. On the screen below her were pictures of the deceased, presumably now that the families had been notified.

Archibald stared at the TV, his hands idly playing with a large golf-ball-size rock that looked more like a dusty piece of quartz than the near-priceless uncut diamond it was. He'd tried more than once to have the diamond cut down. He was, after all, not a sentimental man who would have kept such a valuable find as a keepsake. But the three different men he'd hired to cut it down had all been unsuccessful, their diamond cutting tools shattered the moment they came into contact with the stone. It was a mystery that Archibald could not solve, but he knew one thing—the stone held power, great power. The question that he struggled with was, *What kind of power and how can I use it?*

He had found this diamond in his first year in the jungle when he'd turned twenty-one. Even now, after all these years, he could remember the rush he'd felt at seeing the cave for the first time, stepping inside and flashing his torch over the rocky walls.

The artificial light had made the diamonds on the

ground and in the walls glitter. And there had been more than diamonds in the dark, humid cave. There had been *gold*. Hundreds of pounds of gold fashioned into goblets, plates, and jewelry. Gold had streaked across the walls like shiny paint. It was clear that some ancient culture had left the items there, perhaps the distant ancestors of the now displaced Batwa tribes. The cave had felt more like a temple than a hiding spot, the way the items had been so carefully arranged.

Archibald had stood there for what felt like mere minutes, but later it had proven to be two hours as he'd stared at the treasure, and he could not tear his gaze away.

In that moment of discovery, Archibald had earned his reprieve from the wretched life he'd lived on the streets of Camden in London. He had been born into nothing, and had lived as nothing, yet he'd craved so much more. He had fought hard to leave that world behind, and finally he'd escaped.

At eighteen he'd found work on a cargo ship bound for Africa, and he had never regretted leaving. By the time he was twenty-five, he had amassed enough wealth to buy a townhouse in London and a manor house in the English countryside. The elite of London society now played to *his* tune and were at his beck and call.

But it wasn't enough. He doubted if anything would ever be enough, not when gold and diamonds still whispered to him from a mist-shrouded mountain cave in the jungle. No matter how much money he earned, he could sense that others considered themselves his betters, that he'd never shake his Camden roots. To be found *wanting* was a fate no man wanted to endure.

Archibald set the diamond down and reached for the TV remote, turning the sound on.

"Emergency crews are working through the night to recover the bodies of the park guides and the tourists. There is still uncertainty as to who killed them and why. The bodies of four armed men, not part of the group, were also found, and they are believed to be responsible for killing the tourists. It is unclear at this time who killed the armed men. Theories are already being investigated regarding poachers and rebel activity. Uganda has long been a place of political unrest and has only in the last decade been considered politically stable. It is hoped that this is not a sign of political turbulence that may return."

Archibald muted the TV and leaned back in his leather chair. Killing tourists had been a stupid mistake, one that could have been avoided. If Cash had still been alive, Archibald would have killed the man himself. If the investigation pointed toward Archibald, he would need to make sure there were no loose ends and that he had an escape route.

A picture filled the screen that made him turn the sound back on.

"This isn't the first time the Ugandan national park

has had its tragic mysteries. Twenty-two years ago, the Earl of Somerset, Jacob Haywood; his wife, Amelia; their son, Thorne Haywood; and their pilot went missing when their plane crashed. After months of searching for the wreck site, their bodies were never found. The Haywoods were passionate conservationists who used their wealth . . ."

He tuned out the words and stared at the faces of the Haywoods, his anger only deepening. Twenty-two years ago, he'd killed that family, believing no one would care enough to look too hard for them. Yet their disappearance had upset his excavation work for more than a year. Archibald saw the close-up of the Haywoods' young child and flinched.

Compassion was a word that was alien to Archibald. He had none and gave none. However, he refused to accept the idea that he was no better than the hooligans he'd grown up with. Men of power and means, men of culture, *better* men lived by rules. Killing a child would have made him no better than the swill of his old neighborhood, yet on occasion he wondered if leaving the boy to the forest had been any better.

Upon reflection, he realized it didn't matter. Only the rules mattered. That was how one judged one's place in the world of men. Power and position meant nothing without it, and it was how he knew he was better than those who still looked down upon him.

Still, the thought left him unsettled. He had done his

best to forget that day, to forget those bodies. The last thing he needed was the media stirring up old mysteries, in case it led to new leads.

His phone hummed, and he pulled his cell phone out of his pocket.

"This is Jim. You asked me to keep you informed about the Matthews girl."

"Yes?" Archibald listened to his man on the inside of the US Embassy. Jim Bramble helped him from time to time when he needed information on people.

"She's booked on a private flight to London."

"When does she leave?"

"Tomorrow, midmorning."

"What did you find out about her personally?"

Bramble snorted. "That's going to cost you extra."

"I'll pay." Archibald wasn't in the mood for haggling.

"She's a photojournalist for some nature magazine, *National Park*. She's mainly focused on animals and doesn't seem to have any political leanings in her articles, no skeletons in her closet. Her parents are in Little Rock, Arkansas. She's clean. I found nothing on her you could use. She's a real girl next door, a cute kid."

A squeaky-clean American girl who worked in the media and couldn't be blackmailed into silence? *Unacceptable.*

"Do you know how she managed to charter a private flight to London so quickly? Is the magazine covering that expense?"

"No, definitely not. She's the guest of some hotshot in merry old England, Cameron Haywood. You know him?"

"I'm acquainted." For the first time in a long time, Archibald felt panic. "I'll contact you if I need anything else."

Archibald ended the call and cursed. Cameron Haywood was the brother of the man he'd killed all those years ago. They had even met in passing over the years as Archibald had clawed his way up the social ladder.

How did the girl know him? And why did Cameron charter a plane for her? What had she found?

Perhaps she'd found the Haywoods' plane wreckage. It had been so long ago, however. Nothing tied him to that site, but he couldn't take the chance of having the Haywoods' remains resurface. He needed to silence the girl before she could tell anyone what she knew. It didn't sound as though she'd told anyone at the embassy about it—Bramble was good about finding such things out.

Archibald stared off into space, planning. Thinking. That, after all, was what separated the men from the animals. The stuffed silverback gorilla in the corner of his office suddenly drew his focus. He'd killed that beast when it had been ready to charge the Haywoods. It was a kill that still left him feeling a pulsing of excitement in his veins.

For the first time in days, he smiled.

13

Eden was impressed with how calm Thorne had
been. They had caught a car first thing in the
morning and had driven forty minutes to the
city of Entebbe, which had the nearest airport. There
they had boarded an expensive private jet that they had
entirely to themselves. Thorne had eaten his lunch,
puzzling over the forks, knives, and spoons, and carefully
mimicking her when she used them while they waited
for the flight crew to prepare. Now he was seated on the
plane, watching the ground crew fueling the plane and
preparing for takeoff.

She put a hand on his knee, and he looked away from
the window and toward her, a furrow forming between
his dark brows.

"You okay?" she asked.

"I have memories. Memories of falling from the sky," he said quietly. Eden couldn't even begin to put herself in his place. He had to be frightened of flying, even after all these years, but this was the quickest way to get to London.

"Hey, you survived that, remember? And this plane is much safer." She smiled and placed her hand over his, but he still said nothing as he turned his focus back to the ground crew.

By the time they were cleared for takeoff, Thorne had a white-knuckled grip on the armrests. What he needed, Eden decided, was a distraction. While the plane rumbled down the runway, she retrieved her camera bag and dug Jacob's ring out of the front pocket. With gentle hands, she pried Thorne's death grip from the armrests and slipped it on his finger. He glanced down at it, then to her in surprise.

"Your father is here with you," she said and held his hand as the plane rose into the sky. Thorne sat rigid beside her, and Eden hated that he was afraid. This man was so powerful and confident in the jungle, yet here he was at odds with everything around him. Eden vowed she would do everything she could to erase that fear since he was here because she'd asked him to be.

"Thorne, do you remember much about home?"

He pulled his focus from the window back to her. "Home?"

"In England, I mean. Do you remember?"

"I . . . Yes. A little." He didn't say anything more.

Eden cursed to herself. She had hoped to keep him talking. But now that the plane was high enough, she could pull out her laptop.

"I have some pictures of the jungle. Would you like to see them?"

His face brightened a little. "Yes."

She set her computer on the table in front of their seats. Cameron's plane was fully equipped with all the luxuries a private jet could afford, including polished wood folding tables between the rows of seats, which faced each other.

Eden pulled up the photos and leaned closer to Thorne. His attention turned to the screen, and she showed him how to go back and forth through the pictures. He studied each picture deeply, and would point at things like birds, flowers, or animals he noticed in the background. His favorite photos were those of his family, Tembo, and her. Pictures of himself seemed to hold no interest.

He paused on one of Keza, a close-up portrait of her as she held a mango to her mouth. Her reddish-brown eyes were soft, seeming to hold deep secrets within them.

"Mother," he said, his voice rough with emotion. "I miss her."

She leaned her head on his shoulder. "I know. But you don't have to stay in England forever. You can travel back to Africa to see her and Akika. You have that power now."

His sorrowful expression hardened at the word *power*, and he sighed. "I do not want power."

"And that is what makes you the best person to have it. Believe me, people who want power almost never deserve it." She rubbed her cheek against his shoulder, and he put a comforting arm around her. The unexpected gesture made her smile.

"You learned something new," she said with a giggle.

"I learned many things watching people at the airport." He chuckled. "Men hold their mates like this."

"Yes, they do. That was a very good thing to learn."

He looked through another dozen photos and paused at the one he had taken of her.

"This is my favorite." He pressed his lips to her forehead.

Eden's heart tightened in her chest. Thorne knew just how to get underneath any armor she had put up around her heart. When he reached the photo of himself and Tembo, she stopped him from moving to the next photo.

"And this is *mine*."

"Why?" His eyes were full of boyish innocence. How could he not understand how beautiful he was? How the picture of him and Tembo captured that?

"I see your heart in this picture. I see you and the elephant. You are one, two hearts together. It's the most beautiful thing I've ever seen."

He kissed her again upon the lips, slow and sweet. She lost track of time as the kiss seemed to go on forever. His breath was warm on her cheeks and neck as he breathed deeply, contentedly. She, on the other hand, wanted more of that kiss, more of the languid way his lips moved over hers as though he'd mastered kisses years ago and not just a few days before. The gentle, intimate familiarity between them was growing, and Eden felt as though she had been in love with this man her entire life, as though she'd always known him deep down in her soul and loved him. Was that possible? She didn't know, but she couldn't help but believe it.

"Sleep, Eden. You are weary."

"I'm really not that tired," she argued, but she snuggled closer anyway and fell asleep a short time later, cocooned in Thorne's warmth.

When she woke hours later, it was time for dinner. They still had another few hours left in the flight, but Thorne was adjusting to being stuck on a plane for so long. He smiled at the flight attendant who served them and ate his steak and potatoes au gratin, but when he tried the wine the woman offered, he coughed and shoved the glass back at the poor attendant.

"Would you like a beer instead, Mr. Haywood?" the woman offered.

"Beer?" Thorne glanced to Eden, who shook her head.

"No. Thank you."

"Maybe he can try a soda?" Eden suggested. Alcohol was an acquired taste for most people. Thorne had not had anything but water in twenty-two years and should definitely not start out with beer.

When Thorne tried the soda he grinned. "I remember this taste." He examined the red can with a delighted smile.

"What else do you remember?" Eden asked.

Thorne sipped the soda again. "It is not easy. I only remember when I see things that bring memories back."

"That makes sense." Eden hoped that in time more of his memories would become clear, but being left in the jungle at three years old, it was amazing he could remember anything at all. She then remembered his tree houses and the strange symbols in them.

"Thorne, how did you build those tree houses in the jungle? Is that something you remember seeing as a child?"

"Bwanbale asked me the same thing." He paused in eating, a strange look coming over his face. "I discovered a cave—one deep in the mountains—which had the gold and diamonds I showed you. When I found it, I was overwhelmed by voices."

"Voices? Whose voices?"

"Voices of the old gods, deep in the cave. They do not speak as you or I, but I understand their meaning. They spoke of homes among the birds, high in the trees."

"The old gods spoke to you?" Eden's skin prickled at the thought.

He frowned slightly and played with his fork. "When I sleep, I sometimes see pictures in my head."

"Do you mean dreams?"

Thorne nodded. "I could see the cave, only long ago. The trees were not there as they are now. People used to live near it, in homes on the ground, only they live there no longer. But the cave remains."

Thorne reached across the table and covered her hand with his. "Perhaps they are not gods—perhaps they are the spirits of those who hid their gold. I know so little, but I trust whatever it was in the cave."

"Did you tell Bwanbale about that?" Eden leaned forward.

"I did. He said that long ago, an ancient people lived in the forests. They vanished, and the forest reclaimed all that they had once built. I did not understand all that he said. I know only of one cave. I offered to take him there, but he refused. He said they should be left in peace. I believe the men who killed your friends, they are searching for this cave."

"Thorne, how many are there? How many caves?"

He shrugged. "Only one, but it runs deep inside the mountain."

"And it's full of gold and diamonds?"

Thorne nodded.

"No wonder men are hunting for it. The kind of money they can get from gold and diamonds . . ." She didn't finish, but he seemed to understand what she hadn't said.

"More bad men will come to the jungle." His tone was soft, but a dark edge was there beneath the words.

"Yes, and when they come, they will destroy anything that gets in their way. They might even try to burn the jungle down to make the cave easier to find." Eden felt a deep need to protect Thorne from the greed of men, but she wasn't sure she could.

A strange unnatural blackness burned furiously in Thorne's eyes, clouding the beloved blue, and his voice seemed to deepen even further. *"Then I will stop them."*

"Thorne," Eden whispered, a little afraid. The blackness in his eyes cleared, and he gave his head a small shake.

"I went away," he whispered softly. "I was back in the cave." He seemed puzzled by that, and Eden shivered.

Even if Eden hadn't seen him kill those men a few days ago, she would've seen the promise of death in his eyes and heard it in his voice and knew he meant it. If she believed what Bwanbale and Thorne had told her about the cave and the spirits of the lost civilization and their old gods, she might believe that Thorne really had been chosen to defend the jungle and all things within it. Could she believe that? The evidence was growing by the day, and she would be a fool not to at least consider it. She focused back on Thorne.

"Your uncle may be able to help us protect the jungle and the cave."

Thorne looked doubtful but didn't argue.

They spent the rest of the flight resting quietly, her head on his shoulder. They didn't speak much. Thorne was naturally quiet, but she sensed he still carried a great many worries. She rubbed a hand on his chest, hoping she could soothe him. They spent the remainder of the flight in the quiet comfort of each other's presence.

They landed at Heathrow, and a private car took them to a hotel in London, where they would spend the night. The next day she was going to take him shopping. Cameron had texted her a list of stores that had his card on file and told her to equip Thorne with some decent outfits. Then, around midday, a private car would pick them up and take them to the Somerset estate, somewhere on the outskirts of London.

The car stopped in front of the Mandarin Oriental Hotel in Hyde Park. It was like a white stone castle lit up by gold light. When Cameron had said he'd booked rooms for them here, Eden had nearly fainted. The

Mandarin was one of London's most expensive hotels, with rooms starting at $700 a night.

As she and Thorne walked into the glittering lobby, his eyes widened and his lips parted. She could only imagine what he thought of a place like this. From the towering bamboo and the canopies of hagenia trees to a veritable palace of stone. The Mandarin was decorated in a style reminiscent of the golden age of travel in the early twentieth century. It gleamed with a mix of contemporary London styles and timeless British elegance. Thorne stayed close to her, dragging her suit-case behind him, which he'd found highly amusing when he'd discovered he could spin it in circles.

Eden stopped in front of the check-in desk. A woman in a crisp white uniform and a black vest with a heavy gold nameplate that read *Linda* looked over the tall check-in counter at them. "Name, please?"

"Eden Matthews and Thorne Haywood. Cameron Haywood made a reservation for us."

Linda gasped. "Yes, of course. We've been expecting you." She pulled up their reservation on her computer, then made a couple of key cards and summoned the bellboy to take their luggage. The young man reached for the rolling suitcase, but Thorne jerked it out of reach and glared at the poor man.

Eden's face flushed as she pulled on Thorne's arm. "Thorne, it's okay. It's his job to take it." Thorne stared the other man down, forcing the bellboy to avert his gaze. Only then did Thorne release the luggage to him with a satisfied snort.

Eden nearly groaned. She would have to tip the poor man extra and have a little talk with Thorne about appropriate behavior. He couldn't act like a silverback gorilla whenever someone came near him.

Thorne looked puzzled as Eden led him into the elevator. With one wary look at Thorne, the bellboy chose to follow them up on a second elevator.

"This is our room?"

Eden realized that this was his first time in an elevator. Back at the hotel in Uganda they had taken the stairs down, since they were only on the second floor.

"It is too small. I do not like it."

"No, it's . . . it's going to carry us up to our room."

Thorne frowned and looked around nervously as the elevator shuddered slightly. He stared hard at the ceiling where a small speaker played music. He looked like he planned to climb the elevator wall to investigate. Eden held him back.

"It's just music. There's a speaker in there, like on a phone."

He frowned but calmed down. "There's so much I feel . . . unsettled by," he admitted. "How can I protect you if I do not understand this world?"

Eden moved to stand in front of him in the elevator and held both of his hands.

"You protected me in the jungle, and now it's my

turn to protect you, okay? You'll get used to everything soon and feel safe again." She stood up on tiptoes and pulled his head down to hers for a kiss.

His hands cupped her bottom, and he suddenly moved her back against the elevator wall, pinning her against the wall as he kissed her with ruthless perfection. He rocked his hips into her, and she moaned as her body flared to life with that wild hunger that only he seemed to ignite in her. She curled her arms around his neck, getting lost in him and the kiss that threatened to sweep her away.

At the musical chime of the doors parting, their mouths broke apart only inches, but it was enough. He turned to look out the door, and he looked very confused not to see the lobby.

"It *did* carry us," he said.

Eden bit her lip, trying not to laugh, and gently pushed at his chest. "We should get off."

He backed away and let her leave the elevator first, leading him down the hall. She stopped at the Imperial Suite, which she discovered had two master bedrooms, two bathrooms, and two spacious sitting rooms. The girlish side of her wanted to spin around in a circle. This was ridiculously expensive, and she planned to enjoy every moment of it. She owed Cameron a huge thank-you for booking a place like this. It went a long way to saying that he believed her.

"This is . . . big," Thorne said as he closed the door behind them.

"It's huge," she agreed. "Most hotel rooms are small, like the one you found me in. This is really special, Thorne. Your uncle is treating us very well. Be sure to thank him tomorrow when you meet him."

Thorne went into one of the spacious sitting rooms and ran his fingers over the back of a blue velvet sectional couch. He lifted the cover of one of the heavy coffee-table books, then moved to the tall windows and the balcony doors. He played with the handle until it opened, and he stepped outside, only to stagger back.

"What's wrong?" Eden asked.

Thorne leaned forward toward the balcony and gripped the wrought-iron railing, looking down.

"We are so high up."

Eden smiled to herself. He didn't realize just how high the elevator had taken them. He was quick to adjust, leaning over and looking out as far as he could in every direction. It made her a little nervous for him to lean so far out, and she called out to him to be careful.

"I fell once—from the great rocks on the mountain." He gave a casual shrug. "I was hurt for many days and could not move."

Eden stared at him in horror. "All the more reason to be careful, right?" she asked quietly. If he fell from this hotel, he'd die, but she wasn't sure *he* understood that.

"I will be careful, for you," he promised.

"Thank you."

The bellboy knocked and delivered Eden's suitcase. She made sure to slip the man an extra tip for his troubles. After the bellboy left, she rolled her suitcase into one of the huge bedrooms. When she came back, she found Thorne still standing outside on the balcony. She joined him, and they shared the view of Hyde Park at midnight together.

"It's almost like home," Thorne mused. "So many trees, but yet not the same." He released a slow breath, not quite a sigh, but somewhere in between.

"It's a park. It's like a forest, but we'll see lots of people here tomorrow during the day. Maybe even some people will be riding on horseback."

Thorne suddenly looked at her. "Horses?"

"Yes."

Thorne's face transformed with excitement. "I remember horses. My father . . . he liked to ride. I would sit in front of him."

"I bet he did." Eden smiled and leaned closer to him, and they both went back to studying the dark park. "Hey, are you hungry?"

Thorne touched his stomach with a mild frown. "Yes."

"Then allow me to show you one of the great wonders of the modern world." She looped a finger in one of the belt loops of his cargo shorts and pulled him back inside the room.

"What wonder?" he asked.

"Room service."

TWO HOURS LATER, THORNE SET THE FOOD TRAYS outside their suite as Eden instructed him to, then stepped back inside. Eden had told him there were two bedrooms, and one was his. That made no sense. There was no way he was going to let his mate sleep alone. He listened to her perform her confusing yet adorable cleansing rituals, such as washing her face.

It seemed that females did many complicated things before they slept. Things that Eden hadn't been able to do until now. He enjoyed watching her do the small, puzzling things, trying to understand their purpose. At first it had bothered Eden to bear his scrutiny, but now she simply smiled and tossed tiny towels at his face whenever she caught him doing it. He liked it when she was playful. It meant she felt happy and safe.

Thorne was patient, waiting for Eden to crawl into bed. Once the light in her room was off, he stripped down and crept into Eden's bedroom. The city of London was bright at night, with thousands of electric lights that left a tangible glow in the air that even now illuminated the dark room more clearly than moonlight. While Thorne missed the quiet dark of the jungle, he liked the fact that his vision was clearer at night here.

Thorne pulled back the covers of the bed and slid in beside her, pulling her against him. Whenever he feared he had made a mistake by leaving the jungle, taking his mate in his arms reminded him that he had done the right thing.

Eden settled back against him, her thin pajamas a delicate barrier between his bare skin and hers, but he didn't mind. Clothing made her comfortable, just as he was more comfortable without them. At least at night, he didn't have to worry about the suffocating grip of clothing.

"Thorne." Eden whispered his name, but her eyes were closed and her breathing was steady and slow.

She's dreaming of me.

The thought pleased him. He had dreamed of Eden even that first night he held her, dreamed of a lifetime of nights with her, to cherish and protect her. A life and a future. He longed for an infant of his own someday, and with a mate he had that chance. Eden was the true maker of his dreams.

He wanted to tell her how he felt, that he carried his love for her deep in his heart, but perhaps she wasn't ready to hear it yet. Bwanbale had warned him that he must take things slow with Eden, that women from the outside world would not trust a man who declared his love too early. Eden had tried to tell him the same thing, when she'd explained dating. It would take time, and he would need to be patient.

Thorne kept the words inside him, waiting for the right moment. He hoped he would know when the time was right. Thorne nuzzled her neck and closed his eyes.

Sleep came on swift wings, but soon dreams began to flutter wildly within his mind. He was back in the jungle . . .

The cave was calling to him.

The cave was dark and deep as always, with soft whispers luring him in. The dreams always started this way. He would enter the cave with the land around him exactly as he knew it, and later he would leave the cave to see the world as it once was. But something was different this time.

Thorne moved into the mouth of the cave. He could feel the cold moisture of the craggy rock floor on his feet. The whispers grew louder the deeper he walked into the cave. He could feel the presence of ancient souls all around him, speaking with voices he could not understand. Thousands of voices lived here, or had once. They were but echoes now, and he felt a strong sense of loss tied to them. He wanted to help, but he didn't know how.

In the shadows he heard laughter that made Thorne's blood run cold. He saw a man, obscured by the darkness, pick up a large brilliant stone that seemed to glow from within, casting dim shadows upon his face. The cave wailed as the man took the stone.

The images changed. He was outside the cave, but it

was still his jungle. He was at the white rock, the wrecked plane before the jungle had claimed it. He saw his parents there, a small child in his mother's arms. His father now carried the stone, but unlike the other man, he wished to save it, protect it. He saw his parents carrying him and fleeing the other man, but he knew they wouldn't make it.

He was witnessing the final moments of his parents' lives from a distance, like an outsider. Yet his heart remembered this all too clearly.

The vision jumped again. The sound of a gunshot as his father fell. His mother, pleading for Thorne's safety, only to be shot as well. The men responsible now taking the stone from his father's body and handing it to the man with the cold eyes and hard laugh.

Thorne opened his mouth to howl in rage, but he couldn't make a sound. He strained to see the face of the man responsible, but he couldn't get close enough.

The voices from the cave grew louder and more excited. This murderer was the one they wanted. The one they cried out against. The one who had disturbed the forgotten kingdom.

They wanted Thorne to find him.

No. They were *warning* Thorne. Warning him that the man was coming for him.

Thorne bolted upright, his heart beating so fast it felt as though he might die. He wiped his face and gasped for breath. For a moment he didn't quite remember where he was, but Eden's sweet scent came to him, and he soon relaxed. He lay back in bed, holding her close and shutting his eyes tight. Yet he couldn't chase away the words of worry, or the warning of the voices from the cave.

He is coming.

𝕩 14 𝕩

"Just try this one," Eden begged as she handed Thorne a soft blue button-up shirt. He sighed and accepted the shirt, carrying it into the dressing room of the upscale boutique that had been on Cameron's list of clothing stores. When they'd first come into the shop and Eden had handed Thorne a pair of pants, he'd tried to disrobe right in the middle of the displays. She'd had to rush him to the dressing rooms, explaining that he couldn't take off his clothes like that. He'd given her a long-suffering look before walking into the dressing room and shutting the door.

"That will be a lovely color on him," the young man who'd been assisting them said as he stood next to Eden. They had been making Thorne try on both casual and formal clothes for the last hour, but Eden could tell her jungle man had reached his last bit of patience with this shopping. Earlier that morning they had bought the basics, like boxers, socks, boots, and dress shoes. And now that they were done with jeans and trousers, they were finishing up with shirts.

Thorne stepped out of the dressing room, the shirt only partially buttoned. The top three buttons were undone, revealing his golden-skinned throat and pectoral muscles. Both Eden and the store clerk drew in a breath.

"Help me, please." Thorne lifted his wrists to show the tiny white buttons on the cuffs, which were still undone.

"No problem." Eden stepped toward him, gently threading the buttons through their slits so the cuffs were secure. Thorne gazed down at her, and she blushed wildly. She always got flustered whenever he focused on her like that.

"Thank you," he said softly as she finished the second cuff.

"You're welcome." She tried to focus on the shirt. "I think that blue works nicely." She turned to the clerk. "Can he wear this out of the store?"

"Yes, of course." The young man tore his eyes away from Thorne. "Let me ring everything up. Just meet me at the counter."

Eden helped him secure the last two buttons, leaving open the one at the base of his throat, before they headed to the counter.

"We got all the basics. We should be okay for anything Cameron throws at you."

"He's going to throw things at me?" Thorne's rumbling query was full of sudden distrust.

"No! That's not what I meant. It's an expression. It just means that no matter what Cameron plans to do, I think we've got the right clothing for it."

"Oh. I see." He smiled. "And maybe I should throw things back?"

"Yes. Wait—what? No, no throwing anything, okay?"

Thorne curled an arm around her waist and leaned down to kiss the crown of her hair as he chuckled. She relaxed a little as she realized he was teasing her.

The private car that Cameron had hired arrived and was ready to take them to the estate. It was an hour-long drive, and Eden did her best to teach Thorne about how to behave around his uncle, such as calling him "my lord" unless otherwise instructed. She'd had to google a bit of this herself in order to explain it to him. For her part, Eden was going to do her best to remind Cameron that even though Thorne cleaned up well, he was still getting used to how to use a fork properly.

Thorne listened to her instructions with quiet reserve, but when she was done, his attention drifted back to the rolling green hills and pastures of the English countryside.

"Not many trees" was the only thing he said about it.

He was right. Compared to the jungle, this had few trees.

A light rain settled in, and the distant shapes of sheep and cattle loomed out at them from the misty landscape. Stone walls built waist-high separated the endless emerald fields, which were divided further by small patches of forest. As they passed close to a pair of horses grazing, Thorne's gaze was riveted on the beautiful beasts, as if struck by a memory. He leaned closer to the window before they sped past down a country road.

"Here we are," the driver finally announced.

The car turned down an obscured gravel path lined by poplar trees. After another few minutes, the trees gave way to a pair of iron gates and stone pillars. The name *Somerset* was written across the center of the gates in gold letters. Well beyond, a grand manor house could be seen through the clearing mist, like a home that had been taken into a fairy realm a century ago and only now was emerging back into the modern age.

The Somerset estate was an eighteenth-century red brick home with the corners capped by large gray stones. Stately windows patterned the two-story walls, and wild ivy grew around the main doorway. The abundance of green rippling leaves made the entrance look even more like the entrance to another world. Rounded topiaries decorated a garden to the right of the house, and the base was lined with an explosion of colorful flowers.

The car stopped, and the front door opened. A dark-haired man in a bespoke dark-blue suit and a lovely woman in an emerald green knee-length dress stepped outside to meet them. This had to be Cameron and his wife, Isabelle. Cameron looked so much like Thorne it was startling. The dark hair, the intense blue eyes. If Cameron hadn't been in his forties, it would have been easy to mistake him for Thorne's brother.

"My God," Cameron murmured as he came down the steps to greet them. He held out a hand to Thorne and shook it. "You look . . . I didn't think . . . Can it actually . . . ?"

Thorne nodded respectfully. "Hello, Lord Somerset."

Cameron stiffened. "Good Lord, don't call me that. If you are who I hope you are, then *you* are Lord Somerset, or soon will be."

Eden rushed up to join them. "My lord." She shook Cameron's hand. "I'm so glad you could see us."

"It seems you've had quite the adventure to get here." Cameron looked back behind him. "Isabelle, come my love."

Isabelle was still at the top of the stairs, her mouth covered with her hand and her eyes shimmering with tears.

"This is my wife, Isabelle."

Isabelle seemed to get ahold of herself but then rushed down the stairs and threw her arms around Thorne, hugging him.

Thorne froze, not sure how to react as Isabelle's

body shook with silent sobs. Then Thorne gently embraced her back.

"Why do you weep?" he asked when she finally let go.

Eden watched all this with a lump in her throat.

"I'm so sorry," Isabelle apologized. Cameron gently put an arm around her shoulder. "It's just . . . It's really you, isn't it? Seeing you all grown up . . . I used to read you bedtime stories when your parents were out late. Do you remember?"

Thorne was silent a long moment. "I wish I could. I wish . . ." He said nothing more.

"Perhaps we should all go inside," Cameron suggested.

"Yes, I'll have some tea brewed." Isabelle wiped her tears away and held out a hand to Eden. "Come with me, Ms. Matthews. Let's leave the men alone for a bit."

"WHY DON'T YOU COME INSIDE?" CAMERON volunteered, and then he headed into the house. Thorne followed him, his mind searching for memories of this place, Cameron, and Isabelle. But he had not missed the fact that now that they were alone, his uncle's warmth had cooled just a little.

"You'll have to forgive my wife. She's more convinced about you than I am, but Isabelle always had more faith in the universe. But I believe in what I can see, what I can verify. I'm a man of facts, and frankly the story that Ms. Matthews told us . . . Well, it's hard for a man like me to believe it."

Cameron paused inside a large room with white columns along one wall. The ceiling was the color of a clear sky, and the walls were a soft yellow that reminded Thorne of mangoes, though a little paler. There were two white couches covered in fabrics that Eden had called silk and linen. She had made a point last night to tell him all about the odd furniture in their hotel room and the various fabrics, which he now knew were not animal skins at all.

Cameron waved at a couch. "Would you care to sit?"

"I like to stand. I'm not used to being so . . ." He struggled for the right word. "Still."

"Yes, looking at you, I can believe that. You look as though you never stop moving." Cameron chuckled. "Now, let us get down to business. Eden said you have agreed to a DNA test. I have the kits right here." He picked up two small white boxes and pulled out a white stick with a fluffy white end. He opened his own mouth and rubbed the fluffy end on the inside of his cheek and then put the stick in a clear tube, marking it with a black pen. He then took a second stick and handed it to Thorne. Thorne accepted the stick and opened his mouth.

"Scrape the inside of your cheek. Not too hard, but enough that you feel it," Cameron instructed.

Thorne did as Cameron said, and then he handed the stick back to him.

"Thank you," Cameron said, his tone subdued. "It's not that I don't want to believe you, but we've had many imposters over the years, and neither Isabelle nor I can live with another disappointment."

"Eden told me that men and women have tried to trick you. To take money from you. I want no money. I do this for Eden. If I am to be with her, I must be the man I was supposed to be, not the one from the jungle."

"I see," Cameron said, but Thorne could tell quite clearly that his uncle was more than a little confused. Yet Thorne had no other way to explain things.

"Well, tell me about the jungle. About the gorillas who raised you. Your friend wouldn't happen to be exaggerating about that part, would she?" Cameron leaned against the mantel, and Thorne walked about the room, studying it as he began to speak.

"Ex-ag-er-ate?"

"Is it true?" Cameron asked more bluntly.

Thorne nodded. "My mother, Keza, is a gorilla. She raised me alongside her own son, Akika. He is my brother." Thorne smiled a little as he glanced at Cameron. "I am also an uncle. To Akika's son."

"You're an uncle . . . to a gorilla?"

"Yes."

"I see . . ." Cameron sounded disbelieving, but Thorne had been warned by Eden that this would be the case.

"And you lived with them all this time?"

"Keza rescued me. I remained with her until I was ready to be on my own."

"But didn't you know you were . . . different?" Cameron asked.

"Yes. As I grew older, I could see I was not as they were. As I became older, some of the others were nervous around me."

It was one of Thorne's harshest memories—the day he had left the band and struck out on his own. He could return to visit, but he could never stay very long. He was too different.

It was then he had begun to truly hear the whispers in his head, the calling of the cave. He discovered the cave a few years after he left his family. Once he had set foot inside, visions had flooded his head. He'd fallen to his knees, his body shaking as he tried to understand what he was seeing.

Visions of homes built of wood, how to use shale rocks to cut the wood, how to create ladders, doors, and windows. He could see people much like himself, working and living in the jungle.

All his life he'd wanted to belong, and now he was here in this grand English manor house where he had been born, and he felt no more at home here than he did in the jungle.

Cameron watched him intently, but Thorne now noticed the mantel that the man was leaning against. The fine hairs on his neck and arms rose. A flash of an old memory came back to him. That of a man, his father, touching the underside of that place and . . .

Thorne crossed the room and stood right in front of Cameron. He reached out toward the mantel, and Cameron moved out of his way as Thorne felt around the lip. He found a small uneven indentation and pressed on it. There was a soft hiss, and then the wall next to the fireplace creaked open, revealing a secret door.

Thorne could see it so clearly in his head, his father turning to him, smiling, and saying something to him . . .

"*Avalon.*"

Cameron gasped, pulling Thorne out of his memories. "What did you say?"

"Avalon?" He didn't know what it meant, only that his father had opened the secret door and said that word when he did. Cameron's face drained of color, and he leaned on the mantel as though he needed it for support. Thorne offered a hand to help, but Cameron shook his head fiercely and waved Thorne away.

"There was only one other person who knew that secret door and the word we associated with it." Cameron's eyes widened as he stared at Thorne. "That man was your father. Not even Isabelle knows about the secret library this door leads to. Jacob and I called it Avalon, because we discovered it as boys while we were obsessed with stories of King Arthur."

"King Arthur?" Thorne asked.

"That is a long story for a rainy day," Cameron said. "The point is, there is no way an imposter could know about this door or that word. Which means . . . you *are* Thorne. My nephew." Cameron's once calm voice grew rough with emotion. "My boy, *you've come home.*" Cameron pulled Thorne into a fierce embrace.

Thorne felt changed somehow by this event. Like a static charge from a coming storm had been building in the air ever since he'd set foot on English soil, and now the feeling had eased. Could a person's heart recognize his home even after all this time, even when his mind could not? For the first time since he'd left the jungle, Thorne felt a call, much like the whispering cave in Uganda. The secret room whispered to him too. Both were home to him, both welcomed him.

"My God," Cameron said. "You don't know what it does to a person to live so long on hope and to feel that hope dying bit by bit every day. It's like I've been holding a candle in a hurricane, desperate to keep the flame burning. But you . . . you're here, you're *alive*." He was smiling again, his eyes overbright. "You are a wildfire, my boy, a hope that won't die."

Thorne's throat tightened. He didn't understand all

that his uncle had said, but he could understand the emotion in his uncle's voice.

"*Avalon* told me more about you than any cheek swab ever could." Cameron patted Thorne's back. "I think we need a bit of tea. Let's find the ladies."

EDEN WAS IN A LOVELY SITTING ROOM DRINKING A CUP of Earl Grey tea with Isabelle when Thorne and Cameron entered.

"Did you finish the cheek swabs?" Isabelle asked.

"We did them, but I have all the proof I need already. We'll still have to run the tests to satisfy the courts once we petition to have him declared living, but I'm convinced he is Jacob's son." Cameron shot Thorne a warm smile before meeting his wife's stunned gaze.

"They weren't needed?"

"No. Thorne provided me with clear and undeniable evidence that he is Jacob's son."

"That's wonderful!" Isabelle exclaimed. She leapt out of her chair to embrace Thorne as she had on the front steps. When she released him, she looked between them curiously. "What sort of evidence?"

"It was something Jacob and I knew together as boys. He must have shown it to Thorne. No one else could have possibly known about it."

"Dear," Isabelle sighed. "You're being *overly* cryptic."

Cameron chuckled. "A secret door, my love. That's all."

"A secret door? And you've never told me?" Isabelle didn't appear upset by this, but rather amused.

Cameron bowed and kissed his wife's cheek. "A man must have *some* secrets, my dear." He then turned to Eden and held out his hand. "Ms. Matthews, you have no idea what you've given me today. You've given me back something so precious I cannot even imagine how I could repay you for it, but I will move heaven and earth in the attempt."

Eden shook her head. "No, I don't want anything. I owe Thorne my life. If he hadn't saved me from those men, I'd be dead in the jungle. The least I could do was reunite him with his family."

Cameron cleared his throat, his face a ruddy color. "Right, well, I am still indebted to you, Ms. Matthews, so consider yourself owed a favor."

Eden hesitated a moment. "Actually, there is something you could do, Lord Somerset. The men who killed those tourists weren't simply poachers. Thorne and I believe that his jungle is in danger, and we need help to find whoever those men worked for, and stop them. I was planning to write an article and use my photos to publish in *National Park* magazine. I think Thorne's story would be very powerful, and it could help us gain support in trying to find the men who attacked me and the others. I'm convinced they were hired by an Englishman, from what Swahili I picked up from the Ugandans in the group. They spoke about an Englishman with cold eyes like death. But it was clear they weren't talking about a man currently with them, so it wasn't the man they called Cash."

"If they weren't poachers, then who were they?"

"Why don't we sit, and I'll tell you everything we know."

An hour later, when the last bit of tea had been drunk, Eden was satisfied that she had convinced Cameron of the truth and secured his support to help protect the Impenetrable Forest.

"I have an idea." Cameron toyed with the handle of his teacup. "But it's a rather risky endeavor."

"I am not afraid." Thorne had been quiet during most of the discussion, only speaking to add details that Eden had left out.

"Well," Cameron continued, "what if when Ms. Matthews publishes her article about your rescue of her and the discovery of your identity, she includes some details about the caves and the treasure. It will go viral. Whoever is in charge of the men you encountered in the jungle is likely someone who has influence in London, based on what you've told me. He'll have to see the article, or at least hear about it. I have enough pull that I can make sure that the BBC will heavily cover the story. Unless this fellow is living under a rock, he will hear about you, Thorne. He might send someone to silence you if he thinks his secret about the cave and the gold and diamonds is threatened. We will be ready for him."

"Do you expect danger?" Thorne queried, his tone quiet, but Eden heard the warning in his voice.

"I do, but we'll be smart about it. I doubt he will act quickly. While the story builds attention, we have time to put protection in place. On a much happier side, I think we ought to have a rather big party here at the house, something that we can invite the news crews to and everyone we know. If this man has any influence and power at all, he'll likely hear about this either from the BBC or from the old rumor mill after our party welcoming Thorne home."

"It's a good plan," Eden agreed. They needed to do something to draw out the people behind the gold and diamond thefts. She also wanted to make sure that the Ugandan government was involved in the discussion too, because at some point, they needed to decide if the cave should be accessed for archeological preservation.

"Excellent. Why don't we get you two settled in your rooms, and then we'll talk more this evening over dinner. I'm sure you're both exhausted."

"Thank you." Eden stood, and Thorne held out his hand to her. Eden panicked as she saw Cameron and Isabelle watching with wide eyes.

"My mate sleeps with me," Thorne said to Cameron.

Oh God. She had warned Thorne not to mention the whole mate thing, that it was something his aunt and uncle would likely not understand. How was she going to explain this? No matter what she might try, it looked bad, like she was using Thorne to get close to Cameron and his wife for any number of reasons.

"Eden." Thorne gently took her hand in his, but she tried to pull free.

"I'm sorry, Lord Somerset. He's just teasing, we aren't—"

"We are," Thorne interjected. "Eden feels you will not approve of her belonging to me. But I will have no secrets with you. We are mates."

At first Cameron said nothing, his face an inscrutable mask of English stoicism. Then there was the ever so slight smile that seemed to say, *I won't question love.*

"If she is with you, I will accept that."

Eden didn't know what to make of that response. If she had been in Cameron's shoes, she would have questioned anyone with a journalism background like hers and the circumstances in which she and Thorne had met.

"Let me take you upstairs," Isabelle offered as she led them out of the room. Eden squeezed Thorne's hand. All she could do was hope that this would all work out.

CAMERON STOOD ALONE IN THE SITTING ROOM, HIS cup of tea cold and untouched on the table. Isabelle had taken charge and escorted Thorne and Eden upstairs, but he'd needed a minute to collect himself. It was as though the pieces of his heart, once shattered and scattered upon the winds, were truly tumbling over themselves at his feet and he was trying to collect them all and find a way to put them back together.

He had been ready to believe that Thorne was a fantasy, another well-played ruse to try to take his fortune and his home away from him, along with his hope. But seeing Thorne in person had made his heart cry out, telling him that this young man was blood of his blood. Yet still he had doubts. How could he not?

Cameron left the sitting room and headed back into the drawing room where the secret door was still partially open.

"Avalon . . ."

He whispered the boyhood nickname for his and Jacob's sanctuary. An island of peace and healing for two boys who'd needed to escape the world, even for a short time. There was nothing quite like the bond between siblings, and he and Jacob had been closer than most. They were drawn to legends, drawn to the belief that secrets and beautiful mysteries still existed in the world. Jacob had often said to him that if he could have had one wish, it would have been to witness a legend firsthand.

Today Cameron had seen such a legend in the face of his nephew. The boy who had been raised in the heart of the jungle, and yet he'd grown up to be so like his parents in a thousand small ways. Jacob's intensity, Amelia's loyalty—and he'd known the magic word to break apart the walls of doubt around Cameron's heart.

Cameron smiled and shook his head as he gently closed the door. "Sweet Avalon." That little room contained mysteries for another day, but at least one had been revealed. Thorne was alive. Thorne was *home*.

15

Thorne gazed out of the tall windows of the massive bedchamber. His eyes took in the gardens below the balcony. Colorful flowers bloomed in wild, lovely patterns amidst the carefully arranged green yews and rhododendrons.

The heady scent of roses filling his nose and the delicate brush of petals as he giggled and hid from his mother while she counted to ten. Hearing her call his name as he ran through those gardens and she tried to catch him.

The more he saw of this place, the more small but powerful memories like that came back to him.

Eden came up behind him and wrapped her arms around his waist. She pressed her cheek against his shoulder, and he could feel the heat of her skin through the blue dress shirt he wore. He smiled and covered one of her hands with his.

"Are you okay? That was pretty intense." She was always worrying about him. Even Keza had not worried this much about him. But then, these past few days had been an adventure unlike any other, in equal measures terrifying and exciting to him. Perhaps some worry was justified.

Thorne turned, catching Eden in his arms and holding her close so he could lean down and nuzzle her cheek. One of the best things about being mated was having the right to hold his mate like this. Physical intimacy, even as innocent as this, was a gift he treasured.

"I am fine," he assured her.

"Do you want to rest or explore the house a bit?" she asked, then sighed as he nibbled her earlobe. He knew just how to tease her there.

"You have to stop that or people will think we're sex addicts."

"What is an addict?" he asked. He gently blew on the sensitive spot below her earlobe, and she shivered in his hold.

"People who can't stop doing something, even though they know they should."

"And we can't be addicted to sex?"

"*No*, we definitely can't. I mean, we should find other ways to bond too. At least until . . ." She gave up her protests and wound her arms around his neck. "Oh, fuck it."

He grinned, hearing the soft surrender buried

beneath her sighs as he kissed her. He wanted her to feel how grateful he was to have her, how glad he was that she was here with him. This world had left him feeling out of place, like a fish that had splashed onto shore and couldn't get back to the water.

With Eden, he felt like he wouldn't be lost in the vast currents of this new life. He trusted her guidance. His love for her grew every minute, but he had no idea how to tell her, how to make her see that what he felt for her went above and beyond the sheer bliss of her kisses or her touch or the physical act of mating. From the first moment he'd seen her, it had been something deeper, something that made him feel like he could face anything, so long as she was with him.

Thorne cupped the back of her head, deepening the kiss, enjoying her excitement and knowing he was the cause. Bringing pleasure to her was one of his great joys in life.

But she was right. Their mouths slowly parted, and he held her in his arms, breathing softly as he cherished this moment.

"We should do something else," he said.

"No, no. I'm fine with this, really!" Eden said quickly.

"You are right. If I am always mating with you, we might not bond in other ways."

"Well, I mean, we can always bond *later*." She started to kiss him again.

"No. We should do something now." He couldn't resist teasing her.

"Goddammit," she grumbled. "Of all the times to act all noble."

"Should we not bond in other ways?" Thorne asked, pretending to be puzzled. She was frowning at him, and her face was flushed a lovely red.

"Yes . . . yes, we should," she sighed. Then she added, "How about the house? Should we take a tour?"

"Yes." He did wish to see more of the world he had been born into.

"Okay. Let's go." She stepped out of his arms and led the way, but he heard her mutter under her breath, "Me and my big mouth."

He had to bite his lip to hide his laughter. He would reward her later for being so sweet and letting him tease her like that.

They left the bedchamber and took their time exploring the halls of the house, pausing to study paintings, which Eden had to explain were like photos made by hand.

"Someone made this?" Thorne studied the figure before them, which was surrounded by a beautiful gold frame.

"Yes, with a paintbrush and paint."

Thorne had vague memories of finger painting with his mother, but that was so different than the exquisite portrait he was looking upon now, which depicted a young woman in an elaborate pale-blue gown. He studied the woman's features, looking for any sense of familiarity or likeness to himself. The eyes, perhaps? Yes, she had blue eyes that were like his own.

"She must be an ancestor." Eden leaned against his shoulder, gazing up at the portrait.

"Ancestor?"

"Your parents had parents, and those parents had parents, and so on," she explained, using hand gestures to suggest a series of steps. "She is probably one of them."

"It is strange to be here, to know this was once my home," he admitted.

"I know," she agreed. "To be told that you belong here, after where you've spent your whole life . . ."

"I do not feel I belong here," Thorne said simply. Yet he *wanted* to feel it. He craved that sense of belonging almost as much as he craved Eden.

"Your aunt mentioned horses and stables. Do you want to go check them out?"

That suggestion brought a smile to his lips. "I remember the horses."

"I'll take that as a yes." Eden laughed, and they walked hand in hand out of the house and toward the stables.

"Do you know about horses?" Thorne asked as they walked into the stables. The scent of something rich and wonderful filled his nose, creating waves of old memories.

His father sitting on a tall black beast, his mother lifting him up so he could sit in front of his father. The bouncing feel of the beast as it moved beneath him.

"I rode a little when I was a girl in middle school," said Eden.

"Middle school?"

"School is where children go to learn things. But most girls get obsessed with horses around that time. My mom sent me to a riding school for two summers. I wasn't a great rider, but I was all right. I still love to ride when I get the chance."

Eden moved deeper into the stables and patted a large bundle of some type of gold grass. "I still love the smell of hay." She plucked up a few pieces of dried grass and handed them to him. Thorne lifted them up and inhaled. The rich scent brought back such happy, vivid memories. *Hay.* Yes, he remembered what it was now. His father used to feed it to the horses.

"My father used to take me riding," he said.

"You remember?" Eden asked, her voice lifting skyward with excitement.

"I see images. Certain smells make the images clearer."

Eden tapped the tip of his nose playfully. "That's the power of your nose. Smell can be the most powerful thing when it comes to a person's memory."

Thorne smiled, and he gently touch the tip of her nose back.

"Show me a horse," he commanded.

Eden rolled her eyes. "How can you be so hot when you boss me around? I'm beginning to think I have a submissive streak in me."

Thorne liked it when she talked, even when he didn't fully understand what she meant. He was used to the sounds of the jungle, the chatter of the monkeys, the cries of birds, and the throaty calls of the gorillas.

But there was something innately pleasing about the sound of a human female's voice. Eden's in particular made his body glow like he was beneath the late-summer sun, resting between the cool water of the falls and the heat of the sunlight. It was perfect. Just like Eden's voice.

Thorne fell in behind Eden as she approached the wooden wall with windows placed intermittently down the row. A great beast pushed his head through one of the windows. Thorne tensed, then relaxed when he realized it was a horse. He wasn't a child anymore, yet the beast's size still intimidated him. The horse was like Tembo, but not nearly so tall, yet he seemed more restless, more dangerous with his potential for quick movements.

"Hey there," Eden cooed to the horse and held out her hand. The horse bumped his nose into her palm and snorted softly. Then he nickered and encouraged her to pet him again.

"Need some attention, huh?" She scratched the horse's nose and glanced at Thorne. "Come, you try." She waved in his direction.

Thorne drew closer, holding his breath as he curled his fingers into a closed fist and let the horse breathe in his scent. He imagined he was back in the jungle, and how easy it was to be around animals, to let them speak to him. His shoulders dropped, releasing the tension inside him, and he could in that moment feel the horse's heart alongside his own. He smiled. The horse huffed, and his withers rippled with a little tremor. Then he calmed and nosed Thorne's bent knuckles. He opened his hand and let the horse nudge his palm. The dark, soulful eyes of the beast seemed ancient, much like Tembo's solemn gaze.

"I bet you'll be an amazing rider, like your father."

"My father?"

Eden pointed to the wooden beam above the horse, which held several shaped gold objects. "Those are riding trophies. Your father's name is on all of them."

The thought of a connection to his father filled him with a secret joy. There was so much about this life he didn't know, yet he wanted to. But he feared that the more time he was here, the more he would be expected to stay here forever. To abandon the forest. To give up his life with Keza and Akika. It was an unfair choice between two different worlds, and the world he had left in the jungle was still in great danger.

"There you are!" Isabelle appeared in the doorway of the stables, a warm but cautious smile on her lips. "I found some old photo albums and some videos of you and your parents. I thought you might want to see them."

Thorne nodded. He longed to see his parents.

They left the stables and met Cameron in a cozy library that had a large screen. Cameron had laid out a collection of books on a nearby table and was flipping through them. He grinned as he saw them enter.

"Thorne, come in! Sit." He nodded at a chair beside him.

Thorne sat down, and Cameron slid a book in front of him. It was full of photos of himself. No, not himself —his father. The handsome man stood next to a horse and wore a set of white clothes covered in grass stains and dirt. The rakish grin on his father's face reminded Thorne of how he felt whenever he outwitted a silverback from a neighboring band if he strayed a little too close to their territory.

"He was a master polo champion, your father," Cameron said with pride. He pointed to another man beside him. A happy looking man with laughing eyes. "That's Jordie Lofthouse. We call him Lofty. He was a dear friend of your father's."

Isabelle laughed. "Lofty is such a darling scamp, isn't he, my dear?"

"That he is," Cameron agreed with a laugh.

Thorne saw a dozen more photos of his father before coming across a large photo of a woman in a white dress. She was half-hidden by a large bundle of flowers that she held in her arms. *Roses.* The deep-scarlet blooms were a brilliant contrast against the white of her dress.

"Your mother on her wedding day." Cameron chuckled. "Your father made an utter fool of himself trying to win her over, though one could hardly blame him. We men should all be fools in love."

She was beautiful, so beautiful that a bittersweet ache filled Thorne's chest. It was the face in his dreams, the face that had given him comfort in the dark nights of the jungle in those early days.

"I remember her," he confessed with quiet awe. "I remember them both."

His mother's smile. His father's gentle chuckle. It was all there, buried deep within him. Thorne turned page after page of the pictures in the album, trying to capture more of these memories. When he was done, he looked at Eden, who stood next to the TV with Isabelle.

"Do you want to see the videos?" she asked.

Throat tight, Thorne nodded and stood before the screen. Eden had explained how this worked before they had left Uganda. A TV was like a camera, only the pictures could move and talk. Cameron joined him, gently placing a hand on his shoulder. The screen suddenly flared to life, and he saw a little boy frolicking on the grass. His mother was laughing as she chased Thorne.

"Catch him, Amelia!" A rumbling voice came through the TV's speakers. It was his father's voice.

"He's such a cheeky little thing," Amelia giggled. She caught the child in her arms and carried him toward the camera. Thorne could now clearly see his own face in the child.

"Give him to me, darling," Jacob said. The camera shook, then righted itself, and Jacob was holding Thorne in his arms now, and Amelia must have been holding the camera. The look upon his father's face as he looked at Thorne was one of pure love and devotion. The face of a man who'd been born to be a father.

Thorne had lost his whole world at an age where he could barely remember it. No one should have to face this type of loss. The pain was too great, too cruel.

His breathing changed into deep, harsh inhalations. His fingers curled into fists. Rage swirled within him with a tornadic energy. He had to get out of this house, had to vanish into the wild before he went mad with grief.

He fled the library, ignoring the calls from everyone to stop. He barreled out into the front gardens and toward a distant lake. He needed to be near something

EMMA CASTLE

familiar, something he understood. A place to catch his breath and think.

He skidded to a stop at the wooden dock that extended into the lake and stared at the murky water. Without a second thought, he dove into the water and swam deep down with long strokes until his lungs began to scream. He wanted to drown the memories, erase the dark moments of his past, but he couldn't. Those painful memories were tied too intimately to the moments of joy they had given him.

When he broke the surface, Eden was standing at the water's edge, and the setting sun lit her hair like gold from the ancient cave. He stood waist-deep in the water, gasping for breath.

Eden threw herself into the lake and swam toward him until she had him in her arms. He buried his face in her neck, holding on to her as he cried. His body shaking, he let the grief of the child he had once been and the man he had become bleed into the water around him. His hate, his sorrow, all of it seeped out of him, leaving him hollow inside.

"It's okay, Thorne," Eden whispered in his ear. "I know it hurts. You have to let it out so you can let it go."

She was right. But he didn't want all of the memories to go, just the painful ones. He wanted the happy memories of his parents to return. The rage and the violence that had threatened to consume him eased and started to fade.

"They should not have died."

"No."

"They were murdered."

"I know."

"I hate the men who killed them. I will find them, and I will kill them."

"No, Thorne. They don't deserve your hate. Hate is too great a burden to carry. Choose love instead. The love of your aunt and uncle, the love of Bwanbale and his family. Of Keza and Akika. They deserve your love."

"And *you*," he added. Thorne cupped her face in his hands and gazed into her leaf-colored eyes. "I carry love for you too."

Eden bit her lip and held his gaze. "I love you too, Thorne." He leaned down to touch his forehead to hers and sighed. The light was dying around them, but not within them.

"We should go inside," Thorne whispered. "You are cold."

Eden chuckled even as she shivered. "Hold on a sec. I just want to enjoy this whole *Mr. Darcy in the lake* thing for a minute longer."

"*Misterdarcy?*" Thorne asked, confused.

Eden giggled and patted his soaking wet chest, fingering one of the buttons of his blue shirt. "Never mind."

"Let's go." He scooped her up into the cradle of his arms.

Eden gasped as he effortlessly carried her out of the lake. When they reached the house, Isabelle was there waiting, holding a pair of towels.

"Are you both all right?" she asked.

Thorne gently set Eden on her feet, and they accepted the towels. "Yes."

"Why don't you go shower, and I'll have the cook send dinner up to your room."

"Thank you, Aunt Izzy," Thorne said.

The woman froze. Her lips trembled. "You . . . You said you didn't remember."

Thorne held his aunt's shocked stare. "I do now. You gave me *The Jungle Alphabet* book. That was you."

Isabelle covered her mouth with her hands. "You do remember."

Thorne, uncaring that he was soaking wet, pulled his aunt into his arms.

"Don't cry," he murmured. "Please, Aunt Izzy." He held her, and it was like the last piece of something missing inside him had settled back into place.

"Heavens, look at me, weeping like a watering pot." She pushed at him. "And *you* are cold and wet. Go on upstairs. Wash that lake water off and get some rest. I'll have dinner sent up soon."

Thorne kissed his aunt's forehead before Eden led him upstairs to their room. She was quiet, too quiet, which bothered him. Her towel was wrapped tight around her, and she watched him with wide eyes as he closed the door.

"Eden?" He spoke her name with as much love as he could.

"This is just . . . It's so much, Thorne. Was I right in bringing you home? Would you have been happier if you had stayed in the jungle?" She wiped at the tears that were now trailing down her cheeks. "I came into your life, and now, what have I done? I stole you away from your home. From Keza and Akika . . . even Tembo."

Thorne cupped her shoulders and smiled. "Tembo will remember me, but he does not need me. This is also true for Keza and Akika."

"But you need *them*. You're a part of the jungle. I can't help but think you belong there. I know your aunt and uncle are so happy to see you again, but I feel like I've turned everyone's world upside down."

Thorne put his hand under her chin and lifted it up so she had to look at him.

"I am a child of two worlds, with two lives. You returned that second life to me, Eden. Do not cry." He lowered his head to hers, his mouth gentle as he caressed her trembling lips.

Her towel fell to the floor, and Thorne led her back with him into the bathroom. He paused in his kisses long enough to turn on the hot water in the shower before he turned his focus back to her.

"Take off your clothes," he commanded. His sweet

mate slowly peeled off her clothes, but not all of them. A smaller layer of light-pink fabric remained underneath.

"All of it. I need to take you," he growled in a hungry command.

As he stripped out of his own clothes, he pulled a very naked and beautiful Eden into the shower with him. The steam cocooned them in a private world, while hot water cascaded over them.

Eden's soft curves pressed into him, making him near mindless with lust. His pulse was a rapid staccato underneath his skin as he looked into Eden's eyes, which held a thousand silent questions within them. Thorne's blood surged as he took her mouth, dominating her lips, showing her that he was in charge.

The pull between them was so strong he could feel it locking them together. He turned her in his arms, facing her away from him. She placed her palms on the shower wall, her bottom thrust toward him. He swept his hands over her wet skin, cupping the swells of her breasts and the curves of her ass. She was gorgeous, and she belonged to *him*.

He caged her from behind, pressing his front to her back, his hands on either side of hers on the shower wall as he kissed her neck and nipped her sensitive skin. She gasped and arched against him. He moved his hand down her body between her thighs, parting her slick folds, stroking a fingertip into her wetness.

"Please, Thorne, take me," Eden whispered. "Take me like you did by the waterfall."

He didn't reply with words. Instead, he gripped her hips and pulled them toward him, then guided himself into her body, finding sweet oblivion as he sank into her.

She gasped his name as he withdrew and thrust back in. This position gave him a sense of control that he enjoyed. To take his mate like this brought the animal in him roaring to the surface. He didn't hurt her, but he knew he could be hard and rough in certain ways that would have Eden lighting up like a star with mind-blowing pleasure.

He took his time riding her, and when her legs began to shake, he increased his pace, taking her harder, faster. Their ragged breaths echoed all around them. He fought his own release until she gasped and went limp first. Only then did his pulsing body race to catch up with her, and he released himself inside her. It left him gasping as he held her back against him.

Thorne cradled her to him, nuzzling her neck as she propped herself up against the shower wall with one hand for support.

"Holy shit . . . holy shit . . . holy shit . . ." Eden's breath escaped shakily as she turned to face him. "You have wrecked me for all other men."

He smiled at her. "I'm your *only* man."

She laughed softly and cuddled close to him beneath the hot spray from the shower. "That you are."

Thorne held his breath for a long moment, then spoke the words that had grown too strong to stay caged inside him. He'd said it before in the lake, but not quite so openly, so clearly as he wanted to say it now.

"I love you."

Eden turned in his arms, her lips parted as though to speak, but he kissed her before she could answer him. He spoke without words. He spoke the language of his body and soul, and he hoped that it was a language powerful enough to win her heart.

❧ 16 ❧

The Haywood family and Eden had been busy the week following Thorne's return. The DNA results had come back positive, and the official paperwork to reinstate Thorne as a living person had been filed in the courts. Eden and Isabelle had worked carefully on a special news interview with the BBC where Eden told her story of the jungle massacre and the plight of the gorillas, and she'd teased the interviewer and the audience with Thorne's story, not quite divulging all the details about her miraculous rescuer.

The news about Thorne had traveled fast. Within a day of her interview, camera crews and paparazzi had been buzzing about the Somerset estate gates like bees about a hive. Now a full week later, the print article in *National Park* magazine and the online edition were launching within the next half hour, and Eden was a nervous wreck. So much was riding on this, and Eden knew it could possibly take months, maybe even longer, for the man they wanted to find to make a move so they could catch him. There was also every chance the man would simply disappear—remove all traces of his connections to Africa and the cave and never look back. But Cameron wasn't convinced of that. He said a man wouldn't simply walk away from that kind of wealth.

Eden sat anxiously at the breakfast table with Cameron, even though it was close to noon. Thorne and Isabelle were out riding horses, which they had taken to doing each day right after breakfast. They were usually gone a few hours, since the Somerset estate was large. They had to ride deep into the estate and away from the gates to avoid too many photos from the press outside. Eden's gaze strayed to the windows that overlooked the pasture beyond, but she saw no sign of Thorne or Isabelle. She tapped her foot and bit her lip as she looked back to Cameron.

"Everything is going to be fine, Ms. Matthews. The article you wrote was perfect. Give it time. We know this is a bit of a waiting game. The fellow we're after will be smart, after all, to have been hidden all this time. He won't just walk up to our gates and announce he's looking for you or Thorne. What we need to focus on now is helping Thorne integrate back into society and the good we can do with the international attention this situation has brought us. This is our chance to help the jungle and the life inside it."

"Yes, I know you're right. I just can't help but worry," she confessed quietly. "What if this does more harm than good? You didn't see the bodies. Whoever this is we're dealing with, if he gets desperate, who knows what he might do to cover his tracks, or to steal whatever he can before the net closes on his operation."

Cameron's cell phone suddenly buzzed, and he checked it as he sipped his tea, then lifted his gaze to hers. "I understand your worries, my dear. Have a little faith. You of all people should know that nothing creates change faster than a cause célèbre. I'm getting all sorts of texts and messages and alerts. Everyone wants to know about Thorne. They all want his story."

He set his coffee down to read through a few of the messages. Eden held her breath when Cameron suddenly smiled.

"I believe it's time for the next part of our plan. Thorne's welcome party. Isabelle has made all the arrangements for tonight. All we need do is send out the guest list."

"Will people really come to a party at the last minute like this?" Eden tried to focus on her toast. If she didn't eat something, she would be nauseated all day.

"If there's one thing I know, my dear, it's British society. Everyone in my immediate social circle will be dying to attend tonight and see the living myth, especially since we haven't allowed him to make any television appearances. All they have are a few blurry photos from the paparazzi and the documents we filed in court." Cameron offered a smile. "It's a temptation they won't be able to resist, to come and see him for themselves. This will be one of Thorne's hardest tests, to deal with society."

Eden was concerned, but not just because she was worried that his exposure to the media would overwhelm him, or that they'd eat him alive looking for some angle to exploit. She was all too familiar with the darker side of journalism. That was something she could protect him from, so long as she was able to control who had access to him. She and Cameron had both agreed that TV interviews were not good for him, not yet.

She was worried about those hunting for the treasure cave in Uganda, those who were responsible for the deaths of so many innocent people. She imagined some super-powerful man in the shadows, an archvillain right out of a comic book, with a mustache he twirled while he bathed in a bathtub of stolen gold and ordered the deaths of anyone who stood in his way.

Okay . . . That was definitely not a realistic scenario, but Eden was convinced that whoever was behind this hadn't given up on his hunt. And that meant that Thorne's jungle was still in danger. And depending on how powerful or desperate this person was, Thorne himself was possibly in danger too.

Cameron set his phone aside and cleared his throat. "Ms. Matthews, I believe it's time we had a talk about Thorne and his future."

"Okay." They'd already had a few of these talks, so she wasn't sure what was left to say.

"Actually, what I meant was, we should have a talk about your place in it."

Eden felt the toast she had just eaten surge back up her throat. It took everything inside her not to throw up.

"Oh. I see." She'd been expecting something like this the moment Thorne had said Eden was his mate. She squared her shoulders, ready for a barrage of unpleasant and probing questions.

Cameron steepled his fingers and studied her, his face a mask of inscrutability. "Thorne told me yesterday that he loves you. Are you aware of his feelings?"

"Er . . . yes, I am."

"And do you return such feelings, to the extent that you love him as well?"

"I . . . Lord Somerset, how I feel about him isn't the real issue. Thorne feels things for me because I'm the *first* woman he has seen since he was a child. I imagine any woman he'd rescued would have earned his devotion and interest. But I don't want to hurt him, so I haven't . . ." God, she was rambling, and honestly she didn't even know what she was trying to say. She drew in a steadying breath. "Something happened between us in the forest. I can't explain it, and I know that this is all new to him, so he deserves the right to make a true choice about who he spends the rest of his life with. If that isn't me . . . it will break my heart, but I won't stand in his way. He has lost so much already—I could never hurt him."

Cameron remained silent, and she felt compelled to continue. "I know he'll be the Earl of Somerset someday and that you plan to renounce the title to him. I know that there are better women out there who would make a better countess. I only know that I *do* love him, but if he decides he wants someone else . . . I will respect that decision."

Lowering his hands into his lap, Cameron leaned back in his chair.

"Ms. Matthews, Isabelle and I are perhaps the two people in the world who understand your feelings the most. I never wanted this life." He waved an arm around at the grand old house. "Jacob was the earl, and I didn't want to have the pressure and responsibilities as he did. Isabelle and I didn't crave the power or wealth. We crave happiness. We've had so little of it in the last twenty-two years, until now." Cameron's blue eyes softened, and faint lines crinkled the corners of his eyes. "Now, we are overcome with joy. We couldn't have children of our own, and Thorne . . . He is like a long-lost son to us. I simply want to be sure that both you and Thorne have thought everything through. It is as you said—he knows nothing else save the life he lived in the jungle, and it's possible he may yet change his mind on many things. But for whatever it's worth in a modern age like this, you have my trust and my approval."

Eden swallowed thickly, trying her best not to think about a day when Thorne might change his mind.

"I pray he is like his father. Jacob loved only once and greatly, with all his heart." Cameron patted her hand. "We will trust and have faith that you and Thorne are destined for the same."

Eden tried to smile, but her mind was clouding with worries over the future, not to mention the party tonight.

Thorne found her an hour later working on her computer. He came up behind her to grip her waist and kiss her ear. The aroma of him—male sweat, leather, and hay—was intoxicating.

"Were you at the stables?"

"Yes. I was enjoying the ride, so we stayed out longer than usual. You should have come."

"Sorry, I was working."

He leaned over and closed her laptop, preventing her from typing. "You work too much." He trailed his fingertips down her throat as he kissed her neck, and she relaxed into his attentions with a contented sigh. He was getting really good at this. "I will distract you." He began to pull her off the bed and toward the shower.

"I know you will." She laughed as they stripped out of their clothes and stepped into the shower stall.

Thorne was all seductive smiles and dominance as he captured her mouth and pinned her against the shower wall as the warm water ran over them. But Eden was feeling playful now that he was here, and she pushed against his chest, breaking them apart.

Concern darkened his eyes. "You do not want to—?"

"I do," she said, cutting him off, "but I would like to do something to you and see if you like it."

He raised an arched brow but stood back and let her go. She knelt before him, thankful for the soft rubber mat on the floor of the shower stall. His aroused cock was close to her face, and she took him in her hands. Thorne tensed, and she pushed him back against the wall.

"Eden, what are you—?"

"Hush." She stroked his impressive length with her hands before she opened her mouth and flicked the tip of her tongue against the crown of his shaft.

He cursed low, and she grinned wickedly up at him. "Learned some new words, did you?"

"Yes." He groaned and closed his eyes as she licked him again, this time down the length of his cock. He grew even harder as she stroked him again. She did this a few more times before she took him into her mouth. His naked, muscled body nearly leapt away from the wall, and his eyes flew open. He seemed to have no words for what she was doing and how it made him feel, just reactions.

"Remember how you went down on me? How you licked me? This is what a woman can do to a man. So enjoy." She took him back into her mouth, and he clenched his hands into fists against his sides, showing he was desperate to control himself.

He was too long to fit more than halfway into her mouth, but Eden used her hand in conjunction and opened her throat wider for him. She used her tongue to stroke the underside of his shaft, and a few seconds later Thorne fisted a hand in her hair, pumping his hips madly against her. She nearly choked, and the sound slowed his frenzied pace, but Eden kept taking him in, and soon he exploded upon her tongue. His rough, strangled cry only made her own arousal that much stronger. Being with Thorne was always like the first time, but without any awkwardness. He made love openly, honestly, sometimes ferociously, yet also tenderly in turn. He gasped, trying to catch his breath as he pulled her to her feet and into his arms.

"You are incredible." He said this often when they were together, an expression that had come to represent something special between them. "You make me feel things that . . ." He trailed off and grazed her lips with a soft but hungry look that she adored. A look that promised wild passion, explosive climaxes, and sweet intimacy afterward.

Thorne touched his lips to hers. A river of emotions swept over her, and before she could stop herself, words were escaping her lips like a murmuration of starlings sent into flight.

"I love you . . . I love you . . ."

His lazy, seductive smile was full of leonine confidence. "I know."

"You do?"

"We are mates. Of course you love me." His easy confidence behind that statement felt oddly right. Of course she loved him. How could she not? She had been silly to think she ever could have denied that. But she had been afraid to let herself love him for so many reasons. Now it was too late. She was all in when it came to Thorne. Even if it got messy or painful, she was his to the end.

"Kiss me."

His chuckle turned into a growl as he pinned her against the wall and did just that. He kissed her, loved her, and so much more.

THORNE MET HIS UNCLE IN HIS STUDY HALF AN HOUR before the guests were to arrive for the party. Though it was not uncomfortable to wear, he felt constrained in the dark-blue suit that he'd been told to wear. They called the look "sensible." How could a man move properly when such clothing restricted him? He missed the freedom of wearing nothing but his bare skin.

"Have a seat." Cameron put aside a stack of papers he'd been reviewing and gave his full attention to Thorne. Thorne liked that about his uncle, that as busy a man as he was, he could focus on the person he was speaking with. From what little Thorne had seen of this new world so far, men and women ignored each other and buried themselves in their digital devices. Yet Cameron and Isabelle were different.

"I know you must be worried about tonight, but it's time we had a talk. An important one."

Thorne remained silent, allowing his uncle to continue at his own pace.

"As I'm sure Eden has explained, your father was the eldest son of this family. That meant he became the Earl of Somerset when our father died. That was a year before you were born. As Jacob's eldest and only son, the title now passes to you."

Thorne's stomach twisted, and he shifted restlessly in his chair.

"I don't want it."

"That's not a choice, I'm afraid. These things are like nature. They occur despite our best intentions or desires. You are Jacob's only child. There are ways to leave you without the title if you truly wish, but Thorne, please listen to me. This was meant to be your life. It feels uncomfortable now, but someday—someday this life may call to you as much as Africa does. Your parents lived their lives equally here and traveling the world.

They made it work, and I believe you and Eden could too. You owe it to your parents to try." Cameron cleared his throat. "That being said, I am aware of the shock and pressure this title and its responsibilities will bring to you. That is why I hope you will allow me to share the burden."

"Share?" Thorne didn't understand, but he was glad of any help Cameron could give.

"You will be the Earl of Somerset, but I would be at your side, helping you. You've had no schooling, but we can remedy that. Isabelle and I will help integrate you back into society far better than this little party tonight."

None of this sounded appealing to him. "And if I wish to return to Africa?"

"You can, of course, but you can't escape the title, Thorne. The world knows who you are now, and everyone is interested in knowing more about you. There's no running away from this, no hiding in the jungle forever. You can leave the official title behind, but the world won't forget who you really are."

Thorne looked down at the floor, his thoughts jumbling as he tried to imagine dividing his life like his parents had. He couldn't stay in England forever. He missed the call of parrots, the sound of waterfalls, and the humid feel of the jungle air embracing him. He missed Keza and Akika. But he wouldn't let go of Eden, or this new world that held different joys.

"Were my parents happy? Living in two worlds?" he asked.

His uncle nodded. "Yes, yes they were. Quite happy. Like anything worth having in this life, it required work, but I think you're quite capable of living just as they did." Cameron offered a sympathetic gaze. "I know this is not what you want, but you're British, and you'll learn that if there's one thing we do, it's to keep our chins up and bear anything that comes our way with quiet grace. And the fact is that as an earl you can do far more to help protect the jungle you love than just living there and fighting off poachers, deforestation, and everything else that threatens the wilds of Uganda. You are not alone in all this. Isabelle and I are here for you." Cameron leaned in and touched his shoulder, giving it a gentle shake.

Thorne nodded and stood. He paused at the doorway of the study and looked back at his uncle.

"I am going to marry Eden."

"You mean you're going to propose? We tend to ask our mates for their permission first." There was a hint of teasing in his uncle's tone at this correction.

Thorne nodded.

Cameron chuckled. "My boy, I am not surprised. You have my blessing. Isabelle will be thrilled. She sees much of herself in the girl. Take the advice I gave to your father when he first met your mother."

Thorne waited expectantly.

"Go slow. Take your time. Be sure. Lust is fleeting and can feel a lot like love."

"Did my father listen to you?"

"No, he married Amelia after just one month."

Thorne smiled. "My heart has only one name carved upon it, and I will love her until there is no more breath in me. If I am following in my father's footsteps, then there is no greater honor."

"Then I am happy for you. To love greatly and be loved like that in return is a gift few have received."

Half an hour later, the guests started to arrive. Thorne and his aunt and uncle met them at the door. It was a parade of faces that held no meaning to him, but he smiled, shook hands, and learned the art of what his aunt called "small talk." The description was an apt one. Everything people said to him was of so little importance, and they often repeated one another with the same trivial questions.

Instead of focusing on the names, he focused on faces and the people's tones as they spoke. More than one woman seemed to be interested in him as a potential mate, which he found irritating. They seemed to regard him as some kind of prize to be won.

Some of the men seemed threatened by him and would posture in defensive ways, putting their heads back, their nostrils flaring slightly, and thrusting their shoulders back to make themselves appear larger. These changes were subtle, but Thorne noticed them all the same. He wasn't the least bit worried. Thorne had learned long ago how to gauge his strength against others. It was a vital skill of survival in the jungle.

As the latest group of guests passed by him into the large ballroom, Thorne felt an invisible pull, urging him to turn. He did, and there on the stairs was Eden. She wore a deep-blue gown that touched the tops of her golden sandals and pooled at her ankles like a waterfall. The dress clung to her body and only fueled his desire for her. Her long blonde hair was down and curled in waves that made her even more enticing. Why would a woman dress in such a way? If her intention was to stay and talk with people all night, why dress in a way that would make him want to take her away from all this and remove her clothing as quickly as possible? All it did was remind him how much he enjoyed making love to her and how he wanted to banish everyone so he could do just that with her in their bedroom.

She saw him, and the uncertain expression on her face vanished, changing to a delighted smile. He approached the foot of the stairs and caught her hand in a raised position as she reached the bottom. He'd seen others do this for their mates all evening.

"Sorry I'm late. The curling iron and I are not friends." She laughed, and the sound was sweeter than any music. He didn't know who the curling iron was, but if they were not Eden's friend, then they were Thorne's enemy. But he would deal with them later.

"You look . . . ," he began.

"Incredible?" Eden put her arm in his and winked. "Thank your aunt for that. She loaned me the dress. I definitely didn't pack anything this nice for my trip to Uganda." She squeezed his arm.

Thorne sighed contentedly and escorted her into the ballroom. He noticed his uncle at the front of the room. When he spotted Thorne, he waved him over. Thorne left Eden with Isabelle and then joined his uncle. Cameron clinked his glass with a fork and caught everyone's attention. The room was silenced with a soft hush.

"Thank you for joining us at the last minute. Though I was already convinced that Thorne was indeed our nephew, the lab results confirmed it this week, much to my and Isabelle's joy. Let me start by saying that everything you've heard is true. Amelia and Jacob survived a plane crash and lived for two weeks in the jungle with Thorne, only to be brutally murdered by poachers. Thorne was miraculously rescued by a family of gorillas, who raised him as their own. As to how he was discovered, that story has been extensively reported by most major news outlets by this point.

"I'm sure you all have a lot of questions, and tonight is a chance to meet and talk with Thorne. He is, quite literally, our ambassador to the Ugandan jungle, and tonight he's going to remind you all why it is a land worth protecting. As of today, we have created the Haywood Impenetrable Forest Charity, where you may send donations to protect the wild and beautiful jungles all over Uganda. Please stay and enjoy the wine and hors d'oeuvres."

Thorne answered with a minute nod and began to walk through the room, smiling and speaking with the guests. With his uncle's guidance, he had several stories prepared for them, meant to convey the beauty and importance of his home. Eden had explained to him that if he could win the hearts and minds of the people in this room tonight, the money they would donate would help protect Keza, Akika, Tembo, and all the other animals that lived within the jungle. That alone made Thorne want to do his best to be a man of the modern world tonight.

"Thorne!" A man Thorne didn't know clapped him on the shoulder, holding him in place. "My God, you *do* look like Jacob. Remarkable."

The man, a portly fellow with red cheeks, now thrust his hand out. "I'm Lord Lofthouse. But everyone calls me Lofty, don't you know? Good man, your father, and a dear friend of mine. Went to school with him at Eton." Lofty smiled fondly. "Hell of a cricket player, that man. Don't suppose you ever played? No games in the jungle, eh?"

Thorne could smell an excess of brandy on the man's breath, but he seemed genuinely friendly, and Thorne detected no hint of danger or deception from him.

"Er . . . no." Thorne's solemn reply sobered Lofty up a bit, and a few more people gathered around Thorne.

"What was life really like in the jungle? How did you survive after . . . after Jacob and Amelia were gone? Everyone's been wanting to know," Lofty whispered a little too loudly.

Thorne ignored the pain he felt at having to casually discuss this, but he had to draw attention to the plight of his jungle. The men who would burn it to the ground if it meant getting one more piece of gold. His uncle had said that these people had the power to help.

The crowd around him gathered closer as he began to tell his story. "I do not remember much, not directly. But I know this: The land where I was raised was once home to a great kingdom. Long ago that kingdom was lost, and the jungle swallowed its bones. My parents were killed by men who wished to steal those bones."

"Grave robbers?" Lofty said. "How fiendish. Nothing worse than disturbing a grave, I say."

Thorne's uncle had warned him not to draw too much attention to the gold and diamonds. He'd said that the idea of stealing the past was worse to these people than stealing treasure. Thorne wasn't sure what he meant, but he did understand the difference between treasures that were simply pretty, such as those he kept in his tree house, and ones that held meaning, such as the knife Bwanbale had given him, or his father's ring.

"These men believed my parents would soon be

rescued," Thorne continued, "and would warn people of what they had seen."

Everyone near Thorne was hanging on his every word now, so he continued. "My father was shot first. I saw him die. Then my mother. She stood in front of me and begged for my life, but they killed her too. I was only three at the time, but I remember."

"How tragic," a woman whispered from the crowd.

A man echoed her sentiment. "Yes, bloody awful business."

"Yet you were spared. It seems your mother's pleas worked," another man added. His familiar voice drew Thorne's gaze as he added, "A mother's love—how touching."

Thorne's world shrank to a pinprick, and his head was suddenly full of screams. Thousands of screams receding into the darkness until he heard only his mother's voice begging.

"Please."

"A mother's love—how touching."

Thorne knew that voice. He knew. He *knew* . . .

His muscles grew taut, and Thorne shed the vestiges of civilization and unleashed the beast within him. He launched himself at the man who had spoken those words. He would taste blood tonight. He would have vengeance.

Thorne tackled the man to the ground with a snarl. The tall man swung a fist, catching Thorne off guard. All around them people were shouting and moving back, and some were fleeing the room. But there was only one threat Thorne was concerned with. He roared, the sound exploding around them. The tall man's blue eyes, cold and hard, widened with fear for just a second before he punched Thorne again.

Pain lanced through his head at the blow, but Thorne acted on instinct, the way silverbacks fought. He beat down on the man's chest with his balled fists.

"Stop!" Cameron bellowed, but the sound didn't reach Thorne's rational side. It was just noise.

Stop him. End his evil . . . The voices of the cave howled inside his head.

He was struck in a vulnerable spot below his ribs, and he grunted as the wind rushed out of his lungs. Then several hands grasped his arms and chest, dragging him off the man. He roared again, but the men who hauled him back did not release their hold. Through a red haze, he saw Cameron kneeling by the man he had attacked. His uncle spoke quietly to the man before offering him a hand up. The man smacked Cameron's hand away and got to his feet without assistance.

Blood trailed down his chin and coated his teeth as he sneered in Thorne's direction, "It seems your nephew isn't fully house-trained, Somerset. I suggest you keep a leash on him. He's not fit for civilized society."

Thorne still struggled against the men who held him pinned against the wall of the ballroom.

"I'm truly sorry, Mr. Holt. I don't know what's gotten into him, but you can be sure it won't happen again. Let me see you out."

"No, thank you, Somerset. I'll show myself out."

Only when the man was gone did the voices in Thorne's head still and the choking rage subside. The anger slithered back beneath his skin, but it was still there, deadly but for the moment out of sight.

"Good God, my boy," Lofty snorted at Thorne. "You even fight like your old man. Capital fellow, Jacob. A champion boxer in his day. Never had a taste for the sport, though, competitively speaking, but he was a damned good man to have watch your back."

Cameron ignored Lofty's ramblings as he came to Thorne and made sure they made eye contact.

"I need you to calm down, Thorne. Can you do that?"

Thorne drew in a series of short breaths and finally nodded. Cameron ordered the men holding Thorne to release him. Once Thorne was free, he rubbed his arms.

"You let him go," Thorne growled.

Cameron sighed heavily. "Lofty, be a good man and take everyone here for drinks in the library. I need to speak with my nephew alone."

Lofty marshaled the guests out of the room. "Everyone kindly follow me, thank you, very much. The family needs some time alone." A few of the guests declared they wanted to stay. "Well you can sod off. Out, now, if you please!" He announced cheekily to the crowd who all shot him exasperated looks as they filed out of the front door.

The moment they were alone, Thorne expected Cameron to berate him for his impulsive behavior. But instead, Cameron put a hand on his shoulder and with an emotion-roughened voice, speaking low, he said, "You know that man, don't you?"

Thorne's pulse began to pound harder. "Yes." He could see those awful memories again, too vivid, too full of pain and fear.

"The only reason I could imagine you'd lash out like

that is if he . . ." Cameron couldn't finish the sentence, and instead said, "Are you sure?"

"He said that to my mother before he killed her. Same words. Same voice. He killed them." And as Thorne was able to think more clearly, something else occurred to him. "How is he here? Why?"

Cameron's eyes narrowed as he drew in a forceful breath. "That man is Archibald Holt. His company has interests all over the world, but he spends most of his time in Africa. I've met him only a few times. He expressed interest in coming to this party because of his corporate interests in Uganda. He could have been a powerful ally, but I never imagined . . ." Again his voice trailed off. "But perhaps I should have. He's never been a kind man, and Isabelle always said he makes her nervous."

"Females have a stronger sense of danger," Thorne noted. "They are always the most alert. She must have sensed he was a predator."

Cameron was silent a moment before he spoke again. "You attacked him like an animal."

Thorne inhaled sharply as pangs of shame started to fill his belly. His uncle was ashamed of him—possibly even feared him.

"Just when I believe I understand what you've been through, I see this and it reminds me of all that you survived. You must have . . ." He struggled for words.

"All those nights alone in the crushing dark forest, the dangers you faced. The pain, the scars, the fear . . ."

Thorne realized his uncle wasn't speaking out of shame. He understood.

Cameron met Thorne's gaze. "I wish I had found you, Thorne. I wish none of this had ever happened. You suffered so much because I couldn't find you. Because I gave up." The heartbreak in Cameron's voice hurt worse than any wound he'd received in the wilds of Uganda.

"No. Do not be sad, Uncle Cameron. Life is pain, life is scars, life is fear." Those were the laws of the jungle, but they weren't the only ones. "Life is also love, family, joy, and bravery." He put his hand on his uncle's shoulder in a mirroring gesture. "You cannot live in the past. I had a full life in the forest. The forest brought me to Eden, and she brought me home to you."

Cameron's smile quivered. "You know a good British gentleman never cries."

"Then do not be that. Be yourself," Thorne said simply.

"That's your mother speaking, you know. She was unflinching in her devotion to Jacob, but she never let being a countess change who she was. I've heard people speak of children being living tributes to their parents, but I've never truly understood that until now." Cameron pulled Thorne in for a hard hug, then let him go. "Why don't we find Lofty? It's wise to keep an eye on that man—he can drink a man out of his best brandy."

Cameron and Thorne left the ballroom together. "We'll discuss with Eden and Isabelle later what to do about Holt. If he is indeed our man, it's time to start unearthing evidence against him."

Thorne's hands curled into fists. Then there would be a time for justice.

EDEN LEFT THORNE AND HIS UNCLE TO SPEAK privately. She and Isabelle, along with the amusing and outspoken Lord Lofthouse, escorted those who wished to leave to the front door, after which Lofty headed off to the library to refill his brandy.

"Well, that could have gone better," Isabelle said after dealing with those who'd wanted to leave right away.

"What about Lord Lofthouse?" asked Eden.

"Oh, Lofty's a dear friend. I'm sure he'll want to stick around and make sure we're all right before he goes. I'm more worried about Thorne. What on earth do you think came over him?"

"I have no idea," said Eden. "I've never seen him like that, not even when we were attacked by a lion."

"But what about the poachers?"

Eden hadn't truly seen his expression when he had rescued her from them, but yes, that was the only time she could remember seeing anger on his face. Perhaps someone had triggered a memory of his past?

Only then did Eden realize that someone had splashed red wine over the stunning blue dress she was wearing. It must have happened during the chaos of the fight in the ballroom.

"Isabelle, do you mind if I go change?"

"Of course, dear. Perhaps one of the maids can still save that gown." Isabelle hugged her, careful not to get wine on her own silver gown. Then she headed in the direction of the library to check in on Lofty.

Eden started toward the stairs but halted when she saw the door at the end of the hall start to close. The hairs on the back of her neck rose. None of the servants were here in this part of the house just then. Was it one of the guests? Isabelle had warned her that sometimes British house parties—even one-night parties like this—could be wild. Guests could get drunk and wander into places they shouldn't be. It wouldn't hurt to check and see.

When she reached the door, she eased it open and saw nothing but her own shadow filling the floor—and then a second shadow rose up behind her. She gasped as something struck her, and she fell into darkness before she even hit the floor.

EDEN CAME AROUND SLOWLY, GRADUALLY recognizing the interior décor of a private plane. She was buckled into a seat, and from the sound of things they were already in the air.

"Here, drink this," a voice with a cultured French accent said next to her.

She weakly accepted the bottle of water that was pressed into her hands. The man who'd spoken sat down next to her, and she got a better look at him. He was a fairly attractive man, with light-brown hair and hazel eyes, but there was nothing truly remarkable about him. He was the sort of man Eden imagined could easily walk into a crowd and be forgotten. Eden drank the water greedily, feeling it fill her empty stomach. Her body was stiff and sore, her muscles protesting even the smallest movements. She wiped her mouth with the back of her hand as water spilled past her trembling lips.

She tried to speak. "Who are you?"

"I was worried you'd been struck too hard. Monsieur is not a subtle man when threatened. I fear what he did with you was an act of desperation rather than logic."

Eden didn't recognize the man at first, but then as her memories clicked into place, the water came right back up and she vomited onto the carpet.

"Jesus!" The man leapt up and began to curse in French.

"You're . . . ," Eden panted. "You're one of Cash's men."

"So you do remember me? A shame, mademoiselle. I'd hoped you would not. And I did not work for that oaf." He retrieved another bottled water and handed it to her.

She dragged herself back upright in her seat. "Then who do you work for?"

"Drink, slowly this time, and eat." The man handed her a protein bar. "We had to keep you asleep until it was safe to wake you."

"Who do you work for?" she asked again.

"I work for Monsieur Holt."

Holt. The man Thorne had attacked last night. Cash and this man had worked for *him*? A number of pieces fell into place. Cameron had mentioned him when they were arranging the guest list for the party. Archibald Holt. He had companies all over Africa, including Uganda. Cameron had mentioned that Holt might prove to be helpful to them—how wrong he'd been.

"Holt had those tourists killed? Why?"

"I believe you know why."

"But why kidnap me?"

"Ah, well . . . After your friend attacked him, Holt made that rather rash and impulsive decision on his own. I believe he felt his hand was forced. In all the confusion, it wasn't hard for him to hide out and wait until you were alone. Quite frankly, I'm amazed he wasn't caught. But then, Monsieur Holt did not get where he is without knowing when to take risks."

Eden looked around. "Why isn't he here?"

The Frenchman gave a shrug. "Appearances. Abducting you in the middle of the night is one matter. Taking you through an airport without raising suspicion is quite another. He contacted me and arranged for this little journey. He will be taking a commercial plane to avoid any connection and then meet us at our destination."

"So what's your plan, then?"

"My plan?" He smiled. "I am not the villain of the story, mademoiselle. I care only about the gemstones and evaluating them. Mr. Holt is paying me quite well to escort you to him. When my job is done, I will leave Africa and return to France."

"Where are we headed?"

"Where? Back to the beginning, of course." The man leaned back in his chair, smiling pleasantly. "Do you know why Monsieur Holt sent that brute Cash into the jungle?"

"To steal a treasure that doesn't belong to him," said Eden.

The man waved a hand dismissively. "A treasure of a people that history itself has forgotten. Fair game, as you Americans would say. And he already *found* the treasure, long ago. It's how he started his fortune. But there was so much more to find. However, Holt has never been able to return there. Not in twenty years. And not for a lack of trying."

Eden raised an eyebrow at this, but she said nothing.

"Holt has come to believe that something is preventing him from finding the cave, sending him around in circles. That is why he sent people with no connection to it instead. But that attempt was thwarted by your primitive friend. Holt does not believe that was by accident either."

"What are you saying?"

"What is it that Shakespeare once said? '*There are more things in heaven and earth, Horatio, than are dreamt of in your philosophy.*' Holt believes there is something in that jungle that is beyond anything any of us have dreamt of."

"That's ridiculous. You're saying the jungle has some kind of magical power?" Eden had begun to wonder that herself, but she wouldn't dare tell this man that.

"I am saying nothing. I am simply doing a job. But Holt believes it. And I think, perhaps, you do as well."

Eden tried not to think about all the times Thorne had talked about his strange dreams or how he seemed to understand the animals. The man smiled as if this somehow confirmed his hypothesis.

"Rest, mademoiselle. You have a busy day tomorrow."

"WHERE IS EDEN?" THORNE DEMANDED. THE HOUSE had become quiet since the guests had left, but there

325

was still no sign of her. He had last seen her with Isabelle, but she was not with her now.

"She's not with you?"

"I have not seen her since I attacked that man." He would not say Holt's name. Monsters did not deserve names.

"Eden?" Isabelle called out. When no one answered, she turned back to Thorne. "She was supposed to be getting changed upstairs. Perhaps she's still there?"

Thorne rushed up the stairs. Something was wrong. Eden wouldn't have left him alone for so long, not after what had happened.

The bedroom was empty. No hint of her scent in the air, no evidence that she had been here in the last few hours. Thorne met his uncle and aunt back at the stairs.

"Did you find her?" Isabelle asked.

"No." Thorne tried to ignore the worried hum inside his head, like a hive of bees had been disturbed.

"Call the staff. Let's search the house," Cameron suggested.

They divided up, enlisting the servants to help search the grounds. A maid's shout brought them all running to the ground floor. The young woman held up a piece of paper.

"I found this in the Green Bombay drawing room, Lord Somerset." She handed Cameron a slip of paper. His face turned ashen as he read it.

"What does it say?" Thorne demanded.

Cameron cleared his throat.

"You will take me to the cave, or I will destroy all that you love. Meet me by the plane in two days, or I'll leave her body in the jungle for you to find."

"Holt," Isabelle whispered. "But how? I saw him leave."

"There was a lot of confusion with the guests departing. He no doubt snuck back in and lay in wait." Cameron closed his eyes and rubbed them with his thumb and forefinger.

Thorne was only half listening. His body shook as he tried to keep his rage and fear at bay. Eden was at the mercy of the monster who had stolen Thorne's family from him and left him to die.

"I must go," he said.

"We're coming with you," Cameron said, a hard glint in his eyes.

"Too much danger." The last thing Thorne wanted was to lose the rest of his family. "Get me to my jungle. I will do what needs to be done."

"My boy, you forget that Jacob was my brother. Besides, you'll need someone to watch your back."

Thorne nodded reluctantly, but when he looked toward Isabelle, she crossed her arms. "Don't you *dare* order me to stay here."

"Are we going on a hunting party?" Lofty asked, appearing as if out of nowhere with a billiard cue on his shoulder.

"*Christ*, Lofty," Cameron yelped and shook his head. "Thought you'd gone home."

"Home? Just passing the time in your billiard room, waiting for things to settle. But it seems like intrigue is afoot. Nothing I enjoy more." Lofty's tone then grew serious. "Jacob was my friend, and I'm a damned good shot, especially with a rifle." He patted his slightly rotund stomach. "Don't let this fool you. I can keep up, old boy."

"Whoever is coming, we leave soon," Thorne replied, and he headed to his room to pack his things. Once inside the room, he stood still for a moment, feeling the bedchamber's emptiness and the fear that Eden's kidnapping had left behind.

Thorne curled his hands into fists. His father's ring felt cold and hard, echoing the fury he would unleash upon Holt when next they met. The others could come if they wished, but this was not their fight. He alone would find Holt and kill him.

❧ 18 ❧

Eden struggled through a tangle of blurry nightmares of a man grabbing her in the darkness before she woke up. The last thing she remembered was that awful man on the plane, the Frenchman, jabbing her again with another drug-filled needle just before they landed. No doubt he wanted to keep her subdued, confused, and weak. *The bastard.* She blinked, her eyes dry, her lips chapped, and her muscles stiff as she tried to move. Her blue silk gown slid against soft leather, and she realized she was lying upon a couch.

She was in a huge office with a mahogany desk and expensive-looking oil paintings on the walls. A large stuffed gorilla stood in a corner. Its menacing pose could have been mistaken as threatening, but she saw only a poor creature, afraid, defensive . . . dead.

Its glass eyes were reddish-brown, meant to mimic

the animal's natural eyes if it had been alive, but the sheen on them only emphasized just how dead the poor creature was. Eden repressed a shudder as she sat up and dropped her feet to the ground.

A soft clicking sound and the feel of cold metal against her wrist made her look down at her hands. She was handcuffed. The metal chain between the cuffs was attached to the leg of the leather couch. She tried to lift the leg of the couch to free herself, but the sudden movement swamped her with dizziness and her vision cartwheeled.

Clutching the armrest, she waited for the sense of vertigo to fade. The door to the room opened, and a tall broad-shouldered man stepped inside. He wore no suit, only a black shirt and khaki cargo pants, but she recognized him as the man Thorne had attacked at the party. Archibald Holt. He held a stack of clothes, which he tossed onto the couch. He then removed the key from his pocket and came over toward her.

"Try anything and I will break your jaw." His blunt, emotionless warning sent shivers through her. Eden was not a fool. She would wait. There would be a moment to fight or flee, and she would not miss it.

The man, Holt, unlocked the handcuffs, and she rubbed the reddened skin where the metal had chaffed her. She reached for the clothes left for her on the couch. He did not leave the room and give her privacy, but instead walked over to the tall windows and opened the shutters. Early-morning light broke through the panes, whitewashing the dark, lush office. Holt crossed his strong arms over his chest, exuding an air of barely leashed menace.

Eden quickly stripped out of the dress and put on the khaki shorts and T-shirt, then sat on the couch to pull on the socks and hiking boots. They were all her size. Something about that bothered her. It went to show that he could plan ahead, even when he was being "impulsive," as his lackey had put it.

"You need Thorne, don't you? That's why I'm here."

"Clever creature, aren't you?" His false praise was layered with sarcasm as he faced her. His jaw was purple where Thorne had landed a blow. There was a feral beauty to him, she had to admit, but rather than attract her, it frightened her. He was perhaps in his early forties, which meant he had been barely twenty or so when he'd killed Thorne's parents.

"You can't find the treasure cave from twenty years ago, but you think Thorne can?"

"I'm counting on it. You have only yourself to blame for being involved, you know. Though you never mentioned the cave directly in your interviews, you left more than enough clues for me to surmise that Thorne had indeed found it."

Eden didn't admit that she and Cameron had specifically planned for her interviews to draw Holt out into the open. She just hadn't expected him to come out so soon.

"Is that why you came to the party?"

"Certainly not. I had hoped to curry favor with Lord Somerset, to assure him that I was in a unique position to help his crusade to protect the jungle, and to get Thorne to willingly act as a guide." He snorted and touched his jaw. "When it became clear that would never work, I had to improvise. Which brings us here."

"Why do you need him as a guide? The Frenchman said you can't find the cave anymore. Is that true?"

A tic worked in Holt's jaw. "I found that cave the first time I entered the jungle. It . . . called to me. I took all that I could, along with my men. But we left so much behind." He suddenly pulled out a stone from his pocket. "This was my first conquest, a diamond large enough to choke an ostrich." His fingers curled possessively around the diamond. "When I went back a second time, I couldn't find the cave. I kept going in circles. No matter what direction I started in, I always found myself at the same waterfall over and over. But it sounds like Thorne knows the way and has been there more than once."

"So what happens once he shows you the cave? You'll just kill us and leave us in the jungle? That's what your man who kidnapped me said you'd do."

Holt's pale-blue eyes sharpened. "Jean has a loose

tongue. I shall keep that in mind. People in my employ are valued for their ability to hold their tongues."

"Cameron and Isabelle—?"

"They'll be joining you in the jungle. They insisted on coming with the boy, naturally. It will make it so much easier. Accidents occur all the time in the forest, and there's always a new band of rebels somewhere to throw blame at." Holt picked up a light khaki vest from the back of his chair and put it on. He slipped the diamond inside and patted the breast pocket as if to make sure it was there.

"You think no one will question your involvement? People saw Thorne attack you at the party. Someone will make the connection."

"Perhaps, but my resources and connections make for a very long list, Ms. Matthews. I worked harder than you can imagine for that."

Eden tasted a bitterness in her mouth as panic set in. Thorne, Cameron, and Isabelle were coming here to their deaths. Holt came toward her and gripped her arm, dragging her from the room.

"Where are we going?" she gasped. They exited his office and passed through an elaborate lobby. When they left the building, she found they were standing on a city street, with the jungle encroaching on the edges of the city in the distance. This wasn't Kampala, but it was somewhere in Uganda. She guessed they were in Fort Portal.

He forcibly escorted her outside to a waiting Range Rover. "To find Thorne's other family before he and Somerset arrive. It's time I paid my respects to the apes who took that little brat in."

Keza! Oh God! No!

Holt opened the door to the Range Rover and shoved her inside. Two other vehicles were behind them as they left. Eden saw signs that said they were leaving Fort Portal, and she knew they would have to travel south to reach Bwindi Impenetrable Forest. Holt had at least a dozen armed men with him. Thorne was just one man. Even with Cameron and Isabelle, the numbers weren't good. She closed her eyes, focusing on her breathing, trying to calm herself.

When she opened them again, she had a new sense of clarity. She wouldn't let Holt hurt Keza, Akika, or the others, even if it meant her losing her own life. There was no other choice. Thorne had only one mother left, and Eden wouldn't let this monster take her from him.

IT TOOK A DAY TO FLY FROM LONDON TO ENTEBBE and drive in a car that Cameron rented to Bwanbale's village. Thorne hadn't wanted to bring his friend into this, but Bwanbale knew the forest almost as well as he did, and if he was to leave his aunt, uncle and Lofty behind, Bwanbale would watch over them.

As they exited the vehicle on the edge of the village, Cameron instructed Isabelle and Lofty to stay by the car. Then Thorne and his uncle proceeded into the village. Afiya was in the garden in front of her *shamba*, a basket on one hip as she plucked vegetables from the vines of the plants growing on circular wires.

"Thorne!" She dropped the basket and ran to embrace him. "Where's Miss Eden?" She smiled at him, but her joy soon faded as she looked deeper into his eyes. He held Afiya gently by her arms, glad to see her again, but not under these circumstances.

"She's been taken. I must speak to Bwanbale."

"Oh! Yes, yes, of course. Please come inside." She collected her basket from the ground and rushed indoors.

Bwanbale must have heard the commotion, because he came to the front of the house even as they came inside.

"Thorne." Bwanbale spoke in solemn greeting, and they embraced. "We meet under grave circumstances, yes?"

"Unfortunately, yes." Cameron held out a hand. "I'm Cameron Haywood. Thorne's uncle. Eden was kidnapped while she and Thorne were with us in England."

"Kidnapped? But why return here?"

"The man who took her is the man who killed my parents. He wants me to help him find the cave."

Bwanbale rubbed a hand along his jaw, and he was silent a long moment. "Who is the man?"

"Archibald Holt," Cameron said.

Thorne saw at once that Bwanbale was familiar with the name when his friend's eyes widened. "You know him."

"I know of him. Holt Enterprises. He employs many men, some local, some foreign. He is a man who pays well, and he hires those who are willing to do anything for money. We have a dangerous battle ahead of us."

Thorne put a hand on Bwanbale's shoulder. "You should stay here. Your family needs you. But if we fail, you must tell the embassy what happened to us. He cannot go free."

His friend smiled grimly. "Thorne, my friend, you will not go into the jungle alone. I will be at your side."

Thorne could hear a faint whisper stirring inside his head, like dried leaves rustling along the ground. Bwanbale would come. It was as it should be.

Afiya appeared at her husband's side, a rifle gripped in her hands. She pressed it into his palms and curled an arm around his neck to hold him close. "Say goodbye to Dembe," she reminded him.

He nodded to his wife and went to his daughter.

"I will bring him home," Thorne promised Afiya.

She wiped her eyes and offered a weak smile. "I know you will, jungle man." She hugged Thorne as Bwanbale

returned. Thorne, Cameron, and Bwanbale then joined
Lofty and Isabelle near the rented SUV.

"You have weapons?" Bwanbale asked Thorne.

"We do." He opened the back of the car to show
three rifles.

"I think we need another gun," Lofty said. "Thorne,
old boy, you have no weapon."

Thorne flashed a dark look at Lofty. "I *am* the
weapon."

EDEN FOLLOWED HOLT THROUGH THE FOREST. A ROPE
was knotted around her waist, keeping her tied to him.
Twelve men followed behind in a single column as they
began the ascent into the mist-shrouded mountains.
Eden wiped at the gathering sweat on her brow as the
heat began to build. She managed not to trip when Holt
moved too fast at times and pulled her sharply forward
by the rope.

The tall forest of bamboo proved more difficult to
navigate, since she had to be careful not to tangle the
rope. Holt moved almost as easily through the jungle as
Thorne. Eden realized it was because he had spent
almost as much time here as Thorne had. He knew the
jungle, knew the dangers, knew the lay of the land.
Escape would be almost impossible, assuming she could
find a way to get free of the rope.

They were nearly at the site of the wreck when the rain began, and the mist coiled around their feet in growing clouds like ghostly anacondas. Eden thought that some of the landscape was starting to look familiar. Any minute now they would be near the spot where the Cessna had gone down. Thankfully, Holt had found gorilla nests empty. Eden had breathed a sigh of relief each time he'd cursed when they'd found an empty nest site.

The parrots flying above her were singing shrill warning cries, and for a second, she swore she could understand them. It wasn't so much words as it was visions inside her head.

She could see herself and Holt from far above in the trees, as though *she* were a parrot. Eden pursed her lips together and began to whistle. She'd never been very good at it, but somehow she was able to emit a birdlike call. She imitated their warning song, and the birds took flight in a sudden panicked flutter.

Holt seemed almost as in tune with the forest as Thorne at this moment but rather than being at peace with it, he seemed determined to rule it. He stilled, watching the birds madly scattering above them. The warning cries spread to the monkeys in the canopy. Eden continued to whistle until Holt spun with an open palm, striking her across the face. Pain flashed inside her head, and she went down with a grunt.

"Make a sound again . . . ," he warned in a snarl. He

gripped her left arm and jerked her savagely back to her feet.

Holt pulled a pistol out of his canvas backpack and started walking again. Eden clutched her right cheek, her head throbbing as she tried to keep up with him.

A flash of darkness moving ahead of them caught her eye, and Holt's. He held up a hand, and the line of mercenaries behind her all stopped. Eden held her breath as a soft hooting echoed around them. A welcoming sound.

Oh no. They can't be here. Not now . . .

Eden coughed loudly. It was a human noise, but she hoped it would catch the attention of the band hidden around them. Though Holt didn't move, she could feel the force of his anger at her.

A gorilla emerged from the forest ahead of them. Thorne had called him Sunya, the silverback male who ruled the band. Holt stared for a long moment at the gorilla. Man and beast faced each other down in an ancient ritual that was a prelude to every battle ever fought, but it was a battle that didn't need to be.

"Please," Eden whispered. "Don't hurt them." She moved a step closer to Holt. "They won't hurt you. Not if I'm here."

Without looking at her, he said, "They are in my way. The only way forward is to destroy them."

"You don't have to destroy them to get what you want." All Holt saw was the gleam of gold and the glitter of diamonds, and the power they would bring him. Eden knew a man like him would never have enough to be satisfied.

Sunya stood on his back legs and beat his chest with balled fists, a warning that Holt couldn't ignore. He raised his gun, pointing it at the gorilla.

Eden had half a second to make a decision, but it was no decision, really. She threw herself at Holt, hitting him low around the waist and causing them both to fall to the ground.

"Bitch!" Holt snarled.

Sunya let out a sound of rage and charged Holt. From the bushes around him more males joined him. The men behind her and Holt opened fire upon the gorillas rushing out from the misty forest. Eden screamed, and Holt rolled her beneath him, but rather than shoot her, he fired his gun above her. Eden tilted her head back and saw Sunya halt, stagger a few steps, and fall to the ground.

"No!" She surged up and punched Holt as hard as she could. He grunted, and she reached for the gun. All around them were the screams of men and gorillas, fighting and dying.

One, she recognized with horror, was Akika. He lay on his side, breathing in wheezing gasps. Bullet wounds pierced his chest. Eden couldn't breathe. Thorne's brother was *dying*. The sight of him reaching out toward her with one hand shattered her heart and drove her to a blind rage. She wrestled free of Holt and kicked him in the side again and again. He rallied and countered her, knocking her to her stomach, but she was up on her feet again, lashing out with her fists. She would avenge Akika and his band.

A distant roar vibrating with the force of an earthquake, shook the jungle around them into silence. She knew that sound. Guns stopped firing, and even the gorillas paused in their attack.

"What the hell was that?" one of the men asked.

Holt then looked at Eden, his gun raised to her chest. "You know who it is, don't you?"

Eden wiped her mouth, her hand coming away with blood. "I do. And he's coming for you."

Holt cursed. "Forget the gorillas. We need to get to the plane." He grabbed Eden's arm. "It's time I set the bait."

As though Thorne had heard Holt's words, another echoing call rippled through the jungle.

KEZA CLUTCHED HER GRANDSON TO HER CHEST, panting hard as the females and the surviving juvenile males fled from danger. Her heart was breaking as it had the day she'd seen Mukisa's lifeless body all those many seasons ago.

Here she was again, rescuing another infant who'd

been robbed of his last parent. Akika's mate had been killed by a leopard some time ago. Now the infant had only her. She slung the child up on her back, and his tiny black fists gripped her fur. She led the band north, seeking safety.

When she heard Thorne's roar, she knew Akika would be avenged. The child of her heart had returned, and he would stop this black cloud of evil. Keza had seen Thorne's mate fight, trying to save her son and the others. Keza hoped that someday she would again meet the child of her heart and his brave mate.

Until then, she and the other gorillas would hide in the mist.

Thorne froze in the dense vegetation as the cries of birds reached his ears. All around him the jungle was screaming in terror at the presence of danger.

"What is it?" Cameron asked. He and Bwanbale stood shoulder to shoulder behind Thorne.

"Thorne hears the jungle in a way no one else does," Bwanbale whispered.

"Eden," Thorne said. "The birds see her. Holt has her, and many men are with him. They're heading northeast."

"Toward Ntungamo?" Bwanbale asked. "That is a city past the forest."

"No, they are headed toward the white rock—the plane crash. But first they must pass the falls."

"Falls?" Cameron asked. "I didn't see any waterfalls

on the map, except Murchison Falls much farther north."

"There are things in the jungle no mapmaker has ever seen," Bwanbale explained. Isabelle and Lofty followed, along with Cameron and Bwanbale, as they all traveled behind Thorne, but he was moving swiftly, and it was hard to keep up. The birds' warning had scared him. They had spoken of death. Then the quiet of the jungle was shattered by gunshots not far away.

"Bloody Christ!" Lofty exclaimed and checked his rifle. "I really do wish we had more guns. Sounds like those bastards are well armed."

"Lofty, I quite agree," Isabelle muttered. "But we didn't have time. We could only grab what we had stored at the hunting lodge."

"Three guns? You can't have a decent hunting party with three guns," Lofty muttered.

Thorne broke into their talk by letting loose a deafening roar so that Eden would know he was coming. Then he started to run, leaping through split tree trunks and over fallen logs. He needed to get to Eden, and fast.

He broke through into a small clearing and came to a stop. There were bodies everywhere. Bodies of gorillas and a few of Holt's mercenaries. He rushed among the fallen apes, seeing faces he had known all his life, searching for his mother. Keza was not among them—but his brother was.

"Akika . . ." Thorne knelt beside his brother's lifeless body. His broad chest was splattered with crimson stains, and his once playful, lively eyes were now empty. Grief Thorne hadn't experienced since discovering the fate of his parents came crashing down upon him. The weight of it was enough to make any man fall to his knees. Thorne threw his head back and roared again. But this call was not meant for Eden. It was a cry of sorrow, a bellow of rage.

The voices in his head were whispering, chanting things he couldn't understand. He could only feel their meaning. A sense of coming home, and yet a danger of losing that home forever. A sense of destiny soon to be achieved, or forever lost. He was on a knife's edge, and so much more than the life of his mate was at stake, even if he couldn't fully understand why. He knew what he must do. He got to his feet, his chest rising and falling with harsh breaths.

"Those bastards," Isabelle said as she caught up to Thorne.

"They are dead," he said. "*All* of them."

Lofty and Cameron exchanged glances.

"Take us to them," Cameron said. "We will take them down."

There was no question of morality, no discussion of the lives of the men Holt had hired. Anyone who shot an animal like this—that man's life was forfeit.

"Thorne, my friend," Bwanbale called from behind

him. "Go. You can reach her quicker than we can. We will follow."

Thorne hesitated for only a moment, then ran for the nearest tree. Climbing swiftly, he gripped the long, sturdy vines and swung to a distant tree and another vine, moving faster and faster until he could smell the waterfall. The plane was not far from there. He reached the edge of the thinning woods just as he spotted Holt dragging Eden into the shallows of the river that fed into a massive waterfall below. They were trying to cross but were dangerously close to the falls. The men were clumped around Holt and Eden, all of them knee-deep in the swiftly flowing water.

"Holt!" Thorne bellowed.

The group in the shallows froze. Holt spun in Thorne's direction, pulling Eden in front of him as a shield, one hand around her throat and a gun pressed into her side. She was beautiful, defiant, brave, even in the face of such danger.

Thorne leapt down from the trees, landing gracefully in a crouch, then standing slowly. Perhaps fifty paces separated them, twenty strides, but Thorne didn't mind the distance. It was the men who held all the guns that gave him pause. There were twelve in total. Too many for him to attack alone. But the others were coming, and they too were armed.

"You want the girl? You know my terms. Surrender yourself. Take me to the cave, and I'll let her go."

Eden struggled in his hold. "He's lying!" Eden shouted before Holt squeezed her neck. She gasped as he choked her into silence.

Thorne took another few steps, his hands raised.

"I will surrender if you let her go." Thorne would take his chances once Eden was safe, but he knew Holt had every intention of killing them both.

"Come closer. My men will bind your hands, and then I'll set her free."

"No!" Eden choked, her face red as she thrashed. Thorne stepped into the shallows of the river, his gaze never leaving Eden's face. Her green eyes were full of fear, not for herself but for him. She shook her head at him, pleading for him to go. He held her gaze, speaking to her without words.

You are the mate of my heart, the mate of my soul. I would die for you.

"Bind him!" Holt ordered. A pair of mercenaries approached Thorne cautiously with a short coil of rope. Thorne held still as his wrists were bound in front of him.

"Walk ahead of me, slowly now," Holt ordered.

Thorne waded past him in the shallows. The closer he came to Holt, the stronger that feeling of destiny grew, a crying out, pleading to him for help. He could hear it so clearly now, just as he could hear and understand the animals.

And it was coming from Holt.

More specifically, it was coming from Holt's vest pocket. He could almost see it glowing through the fabric.

Thorne stopped and turned around. "You did not choose to come here."

Holt frowned, not understanding. "I think you have that the wrong way around, monkey boy."

Thorne shook his head. "You were called here to return something that does not belong to you."

Holt laughed. "Again, you have that the wrong way around. I'm here to *take*. When I found the cave, I only got a taste of what it had to offer. I've been trying to get the rest for more than twenty years."

Thorne shook his head. "No. You took something from here, long ago. This land is alive, and you took its heart."

At that, Holt's laugh froze, and his hand almost unwittingly reached toward his upper vest pocket. He opened the flap and pulled out a bright uncut stone that seemed to glow in the sunlight. The voices in Thorne's head were no longer whispers. They were now a steady chant, and he was certain that Holt could hear their words as well.

"You have been called here to return it and to answer for your crimes."

The expression on Holt's face turned from one of confidence to uncertainty, and then to desperation. He knew he wasn't being led to his fortune, but to his execution.

Thorne pointed in the direction they had to go. "Come. The cave awaits you."

As soon as his back was turned, Eden screamed, warning him just in time, but he turned a second too late. A cold blade sank into Thorne's side. Holt held the lethal dagger in him for a long second before pulling it out, a triumphant gleam in his eyes.

"I'll not let you win, you hear me? The treasure in that cave is mine, and I will get it, either from you or from someone else!" he snarled as he held Thorne close in a deadly embrace.

For a second, Thorne could only stare at Holt. It wasn't supposed to happen this way. The cave was supposed to deal with him. *Destiny.* What about destiny?

Eden rammed her elbow into Holt's stomach, and he grunted, releasing her. She swung, punching him in the jaw even as he reached for his gun. Through pain-fogged eyes, Thorne watched helplessly as the gun fired.

Eden cried out, falling back into the water, a bloom of red spreading across the water. Thorne broke through the haze of pain and splashed toward her, but they were too close to the edge of the falls.

"Eden!"

She struggled to stand. "Thorne, look out!" Thorne knew Holt was coming for him, but it didn't matter— only Eden did. She was on her feet now, barely holding her ground against the pull of the water as it vanished over the towering falls.

"I'm coming!" Thorne called out to her, but Holt raised his gun again, aiming at Eden. When he fired, Thorne roared as Eden stumbled back over the edge of the falls.

"Even if she survived the shot, she won't survive the fall." Holt's tone was as cold as his eyes. "You think I'm going to let you waltz me into some kind of mystic ambush? You don't think I know that this stone holds power? More power than you can even imagine."

Thorne faced Holt, every bit of strength in him exploded outward as he tore the rope binding his wrists clean apart.

Holt cursed and slipped in the river as he tried to retreat. "Would one of you guys shoot him already? What am I bloody paying you for?"

Rifle shots exploded from the trees, but they weren't coming from Holt's men, who were falling to the ground or trying to find cover. Thorne looked to the shore. His friends had arrived, half-hidden in the foliage, firing upon Holt's men and pinning them down.

Thorne looked back at Holt, and a grim satisfaction began to fill him as the battle raged along the shore. He advanced on Holt, ignoring the pain in his side.

"Get back!" Holt aimed his gun at Thorne's chest, but when he pulled the trigger, nothing happened. He tried to clear the jam, but the slide wouldn't budge.

"Shit!" With a growl, Holt threw the gun into the water and held up his long knife, still stained crimson with Thorne's blood.

"I should have killed you myself all those years ago. I made a mistake, thinking the jungle would take you."

Thorne felt the voices from the cave escaping his lips in a low growl. "The jungle *did* take me. I am its child, and I will not die here, not by your hand." He could barely feel the deep wound in his side, nor the blood trailing down his body, soaking his clothes and bleeding into the river.

Holt's eyes were wide, fear penetrating the icy-blue depths. "You won't survive. I knew where to stab you. I . . ." His eyes dropped to Thorne's wound, but Thorne kept coming at him.

The spirits of the jungle cave were filling him with strength now. It was time to end this.

Thorne leapt at Holt. Holt tried to stab him, but Thorne gripped his wrist, holding the knife, and they both hit the water. He twisted at Holt's arm until he felt the bones snap. Holt cried out, and Thorne, gripping him, dragged him toward the waterfall.

He couldn't register any pain anymore. Even the gunshots along the bank grew dim in his ears. More and more he could hear only the chant of the cave inside his head, urging him to do what must be done.

"What are you doing? We'll both die!" Holt kicked his legs, trying to slow down Thorne's determined steps forward. When they reached the edge, Thorne grabbed Holt by the vest, gripping the stone tucked inside it and dragging Holt's body around to the waterfall's edge. The chant inside his head was so loud that he could no longer hear Holt's words.

"I trust the jungle. But you took the jungle's heart. And you took away *mine*. And we will both have our revenge," Thorne promised.

He leapt off the falls, taking Holt with him down into the roaring white mists far below.

The impact jarred Thorne's bones. He lost his grip on Holt and struggled through the foaming water, disoriented. It became harder to swim, his limbs exhausted and his lungs burning like fire. When he caught sight of Eden drifting on the surface, he fought with all his might to get to her.

He sucked in a lungful of air as he breached the surface next to Eden. She lay face-up in the water, her body still. Thorne wrapped an arm around her waist and swam to the shore.

He crawled up the muddy bank with her in his arms and laid her flat on her back, staring down at her. Death hadn't trespassed over her face, yet he feared the worst as he pressed his ear against her chest. A faint beating echoed against his cheek.

"Please," he begged the jungle. "Please, I would give my life for her."

The pain that had been so easily ignored before

began to crawl through his body in a slow-burning fire until he collapsed on the bank beside her. As he closed his eyes, he heard the voices of the cave murmuring inside his head, and he swore that his mother and father were among them just before he let go.

EDEN JOLTED AWAKE, WINCING AT THE PAIN SHE FELT all over. She pressed a hand to her shoulder, and warm sticky blood coated her fingertips. She looked down and saw more blood from her side. Both times Holt had shot at her, she'd twisted her body just in time and had managed to only get grazed. It was a small miracle. Cool water lapped at her ankles, and she blinked at the view of the massive waterfall in front of them. It was twice the height of the small waterfall where she and Thorne had first made love.

"Eden! Thorne!" Distant shouts, familiar voices, brought her back to the present, and she glanced around. Thorne lay beside her on the ground, blood pooling beneath his side from the knife wound.

"Oh God, no. Thorne!" She frantically checked his pulse. It was too weak, more an echo than a true beat.

"No! Please don't go. Thorne . . . ," Eden whispered as she lay against him. They were too far away from anyone who could help him. The forest rippled, a rare breeze rustling the leaves and vines of the dark jungle around them.

"Eden!" The familiar voice cried out again, and she recognized it now. Cameron was here, and so was Isabelle. Lofty followed behind, and they were all carrying rifles. Cameron tried to help her up, but she wouldn't move from Thorne's side. Another hand gently rested on her shoulder, trying to pull her back. She cried out in protest.

"Honey, don't," Isabelle whispered. "I think he's gone."

"He can't be. Not after . . . Not . . ." The words fell from her lips as if they were bleeding out of her, leaving her a hollow shell.

Cameron knelt next to Thorne's body, but Bwanbale was on the other side of the pool, next to the body of Holt, which had washed up into the shallows. He dug through Holt's clothes until he found a large uncut stone and held it up, mesmerized.

"What the devil is that man up to?" asked Lofty. "We've got a man down here! No time to be fussing over baubles."

Bwanbale suddenly turned toward them, and his dark eyes now seemed to have a hint of gold in their umber depths. He pocketed it and hurried over to the others.

"We must take him to the cave, now." Bwanbale started to lift up Thorne's body, and Cameron helped.

"Cave? The man needs a hospital," Cameron said.

"He will not survive the journey. This is the only way. You must trust me."

"Bloody hell. All right, which cave?" asked Cameron. "There must be hundreds, and only Thorne knows where it is."

"I know the way." Bwanbale's voice seemed deeper somehow, as though he spoke with a thousand souls. No one questioned him any further.

Eden wiped at her eyes as she followed them into the forest. They soon came upon a cave with a dark, cavernous hole that seemed to be a threatening obsidian abyss, one that made Eden uneasy.

"Stay here. I will take him inside," Bwanbale told Cameron. Seemingly without effort, the man carried Thorne into the darkness, vanishing from view. Eden tried to go after them, but Isabelle put an arm around her shoulders, holding her back.

"What in blazes is he up to?" asked Lofty.

"I have no idea," said Cameron. "But I felt something a moment ago. I can't exactly put it into words, but . . . I think we should trust him."

A minute later, Bwanbale returned from the cave as a deep rumbling seemed to erupt from the bowels of the earth.

Cameron gripped Eden and Isabelle protectively. "Hold on!"

The earth seemed to be speaking with a voice of its own as rocks tumbled down the sloping mountainside, and a heavy rain dropped from the skies only to quickly die away, leaving a rolling mist that shrouded the cave's entrance. Eden stared at the white mists that began to twist and writhe before a figure emerged from it.

"Oh my God!" Eden covered her mouth as Thorne walked out of the mouth of the cave. And then he stumbled, as though whatever strength had been granted to him had fled his body. Bwanbale rushed over and caught him with an arm around his waist.

"Easy, my friend, easy." He supported Thorne until he seemed able to stand on his own and his voice had returned to normal.

Thorne grimaced. He lifted his ripped shirt and stared down to where Holt had stabbed him. The skin was knotted in a deep scar, as though the wound was months old and not minutes.

"How in the world . . . ?" Lofty began, then simply shook his head, removed a handkerchief from his pocket, and wiped the sweat from his face. "I give up. I suppose one ought never to question the magic of the jungle, eh?"

"This jungle has a heart," Bwanbale said with quiet reverence. "And it protects its own."

Exhausted, Thorne looked to Eden. Without a word, he opened his arms, and she ran to him. He caught her with a soft groan and held her close. She buried her face against him, shivering. His scent of river, man, and jungle wrapped around her. She swore she could still feel the rumblings of the earth beneath her feet, faint, dying away, but still present. If this jungle had a heart, she was sure she was feeling its pulse, a pulse that matched the beating of Thorne's heart against her cheek. There had been more than one miracle in the jungle today, and Eden sent up a silent prayer of thanks to whatever power dwelt in the Impenetrable Forest. It was a mystery she would leave alone. The forest had a right to hold its secrets, didn't it? That was what made the world beautiful. There were still unexplored forests, caves of mysteries, and fathomless depths of the sea that men should leave alone. The world needed magic to survive.

"Thank God," Cameron said. "Thank God you're all right, my boy." He placed a hand on his nephew's shoulder. "What happened in there? Do you remember?"

Thorne frowned, not sure what to say. "I . . . I think I saw my parents." His blue eyes were stormy with emotions, but he didn't speak further.

Eden kissed his chin and hugged him tighter.

"We should leave before it gets too dark," Bwanbale said. "It is time for us to go."

"Not yet," Thorne said. "We have one more thing we must do." He turned in the direction that Eden knew would take them to the wreckage of the Haywoods' Cessna.

Cameron's head tilted, as if he was unsure of what he was hearing, but then he nodded his understanding.

"Yes, I think I understand. It's time we brought your parents home."

ONE WEEK LATER

Thorne stood near the shores of Lake Bunyoni, and the Impenetrable Forest lay behind him as he gazed out upon the mist rising from the still waters.

Twenty-nine small islands dotted the horizon of the lake, each of them a private paradise for anyone who wished to feel closer to nature and oneself. The waters of the lake were safe, free of parasites, crocodiles, and hippos. It was a true paradise. A perfect place for him and Eden to live.

Behind them, a fresh pair of graves marked the last resting place of Jacob and Amelia Haywood. It had been an easy decision to make. Jacob and Amelia belonged to Africa. It was in many ways as much their home as it was Thorne's. Their spirits now lived here, helping to protect the jungle.

What Thorne had seen in the cave was something he would never be able to fully understand, let alone explain, but it was true that the stone that Holt had stolen was the heart of this jungle. Bwanbale had told Thorne he'd laid his body down in the center of the large part of the cave, surrounded by raw diamonds that glinted without light to reflect off them. Bwanbale had placed the uncut diamond he'd taken from Holt on Thorne's chest. A strange pulsing beat had filled the cave, like the heartbeat of a mighty god. The earth had rumbled around them, and Bwanbale had known he was supposed to leave, so he'd fled the cave. After that, whatever had happened, Thorne had only flashes of memory that seemed over time to grow more and more dim within him the way dreams faded upon waking. Whatever power dwelt in the cave of that lost kingdom from long ago, it had given him back his life, and he'd had one last glimpse of his parents. That single image of their souls—glowing, endless, infinite—would never fade.

For more than twenty years that stone, the jungle's heart, had been separated from its home. Now that it had been returned, there was a true sense of peace and calm over the land.

Quiet steps close by made him smile as Eden appeared at his side by the lake. She wrapped an arm around his back and leaned against his shoulder. Her free hand played with the gingko leaf necklace that hung around her neck. She only ever took it off to sleep at night. He pressed his cheek against the crown of her hair and closed his eyes as true contentment filled him.

"It's so peaceful here," she whispered.

"It is." She turned so she faced him, and he cupped her cheek with one hand. "Eden, I am told there are better ways to do this, grand gestures a man should make or formal speeches, but I have only the words in my heart. Stay by my side. Be my mate forever."

He paused, letting himself bask in the green of her eyes. "Marry me." He touched the necklace at her throat. "I have no ring—but consider this my promise to you." Thorne smiled. "When I gave it to you, I knew you were my destiny."

Eden's lips parted, and her eyes shimmered. The last thing he wanted was to see her cry. But not all tears were bad, or so he was told.

"Yes," she replied. "*Yes.*" The second *yes* was softer, yet it seemed all the more powerful for the way her eyes glowed with love.

She stood on her tiptoes and kissed him. It was a kiss that burned itself upon his soul. He wrapped his arms around her, deepening the kiss as he let his love for her pour out like the waterfall deep in the jungle, behind which they had first made love. Their love, like those falls, would forever flow wild and free.

EPILOGUE

"IF I HAVE EVER SEEN MAGIC, IT HAS BEEN IN
AFRICA." —JOHN HEMINGWAY

hree years later

Thorne woke just before dawn. With a gentle kiss upon Eden's brow, he slipped out of their king-size bed and padded softly down the hall. He wore light pajama pants, and the slightly humid air warmed him as he opened a door down the hall.

An elaborately carved crib was in one corner. The screened windows were open to allow a light breeze to drift through the room. He smiled at the tiny child as she stirred in her crib. He reached into the crib and picked up the baby, holding her to his chest. She had soft blonde curls like her mother, yet her eyes were blue like his. He nuzzled the crown of her hair, breathing in her scent and feeling the perfect weight of her in his arms. Above her, hanging from a set of ribbons to create a mobile, was his gold leaf crown. The voices of the jungle which still spoke to him, had murmured it was a gift for the child. He and Eden had hung the crown with care above their baby's crib after she'd been born and he would never forget the way her chubby hands had reached desperately for the spinning circlet. Glints of light had lit up her green-blue eyes and the world around Thorne and his family had been quiet with respect.

"Good morning, my love," he said to his daughter.

He could always sense when she woke up in the mornings. It drove Eden to frustration that Thorne always got up before her, worried that she had no motherly instincts. But Thorne always chuckled and kissed away his wife's frown.

"She is a child of the jungle. I will always sense her when she needs me," he'd said, and Eden had sighed with an understanding smile and rolled her eyes playfully.

He carried the child outside and stood on the porch of their home that faced Lake Bunyoni. He and Eden had built this house close to where he'd buried his parents. Half the year they stayed in England, and half the year they spent in Uganda. Though Thorne was still not comfortable with large groups of people, he had become an ambassador of sorts, an ambassador of the jungle, bringing awareness to its plight and the need for its protection.

And then came their daughter, who was a mystery to Thorne. A mystery as to how one so small could create so much love in his heart. That first moment he'd heard his daughter cry in the delivery room, he'd understood how Keza had come to his aid as a child when he had cried. Their daughter was so like him in her fascination with the jungle, and Thorne felt blessed to be able to show her both worlds.

A distant call from the jungle made his eyes turn to the forest. He moved quietly, carrying his child into the edge of the foliage, looking for the one who had summoned him. When he sensed the creature, he stopped and waited.

An aging female gorilla came into view, pulling leafy plants out of her way. Her reddish-brown eyes were soft and ancient as she looked upon Thorne. He watched her approach as he held his daughter carefully. The child was still and peaceful as the gorilla came toward them on knuckled hands.

Thorne reached out to greet his mother in the way of the apes, with gentle brushing knuckles over her brow, cheek, and chest. His daughter squirmed and kicked her chubby legs as she tried to reach for the gorilla. The gorilla hooted softly, a sign of interest and amusement at the baby's reaction.

The child let out a delighted giggle and spoke a few words of child language that not even Thorne could understand. But the gorilla seemed to, and she brushed her knuckles gently over the baby's cheek. She looked up at Thorne. Love made all things beautiful. Thorne's heart was filled with a love so deep that for a moment he could not speak. Then finally, he spoke in the language of the wild to his mother.

"Keza, this is my daughter, Jane."

All around them the quiet forest woke like a sleeping god after a thousand years of slumber as Keza replied, *"Welcome, Jane, daughter of the jungle."*

THANK YOU SO MUCH FOR READING *LOVE IN THE Wild*! My next story is *Devastate Me* where a sexy but oh-so-grumpy Navy Seal falls for the girl who moves in next door. Interfering housewives, a nosy Homeowners association, a loyal service dog and a steamy romance fill this sexy story! Get it HERE!

And don't miss out on future releases from me which will include a sexy retelling of the Labyrinth movie where a dark fae prince steals a woman away by twilight to seduce her.

SIGN UP FOR NEW RELEASE ALERTS AT ONE OF THESE PLACES:

BOOKBUB

NEWSLETTER

TURN THE PAGE TO SEE A LIST OF BOOK discussion questions

BOOK DISCUSSION QUESTIONS

1) What do you believe is the significance of water with regard to Eden and Thorne's relationship?

2) When Bwanbale says that to know Thorne is to love him and to love him makes someone a better person, what do you believe he means, specifically about mankind and the importance of love?

3) What do you think is the importance of the lost civilization to Thorne? What does it represent to him?

4) Do you believe that certain places or certain people attract magic, or spirits?

5) Thorne says he does not matter without Eden, what do you believe he means by that statement?

6) Bwanbale is a pivotal and vital role in Thorne's character and how he sees the world, what do you believe Bwanbale represents in the novel?

7) What is the significance of the gold ginkgo leaf necklace within the story aside from a personal memento of Thorne's mother?

8) What do you believe is the theme behind the gold beyond the representation of man's thirst for power?

EMMA CASTLE
Dark and Edgy Romance

OTHER TITLES BY EMMA CASTLE

Standalones
Love in the Wild- A Tarzan Retelling
Devastate Me
The Lord and the Labyrinth (coming 2021)

Unlikely Heroes
*can be read as standalones
Midnight with the Devil - Book 1
A Wilderness Within - Book 2

Sci-Fi Romance - The Krinar World
The Krinar Eclipse by Lauren Smith - Book 1
The Krinar Code by Emma Castle - Book 2

ABOUT THE AUTHOR

Emma Castle has always loved reading but didn't know she loved romance until she was enduring the trials of law school. She discovered the dark and sexy world of romance novels and since then has never looked back! She loves writing about sexy, alpha male heroes who know just how to seduce women even if they are a bit naughty about it. When Emma's not writing, she may be obsessing over her favorite show Supernatural where she's a total Team Dean Winchester kind of girl!

If you wish to be added to Emma's new release newsletter feel free to contact Emma using the Sign up link on her website at www.emmacastlebooks.com or email her at emma@emmacastlebooks.com!

f facebook.com/Emmacastlebooks
🐦 twitter.com/emmacastlebooks
📷 instagram.com/Emmacastlebooks
BB bookbub.com/authors/emma-castle

Made in the USA
Middletown, DE
02 June 2022

66511936R00224